MVFOL
P9-DXM-305

Also by Philip R. Craig and William G. Tapply

FIRST LIGHT: THE FIRST EVER BRADY COYNE/
J. W. JACKSON MYSTERY

The J. W. Jackson Mysteries by Philip R. Craig

MURDER AT A VINEYARD MANSION
A VINEYARD KILLING
VINEYARD ENIGMA
VINEYARD SHADOWS
VINEYARD BLUES
A FATAL VINEYARD SEASON
A SHOOT ON MARTHA'S VINEYARD
A DEADLY VINEYARD HOLIDAY
DEATH ON A VINEYARD BEACH
A CASE OF VINEYARD POISON
OFF SEASON
CLIFF HANGER
THE DOUBLE MINDED MEN
THE WOMAN WHO WALKED INTO THE SEA
A BEAUTIFUL PLACE TO DIE
GATE OF IVORY, GATE OF HORN

The Brady Coyne Mysteries by William G. Tapply

SHADOW OF DEATH
A FINE LINE
PAST TENSE
A BRADY COYNE OMNIBUS
SCAR TISSUE
MUSCLE MEMORY
CUTTER'S RUN
CLOSE TO THE BONE
THE SEVENTH ENEMY
THE SNAKE EATER
TIGHT LINES
THE SPOTTED CATS
CLIENT PRIVILEGE
DEAD WINTER
A VOID IN HEARTS
THE VULGAR BOATMAN
DEAD MEAT
THE MARINE CORPSE
FOLLOW THE SHARKS
THE DUTCH BLUE ERROR
DEATH AT CHARITY'S POINT

SECOND SIGHT

A Brady Coyne/J. W. Jackson Mystery

PHILIP R. CRAIG
AND
WILLIAM G. TAPPLY

SCRIBNER
New York London Toronto Sydney

SCRIBNER
1230 Avenue of the Americas
New York, NY 10020

This book is a work of fiction. Names, characters, places, and incidents either are products of the authors' imaginations or are used fictitiously. Any resemblance to actual events or locales or persons, living or dead, is entirely coincidental.

For information regarding special discounts for bulk purchases, please contact Simon & Schuster Special Sales at 1-800-456-6798 or business@simonandschuster.com

DESIGNED BY ERICH HOBBING

Text set in Sabon

Manufactured in the United States of America

1 3 5 7 9 10 8 6 4 2

Library of Congress Cataloging-in-Publication Data
Craig, Philip R., 1933–
Second sight: a Brady Coyne/J. W. Jackson mystery/
Philip R. Craig and William G. Tapply.
p. cm.
1. Coyne, Brady (Fictitious character)—Fiction. 2. Jackson, Jeff (Fictitious character)—Fiction. 3. Private investigators—Massachusetts—Martha's Vineyard—Fiction. 4. Martha's Vineyard (Mass.)—Fiction. 5. Terrorism—Prevention—Fiction. 6. Missing persons—Fiction.
I. Tapply, William G. II. Title.

PS3570.A568S43 2005
813'.54—dc22
2004052173

ISBN 0-7432-6067-8

For our kids
Kim and Jamie
Mike and Melissa and Sarah

When the stars threw down their spears,
And watered heaven with their tears,
Did he smile his work to see?
Did he who made the Lamb make thee?

—WILLIAM BLAKE

SECOND SIGHT

Chapter One

J.W.

There are two weekly newspapers on Martha's Vineyard: the *Vineyard Gazette* and the *Martha's Vineyard Times*. Both deal solely with island issues and neither makes much pretense of separating its editorial views from its news coverage. The papers are like dueling banjos, predictably taking opposing views on almost everything. The *Gazette*'s writings are politically correct, brimming with nostalgia for an idealized past, and touched with hauteur, while the populist *Times* relishes muckraking and has asked local pols so many embarrassing questions that sundry boards and town leaders will no longer speak to its representatives unless the questions are first submitted in writing.

I didn't read either paper with hopes of discovering the truth, but merely to get a sense of the issues of the moment and a laugh from the political dissemblers and the more passionate letters to the editors. Between them, the *Gazette* and the *Times* gave strong evidence that Shaw was right when he defined a newspaper as a device unable to distinguish between a bicycle accident and the collapse of civilization.

But both papers agreed on one thing: the upcoming Celebration for Humanity was a very big deal.

It was August and the Celebration had been news all summer. And why not? It seemed that every celebrity, politician, and millionaire living on the island, along with countless others in New York, Hollywood, Washington, and from abroad, was involved, and every one of them would be wrapped in the American flag. It was to be an unprecedented event, bringing together the great and powerful from the entertainment business, Wall Street, religion, and government for one extraordinary weekend of song, speech, prayer, patriotism, and commitment to national and international peace, goodwill, and fearless resolve in the face of terrorism and evil axes.

The Celebration would be broadcast live on national and international radio and television, and taped for viewing by those unfortunate enough to have missed the original show and for the millions who undoubtedly would want to see it all again.

"I just don't think I can stand the tension of it all," yawned Zee, looking at the *Gazette*'s front page. "Less than a week to go, and the island's problems are mounting. Not enough housing, not enough security, not enough tickets to the big event and some outrageous scalping of the ones there are."

"How about we rent out this place for that weekend and use the money to go to Angkor Wat?" I asked. "I've wanted to see Angkor Wat ever since I was a little kid and my father let me read his copy of Halliburton's *Complete Book of Marvels.* Our house isn't much but it should be good for a few thousand dollars during the Celebration. People are desperate."

"I don't know if they're that desperate," said Zee, glancing around the kitchen, where she'd spread the paper on the table.

Maybe she was right. Home sweet home was an old hunting and fishing camp expanded by a couple of modern bedrooms that I'd tacked on since the kids were born. I'd been working in vain for years to fix a leak in the corner of the living room that dripped whenever a strong rain blew in from the east, and the balcony floor was beginning to get a little spongy in one place I'd soon have to fix.

"People will pay anything to stay on Martha's Vineyard," I said, yawning in turn, "and they'll pay twice as much if they get to see a celebrity while they're here. No wonder the scalpers are doing so well. Maybe we should at least sell our tickets. What do you think?"

"As you'll recall, we don't have tickets," said Zee. "Somehow we got left off the VIP list again. I just can't understand it. I see here, though, that Joe and Myra Callahan are among the invited guests. I imagine Cricket will be coming along, too."

Years before, during one of then-president Joe Callahan's several summer holidays on the Vineyard, our paths had briefly crossed, as the paths of commoners and aristocrats sometimes do, but the former president's family and the Jacksons had since walked different roads.

"Maybe you should suck up to some of those Hollywood types who've been after you to become a movie star," I said. "They can probably get us in."

Zee, who had once been an extra in a motion picture filmed on our island, was still being pursued by its director, who considered her, rightly, I thought, to be one of those rare people who light up the screen. Zee, however, preferred to remain a nurse and to live on the Vineyard with our children and me.

"My once promising career as a film star is, I'm glad to

say, a thing of the past," said Zee. "According to this story, though, I actually do know some of the people who'll be part of the show."

"No doubt they'll want you to perform."

"If nominated, I will not run; if elected, I will not serve. We can stay at home like all the normal people in the world and watch the big show on our little TV." She looked at her watch. "The kids should be home any time now. You know, it still feels weird to have them old enough to go play with other kids at a summer camp."

It did seem that way. "Well, their friends come to play here sometimes, so it balances out."

"It feels okay when other kids are here, but it doesn't when ours are someplace else. Does that sound normal?"

"Maybe you should take a parenting class to find out."

"No thanks. I have enough trouble being a parent with just you around. I don't need to be in a class with ten other people who don't know any more than I do. My mother says the secret is to be a grandparent, because by that time you finally know everything instead of always being a year or two behind."

It was a popular notion among grandparents, I knew, and maybe even a correct one, but with luck it would be another twenty years or so before we could either confirm or deny.

Zee scanned the paper one last time and folded it. "Even for this fabled isle where fantasies unfurl like flags almost every day, this Celebration is an eye-catcher. We have as much media here as we did the first time Joe Callahan came down."

During the Callahans' first Vineyard visit, so many security people and media types had been around that every hotel room was full and the island sank about six inches into the sea from the weight of machines and humans. It only rose again when the presidential party flew back to Washington.

"The beginning of that first sentence was quite alliterative," I said admiringly. "But you're right. This is a notable gala even by local standards. I'm going to pour myself a martini and adjourn to the balcony. Would you care to join me?"

She would, so I got the Luksusowa out of the freezer and poured two glasses, adding two jalapeño-stuffed olives to each. I put these on a tray along with crackers and smoked bluefish pâté and went up to the balcony, where Zee was already seated. She was looking eastward over our gardens, over Sengekontacket Pond, over the barrier beach on its far side where families were even now packing up their beach gear and heading home, and over the blue waters of Nantucket Sound to where Cape Cod loomed on the distant horizon.

It was a view we never tired of. Just before dawn all winter long a coral ribbon stretched along the horizon between the dark blue band of ocean and the lighter one of brightening sky. And all year round, as the sun set and our house fell into evening shadows, the barrier beach glowed like a strand of gold before the earth turned and night came down.

Zee sipped her martini. "Not bad, Jefferson. You haven't lost the magic touch."

"The secret of the old family recipe shall never be revealed until my son has reached maturity, and then only to him."

"Diana and I won't be told how to open the bottle, I take it." She handed me a cracker mounded with pâté.

"You know how women are. They just can't keep secrets."

"How true, how true. Certainly none of my women friends can keep herself from saying things about you that should be kept private."

"Like what, for instance?"

"I'm sorry, but my lips are sealed. Besides, you don't really want to know."

"Are you saying you're an exception to the women-can't-keep-a-secret rule?"

Zee lifted her glass. "According to my friends, you're the one who's an exception to certain normal, civilized rules. Several of them, in fact. I'll say no more."

Out on the sound boats were white against the blue water as they headed for harbor. Above them the pale sky was bright and clear. Every shape and color on land and sea was sharply defined by the dry northeast breeze. It was a Babar day.

Behind us I heard the sound of a car coming down our long, sandy driveway and turned, expecting to see Madge or Frank Duncan bringing Diana and Joshua home from an afternoon at their nature studies camp.

But the car didn't belong to the Duncans. It stopped in the yard and a man got out. I hadn't seen him in quite a while. He waved and started toward the house.

"It's Jake Spitz," I said to Zee. It was refill time, so I picked up our empty glasses as I went downstairs with Zee at my heels.

Jake shook my hand and exchanged kisses with Zee, who stepped back and smiled up at him. "Still exercising regularly, I see. Maybe you can have a talk with my husband about the virtues of physical activity other than snoring and surf casting."

"You both look fit as ever," said Spitz. "How are the kids?"

"They're out gallivanting with their friends. They're fine."

I was happy to see him. "How about a little something, Jake? We're ready for seconds."

He hesitated, then smiled and nodded. "Theoretically I'm on duty, but only for a little longer, so what the hell."

"Spoken like a true American. How long have you been on the island, and what brings the FBI to our house?"

I fixed the drinks and the three of us went back up to the balcony.

"Watch that soft spot," I said, gesturing. "I've got some rotten wood there that I have to replace. Your foot might go right through."

"I'm used to rot," said Spitz. "I work in Washington."

We sat and looked at the view. "Mighty fine," said Spitz. "I remember it well."

"It's a nice surprise to have you here to see it again," I said.

Spitz sipped his drink and made an approving face. "Good. But I didn't come here just to drink your vodka and sit on your balcony, much as I'm enjoying both. I've come to offer you a temp job."

On Martha's Vineyard, where prices are high and pay is low, a job is always worth considering. In my case, that was especially true since I had no steady income other than spotty profit from part ownership in a fishing boat and tiny disability pensions from the U.S. Army and the Boston PD, earned absorbing bits of enemy metal into my body during combat. I still carried a bullet next to my spine and small fragments of shrapnel in my legs.

"Let me guess," said Zee. "If you're here on the island, Jake, it means that some Washington bigwigs are too, or soon will be, and that means the job has something to do with the Celebration for Humanity. Am I right?"

"It's hard to pull the wool over your eyes, Mrs. Jackson."

"Well, he's not going to take the job," said Zee firmly and with a hint of anger in her voice.

Spitz and I both looked at her. I opened my mouth but she spoke again before I could.

"My husband has collected a few new scars since you last saw him, Jake, and he's promised not to do any more dangerous things. I'm holding him to it."

"I don't do dangerous things," I said.

"Yes, you do, and Jake here has been involved in security as long as we've known him, so it's pretty clear to me that he wants you to do something that might be dangerous! Well, you won't!"

Spitz lifted his hands. "It's nothing like that, Zee. Let me give you the details before you decide anything."

Zee gave me a hard, wifely look, but nodded.

"Did you ever hear of a singer named Evangeline? Like in the poem by Longfellow?"

"Of course," said Zee, perking up. "Everybody's heard of Evangeline. She's won all the Grammys in the world but she keeps her personal life totally private. Doesn't she live in a castle in Scotland or something? Is she coming to the Celebration? Wow! I haven't seen her name in the local papers."

I could not share Zee's enthusiasm, but even I had heard of Evangeline, although in general I'm not aware of any singers younger than Willie Nelson or Pavarotti. "What about her?" I asked.

Spitz took another short snort. "She's coming to the Celebration, but not many people know that. She doesn't want anything to do with reporters. She wants to stay out of sight, make a 'surprise appearance' onstage, then, when her bit is over, fly back home again. She needs a driver who can keep his mouth shut. We have a safe house for her and you're my choice as her driver. She wants to see the island while she's here, and you know it better than my agents. Also, you were a cop and you can wave a badge as well as the next guy if you need to."

"My shield is pretty much out-of-date these days, Jake."

"I can arrange to get you some official paper. She'll have a Ford Explorer with those dark windows that keep people from seeing inside. And they say that she's got half a dozen different wigs and getups to make herself look different if she wants to go someplace public, so about all you'll have to do is drive her where she wants to go.

"There's money in it," he added, and mentioned a goodly figure.

"Can I get an autographed picture of her for Zee?"

Zee brightened. "That would be excellent!"

"I'm sure it can be arranged," said Spitz, looking relieved. "Well, what do you say, Mrs. Jackson, ma'am?"

"All he has to do is drive Evangeline around the island?"

"And maybe get some take-out clams for her from The Bite, so she can taste the island's finest fries alone on a beach somewhere."

"And that's all?"

"He might have to get her back into the car pretty fast if some fan spots her."

"And that's all?"

"That pretty much covers it."

Zee was never one to miss a trick. "How'd the FBI get involved with Evangeline, Jake? You work for the government, not for people in the entertainment business. Are you sure there isn't more to this job than you're telling me?"

"There's a simple explanation," said Spitz, smiling at her. "Joe Callahan and his family, especially their daughter, Cricket, are big Evangeline fans. He may not be president anymore, but when he asked the bureau to help her out, we obliged. Well, what do you say, are you going to let your husband take the job?"

"Well, all right," she said, smiling back. "But I want that autographed picture."

"Consider it done." Spitz glanced at his watch and took a final sip of his drink. "Come on down to the car with me, J.W., and I'll give you a map that shows where Evangeline and her daughter are staying."

I followed him to the car. He gave me the map, and then said quietly, "I'd like you to carry your pistol on this job."

My eyebrows went up a bit.

"I doubt if you'll need it," he said, "but I think you should have it. Celebrities are targets for some people, and we don't want anything happening to Evangeline." He paused. "We've heard some whispers in the wind, but nothing we can be sure of. I didn't mention this up on the balcony because I wouldn't want Zee to be worried about you."

"Tell me what you know," I said.

"I just did," said Spitz. "You still want the job? It's only for these next few days."

I hesitated.

"You'll be doing me a favor," he said. "I need somebody I can trust."

I glanced back at the house, and at Zee, knowing Jake could be putting me in a difficult—yes, even a dangerous—position. But he was a friend. And I was intrigued.

"All right," I said.

Chapter Two

Brady

Toward closing time on a Friday afternoon in August, Neddie Doyle called me at my office. "Mike needs you," she said.

I started to make a joke out of it. I said, "Hell, Mike doesn't need anybody. Least of all me."

But when she said, "Yeah, Brady, he does, and he insists that it's you," her tone told me that this was no joking matter.

I asked her what was up, but all she'd say was, "It's Mike's idea. He should tell you."

It occurred to me that Mike could've called as easily as Neddie, and the fact that he hadn't gave me a spooky feeling. The Doyles lived in Hancock, New Hampshire, a two-hour drive from Boston. I told her I could be there the next morning.

I hadn't seen Mike Doyle since he abruptly and mysteriously quit his Federal Street firm three years ago and moved to Hancock in the sticks of southwestern New Hampshire. I still remembered him as the idealistic guy I'd known in law school, the Peace Corps volunteer who'd given two years of his young life to teaching African villagers about irrigation. He'd been a whip-smart, handsome, athletic stud who ran rings around Charlie McDevitt and me when we played Sunday-morning touch football at the Yale Law School, argued rings around us in late-night discussions about constitutional law, and picked up girls that snubbed the rest of us in New Haven bars.

After we graduated, the young idealist quickly matured, if that's the word for it, into a relentless litigator. Mike made partner in two years, got his name added to the letterhead, earned about a million dollars a year, and quickly turned stodgy old Fisk, Evans, and Burleson into F. E. B. and D., the top-billing law firm in Boston. When I was still a struggling attorney determined to make it as a lone wolf, Mike threw cases my way that were too insignificant for his big-time firm. In those days, I took anything, and he helped me to get my feet under me.

I was Mike's personal lawyer, and I suppose if I'd ever wanted to sue somebody, I'd've hired him. Smart lawyers always hire other lawyers to do their legal work. Mike and I were both smart that way.

Over the years, we remained friends. Not buddies, the way he and Charlie and I had been in law school, but friends. Mike was a good guy. His success didn't go to his head. When our kids were young, our families would get together a few times a year for cookouts, and now and then Mike and I would meet after work for a drink to talk about old times.

Neddie, Mike's wife, was a gifted watercolorist. She also happened to be gorgeous, of course. Christa, their daughter, was vivacious like her mother and smart and athletic like her dad. And lucky Mike, he managed to retire from the rat race after just twenty years of it. Some guys manage to get it all right the first time around. It was hard not to envy Mike Doyle.

Or at least, that's what I used to think.

* * *

It took a little less than two hours on Saturday morning to drive to Hancock, New Hampshire, from my apartment on the Boston waterfront. I headed for Peterborough, then followed Neddie's directions through a maze of wooded country roads, found the dirt driveway that wound through the pine forest and up the hill to the clearing where the Doyle house overlooked Mount Monadnock.

It was a pretty nice house—all glass and raw cedar and New Hampshire granite—and the way it perched there on the hilltop with its rock gardens and stone walls and fieldstone paths and clumps of paper birch, it looked like part of the rocky landscape.

Neddie greeted me at the door, gave me a hug, took my hand, and led me inside. "Don't be shocked," she said.

But I was.

Mike Doyle was lying in a hospital bed that they'd set up in the big living room. A gray-haired nurse was fiddling with the needle in the back of his hand. Plastic bags filled with transparent fluids hung on the aluminum rack beside the bed, and thin tubes snaked down from the bags to the needle. More tubes sneaked out from under the thin blanket that covered Mike and emptied into bags hanging off the foot of his bed. A blue oxygen tank sat in the corner of the room.

Outside the floor-to-ceiling glass wall, the view of the green, rolling New Hampshire hills and, on the horizon, craggy Mount Monadnock was spectacular on this sunny August morning. But Mike's head was turned away from the vista, and his eyes were shut, and his breathing was slow.

In the couple of years since I'd last seen him, Mike Doyle had become an old man. His skin had that translucent look that you see on very old people, and it stretched so tight over his cheekbones that his face looked more like a skull. His hair had gone white.

Neddie, who was standing beside me, touched my arm. "He's not going to wake up for a while," she said. "It's the morphine. I'm sorry. He's desperate to talk to you. He's usually okay in the morning. Come on. I'll get us some coffee. Let's go out on the terrace."

It was one of those sticky August mornings in New England that promised to turn downright hot, with thunderstorms building in the afternoon, but out there on the Doyles' fieldstone patio high above the surrounding valleys, the breeze was cool and the air smelled sweet.

Neddie poured some coffee, and we sat in the big wooden armchairs.

"I didn't even know he was sick," I said.

"That's why he quit the firm," Neddie said. "It's some damn exotic parasite he picked up in Africa. He was fine for over twenty years. Didn't even know anything was wrong. Then . . ." She shrugged. "The doctors said there was nothing they could do about it. Mike told the partners he was leaving the day after he found out. He didn't want anybody to . . . to watch him deteriorate."

"He's dying?" I said.

"Oh, yes." She smiled softly. "He spent two years trying to convince the villagers they shouldn't wash their dishes in the water downstream from where their animals sloshed around in it. He showed them how to dig wells and irrigation ditches and taught them to boil their drinking water. Ironic, huh?"

"How long?"

"A month. Six weeks at the most. He's gone downhill fast this past year or so."

"Jesus," I said. "I'm sorry."

We were quiet for a minute. Then Neddie said, "He wanted to talk to you himself. But I guess I better speak for him." She looked at me. "This is his idea, not mine."

"If there's something I can do . . ."

"Mike thinks there is," she said. "He's got it in his head that you're the only one who can. It's about Christa."

Christa was the Doyles' daughter, their only child. "What about Christa?" I said.

Neddie looked at me. There was something hard in her eyes. "She's gone. We've lost her. Mike wants her back. He wants to—to understand—before he dies. He wants to know that she loves him."

"What do you mean, 'gone'?"

Neddie spread her hands. "Run away. Disappeared. I don't know how else to say it. She quit school the day after she turned sixteen. That was two and a half years ago last March. Packed up her backpack for school like she always did, left on the school bus, and . . . never came home. We haven't seen her since then."

"You must've—"

"At first she called at least once a week. Said she was okay, she was safe, had a job and a place to stay, had made friends. She was in Eugene, Oregon. She sounded happy. Promised she'd be back. We begged her to come home, of course, but all she said was that she would when she was ready, whatever that meant. Said we had to trust her and made it clear that if we went after her, she'd just leave again." Neddie shook her head. "Mike and I argued about it. He was devastated. Took it personally. He was all for sending the troops after her. Me, I figured, take her at her word, give her a little time, don't spook her, let her get whatever it is out of her system. As long as she kept in touch with us, as long as she was safe, I had faith that it would turn out okay. Christa was smart and resourceful. She'd figure it out. I absolutely believed her, believed she'd come back."

"But she didn't."

"No. After three or four months, the phone calls suddenly stopped. She'd never given us a number. We had no idea how to reach her. So Mike contacted an investigator in Eugene. We paid him a lot of money. After two weeks, he called to tell us that he couldn't find her. Shortly after that we got a letter from Christa. It was . . . terribly hurtful. It blamed us for giving her what she called false values. It accused us of being materialists, of corrupting her." Neddie gazed off toward the mountains. "It was soon after that that Mike started going downhill."

"You haven't heard from Christa since then?"

"No. Not a word. I've come to terms with it. She's gone from our lives, and I just pray she's okay. Mike, though, he wakes up every morning with hope. Maybe today's the day we'll see Christa, he says. That lasts about an hour. Then he just seems to collapse into himself. Waiting for tomorrow, I guess. Another day, another hope."

"Neddie," I said gently, "where do I come into it?"

She smiled. "Remember when we used to get together with you and Gloria, when the kids were little, and we'd have cookouts in the backyard?"

I nodded.

"Christa used to call you Uncle Brady. She thought you were the greatest guy. Always talked about you. Mike was actually a little jealous. I bet you didn't know that."

I smiled. "That was a long time ago."

"Yes," she said. "Mike was healthy then, and Christa was our sweet little girl. A long time ago. Anyway, Mike is convinced that if anybody can talk her into coming home, it's Uncle Brady."

"Wait a minute," I said. "Are you saying you want me to find Christa and bring her home before . . ."

"Before Mike dies. Yes. That's what he wants."

"What about you?" I said. "Is that what you want?"

Neddie looked up at the sky for a moment, and when she turned to me, I saw that her eyes glistened. "I don't know, Brady. If she ever came home and then . . . then disappeared again, I don't think I could bear it. It's taken me a long time to learn to live with this." She nodded. "But I guess it would allow Mike to die in peace. At this point, that's worth everything to me. So, yes, it is what I want."

"Neddie," I said, "I'd do anything for you and Mike. I hope you know that. But I'm a lawyer. I'm not—"

"You know a lot of investigators and police and FBI people, right? You know how it works, finding people."

"Yes, but—"

She touched my arm. "Mike says you've found people before. People who didn't want to be found. That you've done it for other clients. He says you're good at it. He says when you latch onto something, you don't give up. He says people trust you. They talk to you."

I decided not to tell her that several of the people I'd been hired to find had turned out to be dead. Being dead was often the reason they'd disappeared in the first place.

"I'll see what I can do," I said. "Of course I will."

She smiled. "Thank you."

"No promises."

"I understand."

"It'll probably mean retaining some investigators. If they can track down Christa, I'll go to her, talk to her. Then it'll be up to her."

"That's all we want," she said. She stood up and held out her hand to me.

I took it, and as I did, I was thinking: *What the hell have you gotten yourself into, Coyne?*

"Let's go back in," Neddie said, "see if Mike's awake so we can tell him."

The nurse had cranked Mike's bed up and wedged a couple of pillows behind his head. She was holding a glass for him, and he was sipping what looked like ginger ale through a straw and gazing out the big window. Beethoven's Sixth Symphony—the "Pastorale"—was playing from hidden speakers. The music filled the room.

Neddie went over to Mike and kissed his cheek. "Brady's here," she said.

Mike turned his head slowly and looked at me. "Hey," he said. His voice was weak and raspy.

I went over and gripped his shoulder. "Hey yourself."

He smiled. "Thanks for coming."

"Neddie told me about Christa," I said.

He nodded. "Good. You'll do it, huh?"

"Sure."

"I just want to see my little girl," he said. One of his hands crept out from under the blanket. He tapped his cheek with a shaky finger. "I want her to kiss me here and tell me she loves me. I want to say good-bye to her. That's all."

"Fair enough," I said.

He let his head fall back on the pillows, closed his eyes, let out a long sigh, and smiled.

A minute later he was asleep.

Neddie touched my arm, and I followed her into her office. She sat at the desk and pulled out a checkbook.

"What are you doing?" I said.

"Giving you a check."

I shook my head. "That's not necessary."

"We're hiring you, Brady. You don't think we expect you to do this on your own time."

"I'll keep track of it. I'll send you a bill."

"Promise?"

"Sure."

She smiled. "I mean it," she said. "We're not asking you for a favor here."

"I like doing favors for my friends."

"If we don't pay you, the deal's off."

"I'll send you a bill," I said.

"You'd better." She put the checkbook in a drawer. "What's next?"

"I'll need the most recent photo of Christa that you have," I said. "I want that letter she sent you, too, and that Oregon investigator's report. Write down the names of everybody you can think of she might have kept in touch with since she left. And I want to see her room, if that's okay."

"You can if you want," she said. "Mike and I have been through it a hundred times. Looking for clues. Who might help us, where she might go, what was on her mind. She didn't keep a diary or anything. No letters or cards or photos. Nothing like that. "

"I still want to see it."

"Sure. Top of the stairs on your right." Neddie smiled. "Mike insisted we keep the door open. To symbolize how we're always ready to welcome her home, he says. He says shutting the door would be shutting her out. Anyway, go ahead up. I'll get that stuff for you."

Christa's bedroom had a slanted ceiling with two big skylights. A wall-size window offered the same view of the mountains as the one from the living room downstairs. Objectively, it was a really nice room, sunlit and cozy. But it felt cold and unlived-in.

I wasn't sure what a teenage girl's bedroom was supposed to look like. Both of my kids were boys. Young men now. When they were teenagers, their rooms had featured posters of athletes and rock stars, piles of dirty clothes and hockey sticks, perpetually unmade beds, and television sets they never remembered to turn off. If I'd had to guess, I would've pictured a girl's room with a neatly made pink canopy bed piled with stuffed animals, walls hung with posters of movie stars and pop singers, a Princess telephone on the bedside table, and a desk in the corner with a laptop computer and a little color TV.

Christa's bed was, in fact, neatly made, with a patchwork quilt and a crocheted afghan folded at the foot. But there was no telephone, no television set, no computer, no stereo system, not even a clock radio. In fact, what struck me about Christa's room was its emptiness. It reminded me of a guest room in a house that never had guests.

The walls were bare except for one framed picture over the bed—a generic seascape featuring sand dunes and wheeling gulls. A low bookcase under the window held about two dozen Nancy Drew mysteries that, if I had to guess, had been Neddie's from when she was a kid. There were a few Stephen King and Joyce Carol Oates novels, too, and the complete J. R. R. Tolkien, a dictionary, a thesaurus, and a few random paperbacks. There were several empty slots, as if some books had been removed from the shelves.

I pawed through the bureau and looked into the closet. Girl's clothes. No hidden stacks of letters tied up in a ribbon, no videotapes or photo albums or diaries.

I was looking out the window with my hands clasped behind me when Neddie came in. "Find anything?" she said.

I turned to look at her. "Did you clean it up after Christa left?"

She shook her head. "This is exactly the way it was the day she went away."

"It's like . . ."

"I know," she said. "Like nobody ever lived here. Christa hated it when we moved up to New Hampshire. We never told her it was because of Mike's health. Maybe that was a mistake, but he didn't want to upset her. As far as we've been able to tell, she didn't make a single friend around here. The people at school said she was a good student, but a loner. She refused to join any clubs or go out for any teams. They encouraged her, and so did we. She was into everything when we were living in Belmont. After we moved up here, she'd come home on the bus right after school, change her clothes, and walk around in the woods or come up here to her room and read. She refused to have anything mechanical or electronic in her room. No music, no TV, no computer. You noticed that, right?"

I nodded. "Would you say she was depressed?"

"You know," said Neddie, "since she's been gone we've tried to understand. Tried desperately. But honestly, she didn't seem at all depressed. She was pleasant with us. No rebellion, no sulking, nothing like that. She laughed a lot, actually. Helped me cook sometimes. She liked to work in the gardens. Always did her homework. Got excellent grades. Hardly ever got sick, rarely missed a day of school. We were here less than a year when she . . . she left. We figured she was just making a slow adjustment."

"That doesn't sound like the portrait of a runaway," I said. "Are you sure you're remembering it accurately?"

Neddie smiled. "That's a fair question, Brady. It's a question I've asked myself a hundred times. What are we overlooking? What have we been repressing? Where were the hints?" She shrugged. "You know Mike. He's a pretty hard-nosed guy. I'm pretty hard-nosed myself, in my own way. We're remembering it accurately. Her teachers up here remember her the same way. Good kid. Quiet but pleasant. No trouble."

I took one more look around Christa's bedroom. Then Neddie and I went back down to her office.

"I've got what you wanted," she said. She handed me a snapshot. "I took this on Christa's sixteenth birthday. The day before she left. I can hardly stand to look at it."

In the photo, Mike and Christa were standing in their backyard with the long vista of Mount Monadnock behind them. They were both smiling directly into the camera. Mike had his arm around her shoulder, and Christa had hers around his waist, and she was leaning her cheek against his shoulder. Mike looked healthy. Christa looked happy.

She was nearly as tall as Mike, with her mother's ebony hair and flashing brown eyes. Her hair was cut very short, almost a boy's haircut. She wore big silver earrings, a tight white T-shirt, and low-cut blue jeans that showed her belly button. She looked grown-up.

"Here's that letter," said Neddie. It was in its envelope, postmarked San Francisco. I decided I'd read it later.

She gave me a manila envelope. "That detective's report is in there, and I wrote down the names of all the people Christa might've been in touch with that I could think of. I don't have phone numbers or addresses, but they're all from Belmont, from before we moved up here. Is that okay?"

"Sure," I said.

I put the snapshot and the letter into the manila envelope. "Can you think of anything else that will help me?"

"Like what?"

"What kind of job might she take? Does she like to dance, go to concerts, movies, plays? Does she swim, play tennis?"

Neddie frowned. "It seems like so long ago. I mean, to us she was just our smart daughter. She seemed . . . normal, you know? She never had any job except babysitting. She always liked to read. She was wonderfully athletic, but sometime about when she turned twelve, she decided she hated competitive sports. She said competition was destructive. She believed in cooperation. She was idealistic. Like Mike." She smiled. "Christa was a good kid, Brady. Everybody said so."

I nodded.

"I can't think of anything else to tell you."

"Okay. If you do, just give me a call." I tucked the manila envelope under my arm. "I guess I'd better get started."

We went back into the living room. The nurse was sitting in a straight-backed chair beside Mike's bed reading a magazine. Mike was asleep.

At the front door, Neddie put her arms around me, pushed her face against my chest, and said, "This is really stupid, isn't it?"

"It's not stupid," I said.

She tilted her head back and looked up at me. "Hopeless, I mean. Not a word from her in two years. She could be anywhere. Even if . . ."

Even if she's alive, is what I guessed Neddie was thinking.

"There's always hope," I said. I gave her a squeeze. "Tell Mike good-bye for me. I'll keep in touch with you."

She nodded. "Thank you, Brady."

"Understand one thing," I said.

"What's that?"

"If I do find Christa and talk to her, I will tell her that Mike's dying and wants to see her. I'll do my best to convince her to come home. If she refuses, I can't force her. It'll have to be up to her. I may have to promise her that I won't tell you where she is, and I would never break a promise like that."

"I know." She smiled. "That's why Mike trusts you."

Chapter Three

J.W.

My windows on the modern world of television, movies, and contemporary music were in the forms of Jill and Jen Skye, the twin daughters of Professor John Skye and his wife, Mattie. The twins would be going back to college in the fall, but now had summer work on the island and were living with their parents on the family farm. So after Jake Spitz left me with directions on how to find Evangeline the next day, I phoned the farm to discover as much as I could about Evangeline.

Mattie answered and from her I learned that John, having finally finished his magnum opus, a new and definitive translation of *Gawain and the Green Knight,* was now researching his next project: a world history of swordsmanship. John had been a three-weapon man in college, and his old foil, épée, and saber were triangulated below his mask, high on the wall of his Vineyard library.

I also learned that Jen was working an evening shift at an Edgartown restaurant, but that Jill was home. When she came to the phone and I asked her if she could keep a confidence, she assured me that she could, speaking in very grown-up, university tones.

When I told her about my driving job, and asked her to tell me about Evangeline, Jill's college-woman persona instantly vanished. "Evangeline? Evangeline! Is she here? Really? Wow!"

"Zee also said wow," I said.

For the next several minutes I listened to Jill extol the obviously, to her, immortal significance and fame of Evangeline. Evangeline was a comet in the firmament of pop music heaven, a force to be reckoned with since her early teens when she'd first appeared on the music scene. She was totally wild and independent, infuriatingly talented as both a singer and an actress, indifferent to public opinion about both her art and her private life, once poor but now incredibly rich, the owner and inhabitant of her own Scottish castle, the winner of countless awards, the subject of scandalous rumors, and the face on a thousand magazines. At thirty she was twice married and divorced, was the mother of a child by yet another (unidentified) man, and was reportedly now sharing her bed with a movie star whose gender was a matter of great discussion. Was her lover a man or a woman? Evangeline was, in short, the most important singer in the whole world and a star of the first magnitude.

"Are you sure about all that?" I asked Jill.

"Of course! How can you even ask such a thing? You're a hopeless case, J.W.! Evangeline isn't just a star, you know. She has a very spiritual side, too. And she has a tragic past. Some man she can't forget, they say. Isn't that romantic? She can be very deep. I bet you'd like her music if you heard it."

"I think I'll stick to country and western and classical," I said, and switched gears. "Does she have any enemies that you know of?"

"Of course she has enemies! Everyone in the business envies her! And she probably has crazy fans. You know, the kind that shoot you if you're famous! It's dangerous to be famous, you know."

I did know that. "Sad but true," I agreed.

Jill's enthusiasm reemerged. "But you're really going to be her driver? Starting tomorrow? Really?! Can Jen and I see her? Can we be someplace beside the road when you drive by?"

"I don't know where we'll be driving or when. If you want to see her, I think you'll have to buy a ticket to the big show."

She groaned. "Do you know how much those tickets cost? I'd have to spend every cent I've saved all summer!"

"So what? You don't need to go back to college this fall. You can get a job someplace and work all winter instead. There are too many coeds in college already. It's dangerous. Like the guy said, giving an education to a woman is like giving a knife to a baby. You know what I mean?"

"Ha, ha! Very funny. Not!" Then her tone became artificially sweet. "Oh, J.W., do you think that you, my favorite person in the whole world, might be able to get a couple of tickets for us? If Evangeline likes you, maybe she'll get some for you, and you can give them to my sister and me. That would be very sweet of you, dear J.W."

"Are you fluttering your lashes?"

"Absolutely. And I have an adoring look on my face."

"I'm trying to imagine it."

"I can't believe she's here and you're going to meet her!"

"Try not to spread the news. I'm told that Evangeline likes her privacy. If you talk to everybody about her being here, she'll have reporters and photographers following her wherever she goes."

"I don't know if can keep it to myself! I just *have* to tell Jen, and I have to tell Mom and Dad!"

I thought of the old saw that two can keep a secret if one of them is dead, and was sure that knowledge of Evangeline's presence was already being whispered like wind through dry grass. Maybe I'd made a mistake in phoning the Skyes.

"Well," said Zee when I finished the call. "Do you now know everything you need to know about your charge?"

"I know enough to get started, at least. According to Jill, she's the empress of ice cream."

"I never did understand that poem."

"Me, too. And it's not the only one. Anyway, I'll know more tomorrow than I know now. I'll give you a full report."

"She'll probably want to spirit you away to her Scottish castle when the big show is over. She likes men, they say."

"Maybe women, too, according to Jill. But if she tries it I'll just tell her that I've already been spirited away by you, and one spiritization in a lifetime is quite enough, thank you." I leered at her.

"Is 'spiritization' a real word?"

"If it isn't, it should be. May I spirit you to our boudoir?"

She smiled at me and rose from her chair. "You may, but I think that the term, properly used, refers to a lady's private bedroom, not one shared by a man."

"You're very language-sensitive tonight. Have you been reading the dictionary again?"

"It's a good book even though it's short on plot."

In bed, I ran a hand over her hip and down her sleek thigh.

She made a humming sound and put her arms around me. "How long do you think this will take?" she asked, biting my neck lightly.

"No longer than all night," I said. "I have to pick up Evangeline in the morning."

Evangeline, according to Spitz and his map, was staying in a large house on the shore of the Edgartown Great Pond, not too far east from the house where Joe and Myra Callahan had lived during their presidential summer vacations, and not much farther from the Peter Fredericks estate, where the Celebration for Humanity was to be held.

Peter Fredericks was the most notorious castle builder on Martha's Vineyard, where castle building had become a sport among the purchasers of island real estate. The normal pattern of building began with the purchase of some already outsize and highly priced house. The house was then torn down and replaced by one that was even bigger and more ornate. Peter Fredericks had lifted the already high bar by purchasing eighty acres of pond-front land and building a fifteen-thousand-square-foot house on it, plus a five-car garage and various outbuildings.

Even his wealthy neighbors had objected to such a project taking place within sight of their own massive houses, claiming piously that his mansion was inappropriate to its location, since it altered the precious island ambiance in some vital way that theirs did not. Fredericks did not personally stoop to public argument but allowed his lawyers to speak, and prevail, on his behalf.

And now on a onetime sheep pasture beside his three-mile-long driveway, a massive temporary stage was being erected upon which the Celebration for Humanity stars would perform in front of the thousands of fans fortunate enough to have tickets.

The Fredericks estate was actually an excellent choice

for the gala since the Great Pond provided protection from the south and east and the driveway was the only road leading to the sheep pasture. Once the woods and the beaches were filled with public and private security agents, as they surely would be soon, if they were not already, ticketless fans and other intruders would have little chance of joining the celebs and paying customers.

Getting to Evangeline's house proved almost as difficult. The next morning I turned into the road leading to her house and was immediately stopped by a young Edgartown cop who had been sitting in the shade of a tent off to the right. He clearly had the duty of preventing undesirables from intruding upon Evangeline's privacy. He looked serious but happy, and I suspected he was a fan who was glad to make some extra pay guarding his idol.

"Sorry, J.W.," he said, "but this road is closed except to homeowners."

"No, it's okay, Marty," said Spitz, coming out of the tent. "J.W.'s going to be the Lady Evangeline's driver while she's on the island. You're early, J.W."

"I can go home again and come back later. Is Evangeline a late sleeper?"

"Evangeline now has a code name," said Spitz. "She's Ethel Price. You can call her Mrs. Price."

"Price is okay," I said, "but Ethel? Nobody's named Ethel anymore. I think Ethel Barrymore was the last Ethel in America. Anybody who hears me call her Ethel will know right away that it's a fake name."

Spitz looked away, then looked back. "It was her mother's name. She picked it herself, so get used to it."

"Hey, if she wants a name that sounds like a maiden great-aunt, it's all right with me."

"Do you want this job or not?"

"The money's too good to miss. All right, she's Mrs. Ethel Price for the duration."

"Good." He gave me a cell phone and an ID card with my picture on it. I seemed to have become a government agent of some kind.

"Where'd you get my photo and signature?"

"Your tax dollars at work. Wave that at anybody who gives you trouble or call that number at the bottom if you need help for any reason."

I wondered why I might need help.

"Okay," he said, "now follow the signs to the Carberg house and exchange this trusty, rusty old Land Cruiser for the Explorer with tinted windows that you'll find there. Introduce yourself to the lady. She knows you're coming and has a photograph of you."

I rattled down the long sandy road until I came to the Carberg house. Sure enough, there was a new white Ford Explorer in front of the garage. I parked beside it.

The Carberg house was rambling and comfortable-looking. It was shingled in graying cedar and sported at least three fireplaces. By Fredericks standards it was not an impressive structure, but by mine it was a five-star hotel.

Through the open breezeway linking the garage to the house I could see a dock leading out into the Edgartown Great Pond. Tied to it were a small open boat with an outboard motor, and a Laser sailboat. A canoe was pulled up on the beach. They were modest vessels, but ample enough for fun on the Great Pond, where people did not care for large, noisy motorboats.

Clearly the Carbergs were Pond People, one of the Vineyard's cultural subgroups. The Pond People lived on the edges of the island's several great ponds along the south shore and, like other more or less self-contained social groups such as the Campground People in Oak Bluffs, kept to themselves and were generally unknown to the thousands of summer tourists who filled the ferries sailing to and from the island.

Peter Fredericks now had a home on a pond, but he had a ways to go to become a Pond Person. He would have to overcome the size of his new house and the resentment of his Pond People neighbors before he qualified. It would probably take years, if not a lifetime.

I opened the door of the white Explorer and saw that the keys were in the ignition. Tsk-tsk. I put them in my pocket and went to the front door. It was opened by a tough-looking man wearing sandals and a loose shirt over his summer shorts. There was a bulge under the shirt on his right side, about belt level. I showed him the ID card that Spitz had given me.

He looked at it, then at me, then at it, then at me. Then he nodded and showed me his teeth in what was meant to pass as a smile.

"Hi," he said. "Glad to know you, Mr. Jackson. I'm Hale Drummand. Come in. Mrs. Price is on the back porch."

He put out a hand, which I took. His was hard. We had a short gripping contest before calling it a draw and separating.

I followed him along a hall and out into the bright morning sun. To the south, across the Great Pond, was the barrier beach, beyond which the glittering Atlantic rolled away to the horizon.

A woman wearing summer clothes was sitting on the veranda drinking coffee and looking at the water. She turned at the sound of our footsteps and stood up.

My heart jumped. Her eyes were hidden behind dark glasses, but she was the first woman I'd ever seen who was as beautiful as Zee. She smiled and the world brightened still more.

"You're Mr. Jackson. Hello."

She put out her hand and I took it. Some sort of energy passed between us.

"My friends call me J.W.," I said. "And you're Mrs. Price."

"My friends call me Ethel. Please sit down. Hale, will you find another cup for Mr. Jackson, please?"

He left, frowning slightly. While he was gone, she and I studied each other silently. Both of us were almost smiling.

Drummand came back and put a cup down in front of me.

"Thank you, Hale," said the woman.

He made a small bow. I had the impression that his teeth were pressed tightly together. He went into the house.

Evangeline poured coffee into her cup and mine. Even while doing such a simple thing she radiated a glamour I'd rarely experienced. I saw that it would be easy to become a knight-at-arms, alone and palely loitering. Perhaps Hale Drummand already was.

She removed her glasses. Her eyes were a hypnotic pale gray, slanted slightly upward at the corners.

"Agent Spitz has told me about you," she said in her contralto voice.

"I've been told something about you as well," I said.

"He said you know this island well, and that you're married to a woman you love and that you have children."

"That's true."

"He said something else that's even more important. You can be trusted."

I said nothing.

"I want to see your island but I also want to find a man who's living here," she said. "I need someone who can find him and say nothing about it afterward. Someone who can be discreet."

"I can probably manage that."

She sipped her coffee. "You don't make too many extravagant claims about your virtue, do you? Should I have you take an oath?"

"I don't have much faith in oaths. It's the honor of the person that guarantees the power of the oath, not the other way around."

She smiled and nodded. "Very good. Another question, then. Do you have a pistol?"

"Jake Spitz suggested I carry one, but he was pretty vague as to why."

"Because now I can leave Hale at home with my daughter when we go for our rides. He can protect her and you can protect me."

"From what?"

"Rich people and famous people always need protection," she said in a matter-of-fact voice. "And I'm both of those. Let me find a wig and a sweater and we'll be on our way. Finish your coffee. I'll be right back."

It was good coffee. It was true that rich and famous people often needed protection, but I wondered if there might be more to her situation than that.

She was back in a very few minutes sporting a reddish wig that, combined with her huge dark glasses, made her look like a day-trip tourist if you didn't look twice. If you did look twice you could see that she was nothing at all like a day-tripper or any other kind of tourist, but that she was a woman unlike any you'd ever seen before.

"Very Vineyardish, Mrs. Price," I said, getting up. "Where would you like to go first?"

"Call me Ethel, J.W. How about the grand two-dollar tour?"

Hale Drummand did not look happy when Evangeline informed him that he'd be staying at home with little Jane.

I got a map out of my truck, unfolded it, and gave Evangeline a brief geography lesson before handing the map to her. Armed and dangerous, I then drove us to Edgartown and through its lovely, narrow streets, past the flower-filled yards and great captain's houses. I pointed across the harbor.

"That's Chappaquiddick over there. You can get there by that little three-car ferry, the On Time. One story is that it's called the On Time because it doesn't have a schedule and is therefore always on time."

"Is Chappaquiddick worth a visit?"

"It is to fishermen, and the Dyke Bridge is still the most famous tourist spot on the Vineyard. We can go over there later, if you like. Out on the far beaches there's good fishing. Are you a fisherperson?"

"I have a salmon stream on my property in Scotland. I lease some of it to an angling club. Are you a fisherman?"

"I am."

I showed her the twenty-two-million-dollar house out on Starbuck Neck, and she said it was very nice but she didn't comment on the price as most people do. Why should she, when she owned a Scottish castle?

I drove her through the Oak Bluffs Campground and then around East Chop and West Chop, giving her a running commentary as we went. She asked intelligent questions and was interested in little things such as the four-color paint jobs on the campground's gingerbread houses.

Then we went up-island to Menemsha, where I got the island's best fried clams and calamari from The Bite and we ate them in the car. When the fries were gone, we drove on to Aquinnah, where, to my surprise, I actually found a parking space at the cliffs.

"Do you want to get out and take a look?" I asked. "Or would you rather not?"

She adjusted her wig and glasses. "Let's get out."

We walked up between the souvenir shops and the fast food shops until we got to the top. It was a good day for looking, and I pointed out the Elizabeth Islands to the north, Point Judith, Rhode Island on the far western horizon, and Nomans Land to the south. The blue sea was alive with boats.

Tourists, mostly silver-haired or bald, were all around us, but not one seemed to notice that Evangeline was among them.

"This is as far west as we can go," I said to her. "Now we'll head back toward home."

"Can you take me to Indian Hill Road?"

The request surprised me. "Sure. There's a terrific stone wall being built there. My favorite one on the whole island."

"Let's go there."

"Shall we sightsee on the way?"

"All right. You live on a beautiful island."

I drove back through Chilmark and down to West Tisbury, where I stopped and we walked among the dancing statues in the field across from the general store.

"Can I buy some of these? They're completely charming! I know just where to put them on my grounds!"

"I'm sure you can," I said. Everything is for sale if the price is right.

"You can bring me back here another day, and I'll do it." Her smile was brilliant. She took my arm in hers. "I love them all!"

When she became aware of her arm in mine and stepped away, I felt a sense of loss.

"Is it far to Indian Hill Road?"

"No part of the island is far from any other part. Do you want to go there now?"

"Yes."

"I'll show you on the map."

I did that, then drove through North Tisbury toward Vineyard Haven and took a couple of lefts. "This is it," I said.

She seemed both uneasy and excited, and looked this way and that as we drove. I pointed out the long, lovely stone wall that had been under construction for years, and told her how stone wall builders were now in such popular demand on the island that stones had to be imported from New Hampshire to keep them all busy. But she wasn't interested in stone walls, she was interested in driveways.

But she didn't see or didn't recognize the one she wanted. When we came to the end of the paved road, I turned the car around.

"Are you looking for someone or some place in particular?"

"Yes. Alain Duval. I thought he had a place on this road, but I don't see his name anywhere." She touched her teeth to her bottom lip and for a fleeting instant looked like a young girl.

The name was a familiar one. I was sure Duval was the person she had mentioned that morning. "I can probably find him for you," I said.

She gave me a look of gratitude that would have made

a slave of Caesar. "It's important to me that I see him." Then she added, "But I don't want anyone to know. It's . . . a private matter."

"I'll see what I can manage."

She had a sense of distance and space, and she could read a map. By the time we got back to her house that afternoon, she seemed to know where she was and where she'd been.

And I hadn't had to shoot a single person.

"See you tomorrow, same time," she said as I was going toward my truck.

A small girl came running from the house and Evangeline stooped to catch her and swung her up in her arms. In the doorway Hale Drummand watched and then turned back out of sight.

Zee was already home when I got there. I kissed her, then did it again, to make sure.

"Well, well," she said, smiling up at me. "That was very nice."

"I agree. Do you happen to know how to find Alain Duval?" I asked. "My client wants to visit him."

Zee raised her brows in recognition. "The Guru of the Stars? Isn't his summer shrine up-island someplace? His Temple of Light is out in Hollywood, I know. I read once that it's made mostly of glass. He may have an ad in the local papers. Try looking there. Or maybe he's in the phone book. Even holy men have cell phones these days."

Duval wasn't listed in the phone book and I didn't find any ads for his shrine in that week's papers, but I figured I could find him anyway. After all, thousands of other people had managed it over the years. Of course their quests had been spiritual and mine wasn't, but so what?

Chapter Four

Brady

As I drove back to Boston from my visit with Mike and Neddie Doyle, I tried to imagine going two years without hearing from one of my sons. It was unimaginable.

Most runaways, I knew, were fleeing unbearable family situations. They had drug problems, or abusive parents, or the wrong friends, or babies in their bellies. Often all of those things. They headed for big cities. Los Angeles was the number one destination for runaways. More than a million teenagers ran away every year. Three-quarters of them were girls, and nearly half of them ended up as prostitutes. A large number of them were never found. Those that were often turned up dead.

Tracking down Christa Doyle—if she was still alive—and convincing her to go home to say good-bye to her dying father promised to be a difficult and unpleasant job with an unhappy outcome, and I wished Mike and Neddie hadn't asked me to do it. But there was no way I could've turned them down.

When I got back to my apartment on the Boston waterfront, I made myself a tuna fish sandwich, poured a glass of Sam Adams, sat at my kitchen table, and opened the manila envelope that Neddie had given to me.

I looked at Christa's photo again, and again I saw a pretty teenage girl with her arm around her father's waist. Nothing in that photo made me think of drugs or pregnancy or abuse.

The investigator in Eugene, Oregon, was a guy named Harold Rubin. His report was sketchy and designed, it seemed to me, to justify his fee. He charged $200 per hour plus expenses. He claimed to have spent seven hours and forty minutes on the telephone. He racked up 1,459 miles on his car's odometer and fifty-nine hours on the road. He spent three nights in motels and ate thirteen meals away from home. He sent out thirty-two faxes and placed notices in seven newspapers.

Rubin had been dogged enough. He talked with all the police departments, hospitals, and morgues in eastern Oregon, checked out all the bus depots and shelters and youth hostels from Eugene to Portland, showed Christa's photo to all the pimps and predators and street people he knew and offered them a thousand bucks for a lead that panned out.

A bus driver thought he recognized Christa, said he'd taken her to Corvallis. There a cop remembered seeing a girl who resembled her hitchhiking east. A waitress at a café, and then a gas-station attendant, and then a motel clerk, and then a truck driver directed Rubin to what he called "a hippie commune" in the Willamette National Forest.

None of the hippies would admit that they'd ever seen Christa. Rubin didn't believe them. He offered them money for information. They took the money and told him that, well, yes, now that they thought of it, Christa had been with them for a while, but she'd left a couple weeks ago in the company of some man they said they couldn't name or describe.

Rubin suspected they were lying. He figured either they'd never seen her or that she was still there, hiding from the well-dressed stranger who'd pulled up in the brand-new Lincoln Town Car.

Rubin spent two days hiding in the hills with binoculars trained on the grubby settlement of tents and lean-tos and never spied Christa Doyle.

And that was that. The trail had dried up. If she'd ever been there, which he concluded was doubtful, she wasn't anymore.

I put down Harold Rubin's report and stared out the glass sliders that looked down from my sixth-floor apartment onto Boston Harbor. A brisk afternoon breeze riffled the water, and the gulls and terns were wheeling on the thermals.

I found the envelope that held Christa's last letter to her parents. It was handwritten and covered both sides of a sheet of blank typing paper. Most of it was an angry rant that amounted to an indictment of her parents' wealth and their failure to give their daughter spiritual and moral guidance. It sounded canned, as if she were paraphrasing some slick New Age self-help psychobabble.

Was it possible Christa was still with the hippies in the Oregon woods? The fact that Rubin had spent two days spying on them without spotting her didn't mean much. They could easily have known he was still lurking around and kept Christa out of sight until he'd left.

I looked at my watch. Two in the afternoon, which would make it 11 A.M. in Eugene, Oregon. Rubin's phone number was at the top of the letterhead on his report. I dialed it and got his voice mail. It announced that Mr. Rubin was out of the country for the month of August and gave the name of an agency the caller could contact. It didn't say whether Rubin was checking his voice mail or not.

On the chance that he was, I left him a message reminding him of the Christa Doyle case. I told him who I was and what I was doing, and I told him Mike Doyle was dying fast, that time was, as they say, of the essence, and asked him to call me back as soon as possible if he got my message.

I figured I wouldn't hear from Harold Rubin. Strike one.

I went to the refrigerator for another Sam, fetched my portable phone from the living room, returned to the kitchen table, sighed, and took out the list of names Neddie had given me.

There were twenty-seven. Neddie had identified each one with a word or two: "friend from school," "teacher," "neighbor," "cousin." Most of them were friends from school from the days when the Doyles lived in Belmont, Massachusetts. If they were Christa's age, they'd probably be out of high school now.

In my business, I've dealt with a lot of private investigators. They all say the same thing about their work: It's always boring, sometimes dangerous, rarely rewarding, and terminally soul-killing. Private investigators spend most of their professional lives speed-dialing telephones, surfing the Internet, and slouching in parked automobiles. They drink too much Coke, eat too many Tums, tell too many lies, dream too many nightmares, alienate too many of their friends and relatives.

Well, it had to be done.

I took out my Greater Boston phone book, started at the top of the list Neddie had given me, and began calling. More often than not I got voice mail or an answering machine, not surprising in the middle of a Saturday afternoon in August. I declined to leave any messages. I scratched an *X* beside those names. I'd try them again, and keep trying until I talked to somebody.

When anybody answered, I said the same thing: "My name is Brady Coyne. I'm a lawyer working with Mike and Neddie Doyle, and we hope you might be able to help us. We're wondering if you might have talked to or heard from their daughter, Christa, lately."

They all said about the same thing: They remembered Christa but had lost touch with her when she moved to New Hampshire. All of them asked what the problem was. I told them it was a family matter, and I used a tone that suggested I had no intention of elaborating.

I had only four names left on my list when a "friend from school" named Alyssa Romano hesitated a couple beats too many before she said, "Christa? Um, no. I haven't heard from Christa."

"Alyssa," I said, "Christa's father is dying of a terrible disease. He's got about a month to live, and he's desperate to know that she's okay. If you know anything at all . . ."

There was a long pause at the end of the line. I was afraid she was going to hang up. Then, in a soft voice, she said, "I promised her I wouldn't tell."

"Christa? You talked to her? Have you seen her?"

"Is that true? Mr. Doyle is dying?"

"Yes, it is. That's why I'm trying to reach Christa. Please. What can you tell me?"

"Geez. He was a pretty cool guy." She hesitated. "She made me swear I wouldn't say anything to her parents."

"I'm not her parents," I said.

"But you'll tell them, right?"

"Yes, I will. Don't you think they have a right to know? They've been worried sick about Christa for two years."

"I don't know what I should do. I wish you hadn't called me."

"Alyssa," I said, "you have the opportunity to do a good thing. The right thing."

"But I promised."

"You promised you wouldn't tell her parents. Telling me is different."

"Not really."

"Where is she, Alyssa?"

"I don't want Christa to know I broke my promise."

"I won't tell her. I give you my word."

"Her parents must be awfully sad."

"They are," I said. "Terribly sad."

She hesitated, then said, "Christa's down on the Vineyard."

"Martha's Vineyard?"

"Yes. She called me a few days ago. She's been calling me every now and then ever since she . . . she left home. We were best friends when she lived around here."

"What has she told you?"

"Nothing, really. It's like she doesn't want me to know anything. Honestly, I don't know why she calls me. It's like, I don't know, she needs a friend or something. She just asks what I'm doing, that's all. When I ask her about herself, she just goes, 'Oh, nothing much, it's boring,' and changes the subject."

"What's she doing on the Vineyard?"

"Like I said, I don't really know. She kind of let it slip that she was there when we were talking. Said something about the Celebration for Humanity, that world peace thing they're having on the Vineyard, all the singers and famous people. When I asked her something about it, she clammed up."

"Do you have a phone number for her?"

"No."

"An address? The name of somebody? Do you know which town she's in? If she has a job?"

"No, no, Mr. Coyne. Nothing like that. All I can tell you is, she was on the Vineyard a few days ago. I said I'd like to go down, spend a day or two with her, or maybe go to the Celebration with her, and she said no, that wouldn't work. That's all I know."

"It wouldn't work," I repeated. "As if she might be leaving?"

"It didn't really sound like that. More like she was busy, had other friends. I guess she just didn't want to see me. I don't know what's up with Christa. She's pretty weird."

"Weird how?"

"I don't know. When I knew her, when she was living here in Belmont, she was fun, you know? We made jokes and stuff. We laughed a lot. She had a great mom and dad. I used to be a little jealous. Anyways, since she left, whenever I talk with her, it's like, she hates her parents, and everything is so serious."

"You mean you talk about serious things?"

"No, not like that. Just her tone. She *sounds* serious, you know? We don't really ever talk about anything."

I asked Alyssa Romano a few more questions, but she didn't have any more insight. As far as she knew, Christa was on Martha's Vineyard for the Celebration for Humanity, and that was it. I gave her my phone number and urged her to call me if she thought of anything, and I asked her not to tell Christa she'd spoken to me if they talked again. She promised.

I hoped she'd keep her promise to me, even if she'd broken her promise to Christa. Now that I knew where she was, I didn't want to spook her.

For a minute or two I felt triumphant. In about two hours I'd discovered that Christa Doyle was alive, which all by itself was a cause for exultation, and I'd narrowed my search for her down from the entire world to a little island less than a two hours' drive and a forty-minute ferry ride from my apartment. That, I thought, was damn good work for an amateur sleuth.

Then I began thinking about the work I still faced. Finding somebody who didn't want to be found on Martha's Vineyard in August, when the island swarmed with Summer People, was needle-in-a-haystack stuff. And this particular August, when the Celebration for Humanity, or whatever it was called, was coming up would make it even harder.

Well, if anybody could do it, it was J. W. Jackson.

J.W. was an ex–Boston cop who'd gotten shot, retired on his disability, moved to the Vineyard, married a beautiful islander named Zee, and sired a couple of nice kids. If you asked J.W. what he did, he'd tell you he was a fisherman, but I happened to know that he did some investigating now and then. He and I were friends. We fished together a couple times every year. Once we even worked on a case together.

I called his number. No answer, naturally. I didn't really expect the Jacksons to be home on a pretty summer Saturday afternoon. They'd be out with their kids in their catboat or surf casting off the Chappie beaches or raking quahogs in one of the saltwater ponds.

I kept trying, and a half hour later Zee answered. She sounded happy to hear my voice and asked if I wanted to come down, do some fishing. The bonito and false albacore had started to show up, she said, and there were always stripers around.

I told her I'd rather wait till after Labor Day, when the Summer People went back to America, and she said she didn't blame me, it was Grand Central Station down there. Anytime I wanted. They always had a bed for me at their house.

"I bet you want to talk to J.W.," she said.

"Is he around?"

"Nope. He's driving his, um, friend Evangeline around the island."

"Evangeline?" I said. "You mean the singer?"

"Yep. Can you believe it?"

"Sure. Some people have all the luck, and J.W. is one of them."

"Don't tell anybody," she said. "It's supposed to be hush-hush. I'll have him call you when he gets in."

J.W. called an hour later. "What's up?" he said.

"I've got a job for you. Right up your alley."

"I'm retired, remember?"

"So what are you doing driving the world's most glamorous singer around? They paying you for that?"

"Bet your ass," he said. "You don't think I'd do something like this for nothing, do you?"

"Listen," I said. "What I've got is a more important job." I told him about Mike and Neddie Doyle, how I'd tracked Christa down to the Vineyard, and how all I wanted was for J.W. to locate her for me so I could go down and talk to her.

"For the next week or so," he said, "the best I can do is

keep an eye out for her. You want real sleuthing, I can't help you. I'm joined to Evangeline at the hip for about ten hours a day, seven days a week."

"One hip or two?"

"Ha," he said.

"That doesn't sound so hard," I said. "She's an attractive woman."

"Oh, she's attractive," he said. "That doesn't make it easy."

"You can't do this for me, then?"

"Brady, believe me, I would if I could."

"Know anybody who can?" I said.

He was quiet for a minute. "Every cop and spare security man on the island is working overtime, babysitting important people, guarding mansions, stuff like that. You send some PI down here who doesn't know his way around, he'll never get anywhere." He cleared his throat. "There's only one guy I can think of who might be up to the job."

"Yeah?" I said. "Who's that?"

"Stick out your forefinger," he said, "and aim it at your face."

"Me?" I laughed. "Hell, I'm no investigator. Anyway, I did my part of the job. I found out Christa was down there."

"You know your way around here as well as any off-islander," said J.W. "You've got a place to stay and a car to use and a couple of savvy local consultants."

"The consultants being you and Zee."

"Right."

"The place to stay being your place."

"Of course. Anytime."

"Your car?"

"It's just sitting there rusting. They've given me a nice new Ford Explorer to drive the lady around in."

"I really don't want to do this," I said.

"Ah, we'll have a good time. Maybe even get out in the evening, catch some fish."

"You'll help me?"

"Like I said, I'll consult with you, and so will Zee. I'll make some phone calls for you, if you want. I can't sleuth around, except maybe after dark when I've tucked Evangeline in for the night."

I hemmed and hawed, but in the end I told J.W. I'd be on the noon ferry the next day. He said he'd have Zee pick me up at the dock in Vineyard Haven, and he'd meet me on their balcony for martinis around suppertime.

Chapter Five

J.W.

The next morning, while we read the *Globe* at breakfast, Zee agreed to drive me in the Land Cruiser over to the Carberg house so she could bring back my rusty vehicle for Brady's use after she installed him in our guest room.

"I'm delighted to assist you in the performance of your obligations to the world's most famous pop star," she said.

"A man's gotta do what a man's gotta do. The fact that she's one of the richest, most famous, sexiest, and most beautiful women in the world has nothing to do with my dedication to my work."

She looked toward heaven. "Save me, Lord!"

A guy I know says that in California people don't just belong to one out-of-the-mainstream spiritual or medical system or sect, but to at least two and sometimes to more. They pray, meditate, exercise, and eat according to several different disciplines at the same time. Oriental and Native American rituals and healing rites are particularly popular. California, the guy says, is the navel of the New Age.

If so, the New Age has two navels and Martha's Vineyard is the second one. One of its year-round industries is catering to seekers of cosmic comfort and alternate medical cures. If you open any island newspaper or magazine you will find ads and sometimes articles concerning Buddhist meditation, aromatherapy, kung fu, hypnotherapy, acupuncture, alternative psychotherapies, tai chi, past-life regression, Black Elk's vision, sun worship, yoga, animal communication, holistic medical practices, dance therapy, medicine drum therapy, writing therapy, art therapy, palm reading, card reading, tea ceremonies, and other mystical and magical arts and procedures.

One of the most fashionable of such practices was centered at what its adherents called a Temple of Light, more humbly referred to by its founder, Alain Duval, as simply "the ashram."

I had never seen the ashram, and if I'd seen Alain Duval I didn't know it, but I'd certainly heard of both.

Duval, according to his critics, had amassed a fortune by offering dubious spiritual counseling and guidance to a vast number of people from all walks of life. He was also said to have accepted or expected or even demanded sexual favors from the more attractive of his women followers. His enemies took pleasure from recent gossip that the master was beginning to fall from favor, and were quick to circulate and expand upon that and all other negative rumors concerning Duval.

Such criticism and hearsay surrounding leaders both sacred and profane are not unusual, of course, and don't necessarily have any foundation in fact, although it is far from unknown for persons of lofty reputation to have feet of clay and to fall from favor.

According to Duval's aficionados, known to themselves as the Followers of the Light, or simply the Followers, he lived a modest, almost saintly life, and had given all money donated to the ashram to the poor and needy. His personal needs, they said, were few and simple, and to meet them he literally depended on whatever alms were dropped in a bowl at the ashram's doorway. Any donations not needed by Duval that day were passed on to those in greater need, and no woman ever experienced more than a purely spiritual love from the master.

Duval, I'd read in the local papers, was a principal instigator of the Celebration for Humanity. He was not only a religious figure, but was also known to wield influence in the political, the economic, and the entertainment worlds. Who better, in spite of rumors of his decline or womanizing, to persuade the great and the powerful to come together in an unprecedented gathering to dramatize Western civilization's refusal to bow before the world's terrorists, and indeed to promise the inevitable triumph of democracy and freedom?

Heady stuff, but I didn't even know where the ashram was located other than what I'd heard yesterday from Evangeline while driving up and down Indian Hill Road. It was a price I paid for being spiritually undeveloped, not to say irreligious. I only went to church when a good musical program was on the bill.

But you don't have to be religious to find a church, so I made a phone call to Father Joe Gould, who kept track of the island's other religious activities when he wasn't tending to his own.

"You're interrupting my breakfast," said Father Joe. "I suppose you know that."

"You shouldn't sleep so late," I said. "I'll make this quick because I know it's unwise to get between a priest and his orange juice and omelet. How do I find the Temple of Light up in Chilmark?"

"Why? Are you planning on abandoning your sinful way of life and becoming a Follower? If you are, I can offer you a church that's a lot older than Alain Duval's hodgepodge."

"I thought all religions were hodgepodges."

"His is messier than most. A tidbit from India, a symbol from China, a prayer from the Middle East. All very mystical, but not of a piece. If you want consistency, come to St. Elizabeth's."

"Spend more of your money on good music and I might. Where can I find Mr. Duval and his ashram?"

"I believe that's Master Duval, not Mister Duval. His Vineyard shrine is off of Indian Hill Road on the old Exeter estate. I think the whole place has been turned over to Duval and his ashram. Why can't I get a deal like that? Is it because nobody calls me the Truth and the Light, like they do him?"

"That could be it. But how can you ask for more? You already have church ladies waiting on you hand and foot, cleaning your house, cooking your meals, treating you as though you actually know what you're doing."

"I do know what I'm doing. Right now, for instance, I know I'm trying to have a quiet breakfast while I watch the morning news."

"No wonder they say that the church is in decline. I leave you in the hands of God."

"It's a good place to be."

When Zee drove me to the Carberg house, another young Edgartown cop had replaced Marty at the head of the driveway. I showed her my nifty new ID card and she waved us by. At the house, Zee dropped me off and gave me a kiss.

"Do your manly duty, however painful."

"I could not love thee, dear, so much, loved I not honor more."

"Lovelace would be proud. Brady and I will see you tonight for cocktails if you're not too busy with your pop star to join us."

"You might like her if you met her."

"But I haven't met her."

As Zee drove away in my Land Cruiser, Evangeline came out of the house. Behind her, Hale Drummand stared broodingly after her then went back inside.

"Right on time," she said to me, smiling. She was wearing a different wig, different dark glasses, and casual clothes that failed to disguise a figure that I found very fine. She looked after the departing Toyota. "Who was that?"

"That was my wife. My own truck won't be available for a few days, so I'll be taking this Explorer home at night if that's okay with you."

"That will be fine. Hale has a car of his own if we should need it after you're gone in the evening."

"Thanks." We got into the white Ford. "What's your pleasure today? I can take you to Alain Duval's ashram, if you want to go there."

"That's fast work. How'd you locate it?" The pleasure in her voice sounded forced to me.

"I have friends in high places. Shall we?"

She hesitated, then said, "Yes, but later. First, take me to the stage. I want to see the setup and talk with people there about the program, and especially about the sound system. I don't want to work with bad sound."

"You haven't been down there?"

"No. I just got here the evening before we met. Do you know the way?"

"I know about where it is. It won't be hard to find. The road will be the one protected by the First Airborne Division."

In fact, it wasn't guarded by the 1st Airborne but by a couple of police cars, some island cops, and some civilians who looked just like federal agents.

I showed my valuable ID card to anyone who wanted to see it while Evangeline sat beside me pretending to read a movie fan magazine. If any of the guards recognized her, none of them said so.

Finally waved through, we drove down the long paved driveway that led to Peter Fredericks's eighty acres of prime Vineyard property. From time to time we passed other security people, who eyed us as they held their cell phones to their ears. If anyone managed to smash through the security at the front gate, he'd still never make it to the stage in the sheep pasture.

When we came to the pasture and its towering stage, we found a lot of busy people doing things. Carpenters were hammering and sawing, wires were being strung, a crew from the electric company was rigging temporary power lines in from the highway, and another crew was working on a huge generator at the far end of the field, just in case the power lines failed.

Sound people had set up speakers, light people were rigging strobes, and what I guessed was a group of pyrotechnicians was standing by a truck decorated with pictures of fireworks, calculating the best way to detonate the grand finale without starting a forest fire.

The scene reminded me of an anthill. Every person seemed to know what he or she was doing, but I hadn't the slightest idea how to make sense of it all.

Evangeline, on the other hand, knew exactly where to

go and whom to see. I followed her as she went through the many busy people directly to a middle-aged man wearing a tennis cap. He was sitting in a small van totally filled with electronic equipment. A large glass window in front of him looked toward the stage. Beyond him a younger man with glasses and a ponytail was doing something with the dials on a panel.

"How's it going, Harry?" Evangeline swung lithely up into the van. There didn't seem to be much room for anyone else inside, so I stood guard by the open rear doors.

Harry looked up, squinted, and said, "Sorry, lady, but no civilians allowed."

She whipped off her dark glasses and smiled. He squinted some more, then grinned. "Vangie! Is that you, darlin'? Give us a kiss!" She did that and he returned it. "I heard you were coming, kid, but I thought you were still across the briny in that castle of yours. Say, did you hear your pal Flurge and the Bristol Tars are going to be here, too?"

She nodded. "Why do you think I came? Flurge asked me to. The Bristol Tars and I are the last act on Saturday. We're gonna do our thing together and then get everybody else up onstage to join in. People will be dancing in the aisles and screaming so loud they won't even be able to hear us or the fireworks going off. It's going to be something nobody's ever seen before!"

"That's what they say. Beamed around the world."

She peered deeper into the truck. "Where's Scott? I thought you two were joined at the hip."

Harry shook his head. "Scott tied one on and drove his car into a tree just a couple of days before he was supposed to come east and hook up with me here. Busted himself up pretty good. Just lucky for me that Frank, here, came by about that time looking for work. Let me introduce you two." Harry gestured at the man beyond him. "This is Frank Dyer, Ev. This is the one and only Evangeline. Say hello."

Frank had to stare for a moment before he got his hello out.

Evangeline gave him her hand. "Hi," she said. "I always like to stay on good terms with my soundmen."

Frank retrieved his hand and I had the impression that he was never going to wash it again.

"Frank's local talent," said Harry. "Knows his stuff and everybody on the island, so something breaks or we need something, he knows how to get it in a rush. Don't have to fly it in from the city."

"A good man to have." She smiled at Frank, who seemed hypnotized. Then she looked out the window. "I came by to check out the sound system. I'm pretty damn picky, as you know. You want to go over it with me?"

"Sure. You're gonna like what we're doing. No expenses being spared. There's a lot of big money behind this show, and whatever I've asked for I've got, no questions asked. Right, Frank?"

"Right," said Frank, who had gotten most of his voice back.

Harry and Evangeline stepped out of the van and Evangeline introduced us. "You in the business?" he asked.

"No. I'm a fisherman."

"He's my driver," said Evangeline, putting on her glasses.

"You should have professional security," said Harry, frowning. "It's not good for you to be wandering around without a pro."

"I have a pro at home looking after Janie. J.W.'s my security outside the house."

"Is he, now?" Harry looked at me thoughtfully, then nodded. "Well, lemme show you what we have." And apparently he did that, although the language was Navajo to me. Talking steadily, he gestured at the contents of the van first, then led her, with me following, to the stage and around the edges of the field, where speakers had already been installed and others soon would be.

When he was through, Evangeline smiled. "Looks great, Harry. I knew it would be, with you running things, but you know me; I like to see for myself. When I was a kid I had enough sound system fuckups to last me for my whole career."

"That's what happens when you're starting out, kid, but it won't be happening here. This is the best stuff I've ever hooked up to."

"There's sure a lot of it."

"Most I've ever seen for one show. Frank's been worth his weight in gold. Don't know if I could have done it without him. Knows these speaker systems better than I do and set up all of them by himself. When I retire you better hire him. You could do a lot worse."

"You'll never retire, Harry. Say, I want to see Ogden Warner. You seen him around?"

He frowned. "I thought you and Ogden were on the outs. Ever since that fuss with—"

She interrupted. "That was personal. This is business. He's directing this show and I want to talk to him."

"Okay, Vangie, if you want him you'll find him over yonder in that RV. He's made one end of it into his office. But I warn you: He works at his desk this time of day, and he doesn't like being interrupted."

"Too bad. He give you any grief on this job?"

Harry scowled then grinned. "Does he ever not give people grief? He took one look at Frank and told me to get rid of him. Wouldn't say why, of course. I've seen him do that before: ax somebody he didn't even know just to prove he's boss. But he can't have a show without sound, and I'm the best there is, so I told him I did my own hiring and if he didn't like it I was on my way home. He didn't like that at all, but he walked off."

"Good for you, Harry. Ogden can be a real pain in the ass, all right, but he's like you: the best in the business."

"Yer right, kid, but don't let him pull any fast ones on you."

"That's why I want to see him. To make sure he doesn't. I want my act done the way I want it, and I'm not interested in Ogden's opinion. If you're in touch with Scott, give him my regards and tell him to get well soon. Come on, J.W., let's continue your musical education."

I followed her to an RV parked near the edge of the field. Beyond it, rising above the trees, I could see the top of what looked like a fair-size hotel. I presumed it was Peter Fredericks's famous house. My own house was just barely too big to fit inside one of its chimneys.

Evangeline knocked on the rear door of the RV. There was no response. She didn't hesitate but pushed open the door and went in. I followed.

She stopped just inside and shook her head as she looked at a man seated in a swivel chair, his upper body lying motionless on a desk fronting the chair.

"So that's the kind of work you do at your desk, eh? How can you sleep like that when there's so much to do and all this commotion outside? Hey, Ogden, wake up! Time to go to work!"

But Ogden didn't wake up.

I looked at him, then put my hands on Evangeline's shoulders.

"Stay right here," I said.

I went to Warner and put a finger on his throat. There was no pulse. His eyes were wide and empty. There was a bloody mark around his throat. I went back to Evangeline. She was staring at the man.

"Go to Harry," I said. "If there are any medics around, have him get them over here. Tell him to call the cops, too, and have them bring an ambulance. I think you'll be needing a new director. This one is dead." I kept my gaze level and my voice calm. "I'll wait here until the cops come. Walk, do not run. No reason to get people excited ahead of time."

She never said a word. Instead, she nodded, went out the door, and walked toward the sound truck.

Chapter Six

Brady

After I hung up with J.W., I called Julie, my secretary, at home and told her I was taking a few days off next week and she might as well do the same. She started to protest—we had clients to tend to, after all, court appearances to keep, hours to bill—but when I explained my mission for Mike and Neddie Doyle, she suddenly went silent.

After a minute, I said, "Julie? You there?"

"I'll take care of everything," she said. "You go find that girl and bring her home to those poor parents. Any idea how long you'll be gone?"

"No idea. Until I give up, I guess."

"Don't you even think about giving up, Brady Coyne. You find that girl. I'll clear the calendar for the week, and if it looks like you'll need more time, you just let me know."

I hung up smiling. The only thing Julie considered more important than accruing billable hours and making money was nurturing parent-child relationships, although getting me married and settled down was high on her list of priorities. After several disappointments—Julie's, not necessarily mine—she now had high hopes for Evie Banyon.

Which reminded me: Evie would be arriving around

seven for our regular Saturday-night sleepover. Usually we spent the weekends together. We never planned them. We let them evolve from our moods and the weather and whatever whim occurred to one of us. Just being together was the main point.

Whatever we ended up doing, we always managed to find time to make love.

My first thought was that Evie would be upset when I told her I had to drive down to Woods Hole and catch the ferry to the Vineyard early Sunday morning. Women depend on routines. They like their men to be predictable.

My second thought was that I was projecting. Evie had taught me that I shouldn't base my expectations of her on my experiences with other women. That was unfair to both of us. Evie was Evie, she kept telling me. She wasn't Gloria or Alex or Terri or Sylvie or any of the other women I'd been involved with, and lumping them all together was the worst kind of stereotypical thinking.

Well, we'd see how she reacted.

I had a couple hours before she was due to arrive. So I tucked Christa's photo in my shirt pocket, took the elevator down to the lobby, and headed up Commercial Street to the photocopy shop.

I used the machine that made color copies. I set it for high magnification, and after a couple of experimental tries I was able to block out the foreground and background and Mike Doyle and completely fill the letter-size sheet of paper with Christa's face and the upper half of her body. The original photo was well focused, and the enlargement came out sharp and clear. You could see that Christa had eyes the color of hot fudge and one slightly crooked incisor.

I ran off fifty copies, paid with my credit card, tucked

the copies into the transparent plastic envelope they gave me, and headed home.

I still had an hour before Evie would arrive, so I threw a few days' worth of casual clothes into my small duffel. Jeans, shorts, bathing suit, a few T-shirts and boxers and pairs of socks, a couple flannel shirts, a windbreaker, an extra pair of sneakers, my dop kit, and my dog-eared copy of *Moby-Dick*, my regular bedtime reading.

I also added my good Canon with the zoom lens, my bird-watching binoculars, and my little battery-powered tape recorder, just because it seemed to me that any sleuth, however amateur, should have some gadgets with him.

I decided not to bring my fly-fishing gear. I wanted to travel light, and I figured that if J.W. and I ended up going fishing, I could use one of his surf-casting rods.

I realized I had no idea how long I'd be staying on the Vineyard. Screw it. If I ran out of clean clothes, I'd use the Jacksons' washing machine. If I needed something I didn't have, I'd borrow it from J.W. or buy it down there.

It took me about ten minutes to pack. I used to drive Gloria, my ex-wife, nuts when we were heading for a vacation. She'd spend weeks agonizing over what to bring, trying things on, rejecting them, buying new things and taking them back, packing and unpacking and repacking, and when she was done, she always moaned that she knew she'd forgotten something. Me, I just threw some stuff into a duffel, and when we got to where we were going, I made do with what I had.

I left my bag beside the door, got a beer, and took it out onto my balcony overlooking the harbor, and I guess I dozed off with my feet up on the railing, because the next thing I knew Evie was kissing the back of my neck.

I opened my eyes and she pressed her forehead against

mine. "Hey, big guy," she whispered in that husky voice that never failed to make me shiver.

I kissed her mouth, and we held it for a while. Then she pulled away and sat beside me. She'd fetched two cold bottles of Sam Adams from my refrigerator, and we sat there for a few minutes, sipping beer and watching the airplanes swarm around Logan Airport across the harbor.

"You running out on me?" she said.

"Huh?"

"You're all packed and ready to go. What's up?"

I told her about Christa Doyle and about my meeting with Mike and Neddie and talking to Alyssa Romano. "So I gotta go to the Vineyard," I said. "I'm leaving tomorrow morning. Early."

Evie was quiet for what seemed like a long time. Then she said, "Well, I'll drive you to the ferry."

"Oh, hell, that's not necessary," I said. "I've got to get up early, and it's a long drive. I can leave my car in one of the lots, take the shuttle bus. I have no idea how long I'll be down there."

"You don't get it," she said. "I *want* to drive you. And I want to be there to pick you up when you come back. Do you understand?"

"Me?" I laughed. "Understand women? Ho, ho. I thought you might be upset."

Evie blew out a breath. "There you go again, lumping us all together. I'm me, remember?"

I turned and kissed her cheek. "Yes, you are. And that's why I love you."

She stood up and held out her hands to me. "Come on, then. Prove it."

* * *

We had a late dinner at the Union Oyster House, and when we got back to my apartment, Evie picked up the envelope of photocopies that I'd left on the kitchen table. "Is this Christa?" she said.

I nodded.

"Pretty girl. She looks all grown-up. I would've said she was twenty-two or twenty-three at least."

"She was sixteen in that photo. She's eighteen now."

"She's into body piercing in a big way," Evie said. "Look." She touched Christa's ears. "Looks like at least half a dozen rings and studs in each ear. And look." She put her finger on Christa's belly button. "She's got a stud here, too."

"I didn't notice that," I said. "It wasn't apparent in the photo. It's pretty clear in the enlargements, though." I looked at Evie. "Do you see anything else?"

She squinted at the picture. "You got a magnifying glass?"

I went to my desk and fetched my round Sherlock Holmes magnifier for her. She held it over the photo. "I thought so," she mumbled.

"What?"

"Look. Her necklace."

I took the glass. Christa was wearing a gold chain around her neck, and dangling from it on the outside of her T-shirt was a gold charm. It was a bent-over, more-or-less-human figure. It looked like he was playing a flute, and he had . . .

"Is that what it looks like?" I said.

Evie smiled. "Oh, yes. That is a penis. A very large, erect penis. This is Kokopelli, the wandering flute player, the trickster, the seducer with his bag of songs on his back. He's a beloved pagan deity of fertility. Kind of a universal figure. You see him a lot in pictographs and glyphs on rocks and in caves in New Mexico and Arizona. He brings new life and joy wherever he goes." She poked at the photo. "This guy is the real deal. Nowadays you'll see a lot of Kokopellis without the giant dick."

"Do you know everything?" I said.

She smiled. "I know a lot."

"So what would you say about a sixteen-year-old girl who wears one of these fellows around her neck?"

Evie shook her head. "I wouldn't try to read too much into it, Brady. Native American stuff is very popular nowadays. Kokopelli stands for love and music and happiness. He makes you smile, doesn't he?"

"Mainly he makes me feel inadequate," I said.

She wrapped her arms around my chest and wiggled her pelvis against me. "I think we'd better address that issue," she said.

We left my apartment on Lewis Wharf in Boston around eight-thirty in Evie's Volkswagen Jetta, and at quarter of eleven on Sunday morning I was climbing the ramp onto the ferry that would take me to Vineyard Haven on Martha's Vineyard.

As I handed my ticket to the Steamship Authority guy, I noticed another man standing beside him. This other guy had a short, federal-issue haircut and a smoothly shaved face. He was wearing sunglasses and a white short-sleeved shirt and pressed khaki pants, and from behind those glasses he appeared to be scrutinizing the people coming aboard. He was holding a two-way radio.

He ran his eyes over me. Hmm. A single man carrying a well-worn L.L. Bean duffel bag and an ancient briefcase.

I gave him a smile, and his eyes slid away to the person behind me.

Before September 11, I'd never been aware of security precautions on the ferry, although I'd always managed to time my visits with the Jacksons to avoid conflict with presidential vacations.

I went up to the top deck. It was mobbed. Summer People. There were young couples with toddlers, middle-aged couples with dogs on leashes, college-aged kids in clusters. With the Celebration for Humanity just a week away, I figured the island would be even more of a zoo than it normally was in August. I'd been reading about this event for several months, thinking how the Vineyard would be number one on my list of places to avoid during the Celebration—and here I was, heading straight into the fray.

I found a place at the ferry rail from which I could watch Woods Hole on Cape Cod grow small behind us and the green mound in the ocean that was Martha's Vineyard grow larger. The ferry ride took less than an hour, but it always felt like traveling to a foreign country—which was probably why islanders like J.W. and Zee always distinguished the Vineyard from the mainland, which they called "America."

We'd been chugging across the Vineyard Sound for about fifteen minutes when someone touched my shoulder. I turned. It was the guy in the sunglasses who'd been giving passengers the once-over as we climbed aboard.

"May I ask your business on the Vineyard, sir?" he said.

"Is this a random check," I said, "or do I appear unduly suspicious?"

"Your business, sir?" he repeated without a smile.

"It's because I'm alone, isn't it?"

"Random," he said.

"Who are you?"

He frowned for an instant, then dug into his pocket and showed me a card with his picture on it. Massachusetts State Police. Sergeant Robert Lamm.

I nodded. "I'm looking for a girl."

He arched his eyebrows. "Oh?"

I opened my briefcase, took out one of the copies of Christa's photograph, and handed it to him. "You're a trained observer," I said. "Do you remember seeing her?"

He glanced at the picture. "No." He handed it back to me.

"Would you keep it?" I said. "If you see her, call me? I'll give you a number where—"

"No," he repeated. And then he moved away from me and disappeared in the crowd.

Oh, well.

The ferryboat docked at the wharf on Vineyard Haven at quarter of twelve. It took me ten minutes to shuffle down the stairs from the top deck to the ramp, and when I got to the bottom the state cop with the sunglasses was there, watching us all get off.

As I started to move past him, he gripped my arm and pulled me aside. A wisecrack came to my tongue, but I swallowed it. These security guys were never noted for their sense of humor. So I said, "What's up?"

"Why don't you let me have that picture," he said.

"You'll keep an eye out for her?"

He shrugged. "I've got a daughter."

I took out one of the photocopies and wrote my name and the Jacksons' phone number on the back of it. "Her name is Christa Doyle," I said. "The photo is two years old. She's eighteen now."

"My daughter's six," the guy said. "I can't imagine losing her."

"I appreciate it," I said.

He nodded, and already his eyes had shifted to the crowds that were coming down the ramp from the ferry.

I spotted Zee Jackson's little red Jeep Wrangler double-parked on the street. Zee was leaning against the side. I waved, and she smiled and waved back, and when I got there, she wrapped her arms around my neck and gave me a big hug and kiss.

Diana and Joshua, the two Jackson kids, were buckled in the backseat, and when I leaned in they both held out their hands to be shaken and said hello to Uncle Brady.

I slid into the passenger seat and Zee climbed in behind the wheel. She was wearing shorts and a sleeveless jersey. A pink ribbon held her long ebony hair back in a ponytail, and she had her usual all-over summer tan. She was stunning. J.W. had lucked out.

As we drove to the Jackson house at the end of the dirt road in Edgartown, I filled Zee in on Christa Doyle. "It feels like the wildest possible kind of goose chase," I concluded. "But I've got to do it."

"J.W. and I talked about it last night," she said. "He thought you should start by talking to the police. All the towns on the island have hired on extra part-time help for the month. Everybody's superconscious of security with all the bigwigs coming down for the damn Celebration. The place is swarming with feds and local law enforcement types. You've got a picture of the girl, I hope."

"Fifty copies," I said. "Getting cooperation from the police would be great, if I could manage it. I'll try to get around to them this afternoon. After that, I have no idea what to do."

Zee nodded. "She could be anywhere. It's not a big island, as land masses go, but people are coming and going by ferry, boat, airplane, and helicopter, and they figure there will be close to a quarter of a million people here this week. Just get as many eyes and ears working for you as you can, I guess."

The Jacksons lived at the end of a sandy driveway off an unpaved road through the scrubby woods. When we got there, Zee insisted on making me a bluefish-salad sandwich. To sustain me for my afternoon's quest, she said. I ate with her and the kids up on the balcony, which gave a long view of a big salt pond and beyond it, Nantucket Sound. If you ignored the sailboats and the lines of traffic creeping along the distant causeway, you might think you were one of the Swiss Family Robinsons, utterly alone on some deserted tropical island.

When we finished eating, Zee said, "Why don't you give me a look at the girl's picture."

I handed a photocopy to her.

She squinted at it, then shook her head and said, "Nope."

"You were thinking she might've been to the hospital?" Zee was an emergency-room nurse at the Martha's Vineyard hospital.

"Always a possibility," she said. "The ER's been awfully busy this summer. She's quite a striking girl. I think I'd remember if I'd seen her." She gave the picture back to me. "You might want to talk to Ilsa Johannsen. She works the desk at the ER. I can give her a call, if you want. Tell her to expect you."

"That would be great," I said.

Zee went downstairs. I stayed up on the balcony, sipping my coffee and looking at Christa's picture, as though she might speak to me if I stared at it long enough.

She didn't.

A few minutes later Zee came up. "Ilsa's expecting you," she said. "I also talked to Kit Goulart. She's on duty at the Edgartown Police Station this afternoon. Remember Kit?"

I held my hand about a foot over my head. "Big woman, right?"

Zee smiled. "Right. She and J.W. are friends. She likes our kids. I'm not telling you what to do, but Kit's got a soft heart, and Ilsa's a peach. That's a start, anyway, huh?"

"That's a great start," I said. "Thank you."

We went downstairs, and Zee gave me a thermos of coffee and the keys to J.W.'s ancient Toyota Land Cruiser, which was parked in the driveway.

"J.W. should be home around six," she said. "There'll be martinis and bluefish pâté on the balcony and seafood St. Jacques on the table."

"I'll be there," I said.

Chapter Seven

J.W.

It was almost noon before Evangeline and I could get away from the sheep pasture and the questions of Sergeant Dom Agganis of the state police. In Massachusetts, the state cops handle all murder investigations outside of Boston.

Dom had shaken his head when we met. "They told me you're the one who found him. I should have guessed. What is it about you? Why don't other people find bodies?"

"Mrs. Price found him," I said. "I was just following her."

"That would be Mrs. Ethel Price, better known to a hundred billion fans as Evangeline, would it not? What are you doing following Evangeline around? You and her move in pretty different circles."

"Jake Spitz got me a job as her driver."

"I'll talk with Jake. You gotta be dressed for the job?" He flicked a thick finger toward the slight bulge under my shirt where my old .38 was stuck in my belt. He had sharp eyes.

"The gun was Jake's idea and she approved. She has a real bodyguard, but since she got here she has him staying home looking after her daughter. Name's Hale Drummand."

He scribbled in his notebook. "You touch anything at the crime scene?"

"So it's officially a crime scene."

"That's how we're treating it. Looks like he was strangled from behind. Wire or cord, I'd say. The ME will make it official, one way or another. Well, did you touch anything?"

"I put a finger on Warner's throat to see if he had a pulse. I didn't touch anything else and I got Mrs. Price out of there before she could. Then I stayed at the door until the cops came. Nobody got in while I was there."

He grunted. "Cops can mess up a crime scene as well as anybody else. You know anything about the deceased Mr. Warner?"

"Never heard of him before today."

"They tell me he was a big shot in the entertainment biz."

"I wouldn't know. I don't pay much attention to the entertainment biz."

"You get to be a big shot in most businesses by stepping on a lot of people on your way up the ladder. I hear that your Mrs. Price and Warner had some kind of falling-out a while ago. You know anything about that?"

"She didn't kill him, if that's what you're thinking. He was dead when she got here."

"Maybe she snuck in last night and did the job."

"She said she'd never been here. Besides, sneaking in here is pretty tough. The woods are full of security. I think you better look for somebody else."

"I got plenty of suspects, all right. Everybody in show business. But I think I'll start with your Mrs. Price, in spite of your wise advice."

He went away and an hour later Evangeline found me

waiting by our car. She looked tired and troubled. By that time rumors of Warner's death had spread and people were doing more gossiping than working.

"Get in," I said. She did, and we went out the long driveway. "Dom Agganis is okay," I said. "He's tough, but he's fair and he's good at his job."

"They say it was murder. I never saw a murdered man before. It's quite a shock."

"I didn't notice anybody crying at the news. Did Agganis give you a hard time?"

She stared out through the windshield. "He wanted to know about Ogden and me."

My nose itched. "What did you tell him?"

Her voice was flat. "It'll come out anyway, I suppose. Years ago Ogden and I were an item for a while. Then I went in another direction. I was pretty young at the time and he was an important man. He didn't want to break it off."

I waited for more, and when it didn't come I said, "But you did, so you left."

"Something like that."

"A grilling can take a lot out of you," I said. "Let's get some lunch. It'll make you feel better."

"I don't feel hungry."

"I do. I'll take you to a bar where nobody will know who you are."

She tried a smile. "All right."

I took her to the Fireside, in Oak Bluffs. It wasn't full yet, so we found a booth. Evangeline kept her dark glasses on.

Bonzo spotted me and came right over. He stared at Evangeline and smiled his childlike smile.

"Hey, J.W.," he said. "How ya doin'?"

"I'm fine," I said. "Bonzo, this is Ethel Price. Mrs. Price, this is my friend Bonzo."

"Call me Ethel," said Evangeline, smiling up at him.

Bonzo beamed. "Glad to know you, Ethel. You ain't been in before, or I'd have remembered. I never forget anybody as pretty as you. Say, J.W., I hear they're catching bass up at Lobsterville. Maybe we can go up there sometime. What do you think?"

"Well, I'm pretty busy for the next week, but after that we'll do it."

"Hey, J.W., that sounds good. Now, what can I getcha?"

I ordered a Sam Adams and a hamburger, and Evangeline, to my surprise, did the same. I don't know what I expected, but that wasn't it. A salad and diet soda, maybe?

"Your friend seems nice."

"He got the way he is by using some very bad acid, but he's a sweetheart. Loves birds and fishing. Lives with his mother. I'd trust him with my life."

She nodded. "I know some people like that. Could have happened to me, I guess. I haven't done dope for years. It scares me to think of the chances I took."

"We all did things once that scare us now."

The beer and sandwiches came and by the time we were finished with them and headed for the door she seemed to be feeling better and the place had filled with its typical summer mixture of working stiffs and college kids pretending to be working stiffs.

"Hey, J.W., who's the looker? I thought you were a married man, and here you are out with another beauty."

Nate Fairchild was as wide and rough as a barn door. He and I had gone nose to nose a few times in the past, but now had more or less struck a truce.

"Why, Nate," I said, "I thought you'd be fishing on a nice day like this."

"Well, I ain't. Who's your good-looking friend? Does Zee know about her?"

"Nate, let me introduce my sister. Ethel, this is Nate Fairchild. Nate, this is my sister, Ethel Price. Like you noticed, she inherited the family genes for looks."

"I never thought there were any Jackson genes for looks, but of course you're the only Jackson I ever met. Howdy do, Miz Price. Nice to meet you." He showed his strong yellow teeth.

She gave him a swift but charming smile. "That's Mrs. Price, Mr. Fairchild. Nice to meet you, too." She took my arm. "Now, if you'll excuse us, we really have to go. I'm forcing my brother to take me shopping, and he just hates it."

As we went out I could feel Nate's eyes following Evangeline.

"My, my," she said as we found our Explorer. "Now we're siblings. You handled that well. He looked like a bruiser."

"He is a bruiser, and you handled him quite well yourself. We have an afternoon in front of us. What's your pleasure?"

"How about shopping?" She arched a brow.

"You'll really be making me earn every cent of my salary, but okay."

She laughed. "Just kidding."

"I can take you to see the ashram. We were pretty close to it yesterday."

She put her lower lip between her teeth.

"Or I can take you back to West Tisbury. You were interested in buying a statue. Or I can take you someplace else. You're the boss."

"West Tisbury, then. I love those statues. A couple of them would look wonderful at Cragmoor!"

Cragmoor, I guessed, was her Scottish castle. I'd never been to Scotland, but I liked singing Scottish ballads while I thumbed my guitar. I also liked the Loch Ness Monster and had opted to believe everything that supported its existence and disbelieve everything that didn't.

Zee noted correctly that this position was totally contrary to my normal skepticism about lots of things other people believed in, and to my definition of truth as that for which there was the most evidence at the moment.

Confidence in the reality of Nessie didn't quite qualify by this test, but so what? A foolish consistency is the hobgoblin of little minds, as Ralph Waldo observed.

We drove to the Field Gallery in West Tisbury and walked among the dancing statues so Evangeline could make her choices. Then, while I looked at other art on display and at the outdoor workshop where the statues were made, Evangeline arranged for her purchases to be shipped across the sea.

When that wa done, and we were again in the Explorer, she said, "I guess I've procrastinated as long as I can. Let's go find the ashram."

"Are you sure you want to go there?"

"I'm sure I have to, so it may as well be now."

We drove to Indian Hill Road, where I found a narrow, unpaved driveway beside which was a small sign bearing the single word EXETER.

There are a lot of such modest driveways on Martha's Vineyard, and many of them lead to very substantial homes owned by people who, unlike Peter Fredericks and the Vineyard's other recent palace builders, are not interested in making a display of their wealth. This one wound over a hill and then down toward Vineyard Sound, ending at a large, early-twentieth-century house and a number of outbuildings. Lawns flowed away from the house on three sides. On the fourth side, a walkway led to wooden steps that in turn led down to a private beach. Across the sound, the Elizabeth Islands were part of the house's excellent view.

There were several people in sight, and they, like the buildings and the grounds, seemed to be in excellent condition. They paused and looked at us as we drove into view. As I parked in front of a five-car garage, four of the larger men approached. They were wearing black summer shirts over black summer shorts.

"Alain calls them Simon Peters," said Evangeline. "Ashram security."

"After Simon Peter, the guy who cut off somebody's ear when they came to arrest Jesus?"

"That's it."

We stepped out of the car and she took off her dark glasses.

"Welcome," said the first Simon Peter. "May we be of assistance?" His eyes flitted between my face and the lump made by the gun in my belt, and he made a small gesture. The other three Simon Peters silently surrounded me.

"I've come to see Alain," said Evangeline. "Do you know who I am?"

He spoke in a formal voice. "I recognize you, madam. Yours is a famous face. How may I help you?"

"You can tell Alain that I'm here."

"I'm sure he will be delighted to see you." He gestured toward the house. "At this hour he meditates, so it will be a short time before he'll be free. May I suggest that you wait inside?"

"I'd prefer the porch. I've always loved a view of islands. Come on, J.W."

She turned toward the house, but the Simon Peter held up a hand. "I'm sorry, madam, but your companion must stay here. Arms are not allowed in the ashram."

"I want him with me." Her voice was hard.

"I'm sorry, madam, but it cannot be. Your companion may go no closer."

"Is it the pistol?" I asked.

He placed his palms together. "This is a house of peace and prayer. Weapons have no place here."

His body, like those of the other three Simon Peters, looked like a weapon to me. I said, "I'll leave the pistol in the car. I think there's enough security here already."

"Very good, sir. I regret the necessity of asking if you have other arms. The threat of terrorism has reached even sacred places such as this, and we must all be more careful than we were in more innocent times."

"I also have fingernail clippers, a pocketknife, and a Leatherman tool. I don't think of those things as weapons, but the airlines do, and maybe you do, too."

He placed a smile on his face. "Perhaps you will be kind enough to leave those items in your car as well."

"No problem."

I carefully lifted the hem of my shirt and with thumb and forefinger took my pistol from my belt and put it under the seat of the Explorer. Then I put the items I'd mentioned on the seat itself.

"You'll feel better if you double-check," I said. And spread my arms and legs.

A Simon Peter patted me down expertly from behind.

"Thank you," said the one in front. "Please follow me."

We went to the house and Evangeline and I sat on comfortable chairs on the north porch and looked out over Vineyard Sound. The Simon Peter went away.

A square-rigged ship that I guessed was the coast guard's *Eagle* was tacking west into the wind, looking like something out of ages past. Down at the beach below the stairs people were in the water or lying on blankets and mats. Most of them were young and many were women in very small bathing suits. As I looked at them, a beautifully shaped girl wearing a bikini and sandals and carrying a large towel came from behind the house and walked past us toward the beach. As I watched her go down the stairway, I finally noticed her hair and realized that my eyes had not previously gotten higher than her neck. I wondered if her face was as lovely as the rest of her.

"Not bad, as religious sites go," I said. "Nothing monastic or nunnish about this place."

"The spirit and the flesh are one, according to Alain," said Evangeline. "Balance between them is the key."

"Who are all these people?"

"Followers of the Light and novices considering whether to take their vows."

"Vows?

"Not the Benedictine Rule or anything like that. Just to practice virtue, to be true to the Light."

"To love God and to follow the golden rule. Not a bad vow as vows go."

"You told me what you think of oaths. I presume you think the same of vows."

"I've taken some. When I joined the army, when I joined the Boston PD, both times I got married. I think that's enough vows to last a lifetime."

I felt her eyes. "You've been married twice?"

"My first wife couldn't stand being married to a policeman, never knowing if I'd come home alive. When I got shot, she stayed until she knew I'd get well, then left me and married a schoolteacher."

I felt her turn toward me. "You got shot?"

"It happened a long time ago. A thief got trapped in an alley and shot me trying to get out."

"My God! Did he get away?"

"It was a woman, although I didn't know it at the time. I killed her." I looked toward Evangeline and found her wide eyes boring into mine. "When I got out of the hospital I quit being a cop and came down here to be a fisherman. Now I'm doing cop work again. Security detail. Life loves a jest."

"I had no idea."

Footsteps came toward us and we turned toward them. A man wearing loose, casual summer clothing approached us with a smile. He looked to be about my age and he walked like a cat.

Evangeline was on her feet. Her face was pale and she seemed to be trembling. She didn't look like the tough, self-made international star I'd heard about. She looked like a lost girl.

His voice was soft and deep, and I had a flashing thought of Mesmer. "Evangeline. You've returned. Our house is blessed by your presence. I was delighted when I learned you'd be performing at the Celebration. It was good of you to come so far for such a good cause. Alas, I'll miss your performance Saturday night because I have to return to California that morning." His smile was melancholy but not without humor. "Duty keeps one humble, and that is no doubt a fine thing."

He took her hands in his and beamed at her, then turned to me.

"I'm Alain Duval. Simon Peter tells me that you brought Evangeline to me. You have my thanks."

He released Evangeline and put out his hand. I shook it and gave him my name. His was a gentle hand, but there was sinew in it. I looked into his pale blue eyes and could feel myself being drawn into them, as though I were falling into the sky.

I pulled myself back to earth, but in that instant understood his power as a proselytizer. Beside me, Evangeline took a deep breath and seemed to gather scattered strength of her own.

"Come inside," said Duval, spreading his hands in an encompassing gesture. "We'll have tea and conversation. You and I have much to talk about, Evangeline."

But she shook her head. "No. I don't want tea. I came back for just one reason, Alain. To apologize."

His smile was beatific and his eyes were bright. "You owe me no apology, my dear."

"But I do. When I left you I hadn't the courage to say good-bye. I owe you an apology for that. Now you have it. Good-bye, Alain. Come on, J.W."

But his eyes seemed to hold her where she was, and that hypnotic voice said, "You were always free to stay or go, but we really should talk. Come, my dear. We'll have some tea. I'm sure you have something more to tell me."

"No!" But her feet didn't move, and her eyes were staring into his.

Why so great a no?

I took her arm and turned her away. "We'll go, then," I said. "Very nice meeting you, Mr. Duval. Maybe we can have that tea another time."

His eyes glowed with some inner flame. But then he

stepped back and smiled the smile of a saint. "Anytime, Mr. Jackson. You'll both be more than welcome."

Holding Evangeline's arm firmly in mine, I walked her back to our car and put her in the passenger seat. I repossessed my tools and pistol and drove away from the ashram. Alain Duval was still on the porch, and on the lawn the four Simon Peters stood watching.

"I'll take you home," I said. "I think you've had enough excitement for one day."

"Yes. Thank you."

About halfway back to Edgartown she reached into herself and found that strength that women can muster when many a man would still be weak.

"Alain is a man who doesn't give up easily," she said. "He doesn't like it when women leave him. He wants them back so he can leave them."

I thought there was more between her and Duval than that, but I only said, "You're already gone. If you hadn't left before, you did it today."

"With your help. If you hadn't been there . . ."

"I just made it easier for you to go. If you'd wanted to stay, you would have."

"I suppose." She was silent for a while, then said, "Your wife is a lucky woman, I think."

"I'm the lucky one. I'll introduce you sometime. Incidentally, our daughters are the same age, if Jane ever wants a playmate."

"That's a very kind offer. Thank you."

"Give it some thought. Ask Jane."

"I will."

We drove past the guard at the head of her driveway and went down to the Carberg house, where I parked the white Ford.

She thanked me, then smiled and gave a small wave as she walked into the house. I watched her go inside, thinking about what I'd heard and seen. I was turning the Explorer toward the driveway when the door of the house burst open and she came running toward me, her face awash with fear.

I stopped, got out, and went to meet her.

"Janie's not here and neither is Hale! They should be in the house! Something's wrong! We have to find them!"

Chapter Eight

Brady

I climbed into J.W.'s old Land Cruiser, drove to Edgartown, and found Officer Kit Goulart talking on the phone at the reception desk inside the police station. When I walked in, she smiled and held up a finger. I smiled back.

I'd met Kit a couple of times when I'd been on the Vineyard fishing and hanging around with J.W. She was a giant of a woman, several inches taller than me and built like a linebacker, but she had an incongruously soft, little-girl voice. I wondered how the person on the other end of the line was picturing her.

When she hung up, she stood and held out her hand to me. I took it. It was the size of a first baseman's mitt.

"Mr. Coyne," she said. "Nice to see you again. Zee Jackson told me you'd be stopping by. What can I do for you?"

I gave her a condensed version of the story, then took one of Christa's pictures from my briefcase. "It would be too much to expect, I know, but I wonder if you recognize her?"

She frowned at the picture, then shook her head. "I'm pretty good at faces," she said. "I can tell you that she hasn't been arrested or anything. At least not here in Edgartown. Otherwise . . ." She blew out a breath. "I can't guarantee I haven't seen her. The island has never been this mobbed. Crowds everywhere. I see thousands of faces every day I'm out on the streets."

"I wonder if you could keep an eye out for her," I said, "and call me if you see her. I'm staying with Zee and J.W."

"Can I keep this?" She touched the picture.

"Of course."

"I'll make copies and give them to the other officers," she said. "We've got a bunch of auxiliaries and part-timers on for the summer. We're trying to be a presence, what with all the people and all the excitement over the Celebration."

"That's great," I said. "Thing is, though, I wouldn't want anybody to confront her. Christa doesn't want to be found. Our best chance is if I can speak with her myself, if we can just locate her."

Kit smiled. She had a surprisingly pretty smile. "I'll make that clear to everybody." She looked away for a moment. "I could fax this picture to the other departments on the island, if you like. Tell them if anybody sees this girl, they should call you at the Jacksons' house. How would that be?"

"That would be a wonderful help," I said.

"Have you checked the hospital?" she said.

"That's where I'm going. Can you suggest anyplace else?"

She looked up at the ceiling, and at that moment the phone rang. She answered, spoke briefly, then hung up. "There are kids all over the place," she said to me. "Most of them don't have any money. They're all here to gawk at famous rappers and crash the Celebration. If we arrested all of them, we'd have to build a prison the size of the Fleet Center."

"Arrest them for what?"

Kit Goulart smiled. "Peeing in parking lots. Throwing up on the sidewalks. Camping in the state forest. Building bonfires on the beaches. Running each other down with motor scooters. You name it."

"You're letting them do those things?"

"You get caught peeing on somebody's BMW, you get what we call a stern warning." She shrugged. "You can only do so much."

"So the kids are camping out in the state forest?"

She nodded. "We've been, um, advised to look the other way. The Chamber of Commerce likes it. They're happy to get the kids out of the way. Out of sight, out of mind, you know?" She waved her hand in the air. "They're good kids, most of them. They just like to party, and they say this Celebration is gonna be the biggest party of the new millennium. The local police forces take turns putting a couple of auxiliaries in the forest at night, just to keep an eye on things. The kids drink, they smoke stuff, they play guitars, they have sex. So far, nobody's stabbed anybody."

I was nodding. "Christa could be there. In the forest."

"Mr. Coyne," said Kit, "Christa could be anywhere."

It took me nearly half an hour to drive the few miles from the Edgartown police station to the hospital in Oak Bluffs. The traffic was bumper-to-bumper on this Sunday afternoon, and the streets and sidewalks were thronged with bicycles and scooters and joggers and people walking their dogs. I couldn't imagine why anybody would be here voluntarily, but here they all were, having what I guess was their own version of a good time.

Ilsa Johannsen turned out to be the woman who took

insurance information and admitted emergency room patients at the island hospital, which she was doing when I got there. When she finally had a minute to talk to me, she told me they'd already set a season's record for motor scooter accidents and drug overdoses and sunburns, and there was still almost a week to go before the Celebration. They were bracing themselves for that.

"We're just not equipped," said Ilsa. She was a small, sixtyish woman with permed grayish hair and big round glasses and quick, nervous hands that kept fiddling with her computer mouse. "Every Boston surgeon and Manhattan psychiatrist with a summer home here will be on call next weekend. It's gonna be Woodstock all over again." She picked up a pencil and poked her hair with it. "Anyway, Zee said you were looking for a girl?"

I gave her Christa's picture.

She squinted at it. "Nope. Don't recall seeing her. Course, I'm not here twenty-four hours a day. It only seems that way. What'd you say her name was?"

"Christa Doyle."

Ilsa Johannsen tapped at some keys on her computer, squinted at her monitor, then looked up at me and shook her head. "She hasn't been in." She glanced past me. "Sorry, Mr. Coyne. I got people waiting."

"Would you mind keeping that picture?"

"Sure. If I see her, I'll call you. You're staying with the Jacksons, right?"

"Right," I said. "Thank you."

When I turned to leave, I saw that there were five or six people behind me. There was a man in a bathing suit holding a baby in his arms, a teenage girl holding a bloody towel against the side of her head, and a woman pushing a very old man in a wheelchair, and as I walked out through the sliding doors, a man helping an extremely pregnant woman squeezed by.

Back in J.W.'s Land Cruiser, I poured a mug of coffee from the thermos Zee had given me and looked at my watch. It was a little after four o'clock. I felt pretty good. I hadn't found Christa, but I'd touched base with the local police and the only hospital on the island, which was the first thing any competent private investigator would have done. With luck, somebody might spot her in the next day or two.

Well, I couldn't depend on luck. I knew how it worked. Good investigators—mediocre ones, for that matter—just kept at it, turning over rocks, kicking at bushes, flailing around stubbornly and persistently until something happened. I could do that. I was as stubborn and persistent as the next guy.

I had no idea where Christa might be staying. The most populous towns on the island were Oak Bluffs and Vineyard Haven, where the ferries docked, and Edgartown. But she could be anywhere.

Since I was already there, I headed for the waterfront at Oak Bluffs. I knew there were lots of shops and restaurants and bars there. Oak Bluffs was one of the two towns on the Vineyard that sold booze, which made it a focal point of island nightlife. The other wet town was Edgartown.

I figured I'd find a bartender to talk to. Bartenders saw everything, knew everyone. While I was at it, I'd have a beer.

The commercial section of Oak Bluffs by the harbor was worse than Copley Square at four o'clock on a Friday afternoon, and I drove around for about half an hour before I finally spotted a shiny Audi pulling out of a parking space down near the ferry landing. It left a slot big enough for J.W.'s Land Cruiser, and I grabbed it.

I wandered up and down the narrow streets, studying every face I saw in the sidewalk crowds and peering into the shops and restaurants, and I was about to step into a dimly lit bar when something on the sign over a shop doorway across the street caught my eye.

Painted on the sign was an expurgated Kokopelli—that is, minus the erect penis—and the words "Four Winds Trading Post." I smiled and crossed the street.

The window display featured silver and turquoise jewelry and bright woven blankets. There were corn-husk dolls and beaded moccasins and buckskin vests, painted pots and clay pipes and hanging dream catchers, miniature badgers and mountain lions and moles carved from stone. Propped on a stand inside the window was a hand-painted sign that read, FORTUNES BY PRINCESS ISHEWA.

Hmm. Why not? I went in.

There were six or eight tourist types in Bermuda shorts peering into the display cases, and behind the counter with her arms folded across her chest stood a tall woman with long gray-streaked blonde hair. She wore jeans and a pale blue T-shirt. She seemed to be scowling at her customers, as if she hoped they wouldn't try to buy any of her wares.

I went up to her and said, "Are you Princess Ishewa?"

"Not hardly. She's out back." She jerked her thumb over her shoulder at a doorway hung with a beaded curtain. "Do you need your fortune told?"

"I need help," I said, with what was intended to be my most disarming smile. "That's for sure." I pulled out a picture of Christa. "I'm looking for this girl."

She glanced at it, then shrugged. "I don't know her."

"I thought she might've come into your shop. She wears a Kokopelli." I pointed at Christa's necklace.

"Lots of people wear Kokopelli. Most of them have no idea who he is." She glanced at the picture. "Is this your girlfriend or something?"

I laughed quickly. "She's eighteen."

The woman shrugged.

"It's my friend's daughter," I said. "She's gone missing. We think she's here, somewhere on the Vineyard."

"And you?"

"Me? I'm the family lawyer. Would you mind keeping the picture, and if you should see her, call me?" I wrote my name and J.W.'s phone number on the back of the photo.

"I don't see why not." She took the photo, glanced at it again, slipped it under the counter, then looked up at me. "So did you want the princess to tell your fortune?"

I smiled. "Is she really a princess?"

"In fact she is."

"And she has a psychic gift?"

The woman smiled. "Oh, indeed. She's got the second sight. She's quite uncanny."

"Well," I said, "why not. I can use all the help I can get."

"She's with somebody right now. She should be done soon."

"Okay," I said. "I'll wait."

I stepped outside the shop and watched the faces in the crowd. I was tempted to just walk away. Me, a hard-headed attorney, a confirmed agnostic, visiting a damn fortune-teller. It was ridiculous. As far as I was concerned, all psychics—card readers, astrologers, crystal-ball gazers, mediums, channelers—were fakes and rip-off artists. Some of them, of course, were pretty clever at it. They knew how to size up a sucker, make a few educated guesses, and then tell him what they figured he—or more often she—wanted to hear.

I'd run into a lot of women—and a few men, too—who sincerely believed that the alignment of the moon and stars and planets at the moment of your birth determined the course of your life. It seemed to give them comfort, and I sometimes envied them. Anything that gave you comfort was a good thing, as far as I was concerned. The trick was believing in it.

Several years ago I got into a conversation about racial profiling with an attractive female lawyer while we were waiting for a taxi outside a courtroom. We decided to continue our discussion over a drink, and we were on our second old-fashioned when she reached across the table, picked up my hand, and began tracing her forefinger across my palm. She told me I had a long life line that featured many intriguing side streets and detours. Then she rubbed the base of my thumb, looked up at me, and proclaimed me a "passionate person," and two hours later she proceeded to prove her clairvoyance to both of our satisfactions.

Well, I didn't care about my fortune. If I had a fortune, I certainly didn't want to know it. But I did care about Christa's fortune. Maybe this Princess Ishewa had seen her, and if she wanted to pretend to conjure up Christa's image in tea leaves or talk to her spirit as it floated around on the ceiling, it was okay with me. I'd take a little truth any way I could get it.

A few minutes later the blonde woman from the shop beckoned me inside. "The princess is waiting for you," she said. "Go ahead in."

I pushed my way through the beaded curtain and found myself in a square, windowless room about the size of my bedroom back home. There was burning incense in the air, and some kind of music featuring flutes and bells was playing softly. The room was lit by dozens of candles lined up on shelves on the walls, and I had to blink a couple of times before I saw the woman standing in the corner next to a small round table. She was looking at me without expression from large, dark eyes.

She wasn't as old or as fat as I had, for some reason, expected. In fact, she looked to be no more than thirty. She had an angular face, with high cheekbones and a magnificently long, slightly off-center nose. Her black hair was braided and wrapped around the top of her head. She wore a sleeveless pale orange blouse and tight-fitting blue jeans, with enormous silver hoops in her ears and a silver-and-turquoise necklace around her neck and many silver bracelets on her wrists and rings on her fingers.

"I'm Princess Ishewa," she said in a soft, low-pitched voice. "Please come in."

She held out her hand, and I took it. It was small and soft, and she held on to mine longer than a normal handshake would warrant.

"I'm Brady," I said.

"Please sit down," she said. "Try to relax. I'm not going to hurt you."

"I am relaxed," I said.

She smiled. "No, you're not. I'll get you some tea."

I shook my head. "No, thanks." I sat at the table.

She ignored me. There was a hot plate on a table, and she poured from a kettle into a tiny cup and put the cup in front of me. "Try it."

I took a sip. It was sweet and herbal, with a little afterbite to it. "It's good," I said. I drained the cup.

She sat down across from me. "You're not here on vacation," she said. "You're on a mission. It's a serious mission."

"I want you to know," I said, "I don't believe in fortune-telling."

"Oh, I know that," she said. "I wasn't telling your fortune. I was observing."

"So how—?"

"You're carrying a briefcase." She smiled.

"Well," I said, "you're right. I am on a serious mission. I don't really care about my fortune. But there is a fortune I do care about. Can you tell a person's fortune from her photograph?"

"Maybe. But let's start with you."

"I told you—"

She reached across the table. "Give me your hands."

I shrugged. "Why not?"

I held out my hands, and she turned them palms down and held them in hers, palm to palm. "Usually," she said softly, looking down at our hands, "people come to me with problems and questions. They want answers. They want to know about money or love or health. You don't have any of these questions."

"I really don't want to know my future."

"There is a lot of change happening in your life," she said. "For a long time there has been no change. Now there is. Or there soon will be. You are worried about it."

I said nothing. But I thought about Evie. We'd been talking about living together. That would be a gigantic change in my life, and I was apprehensive about it.

"It has nothing to do with money," she continued. "Or

health. This change. It is love. You find yourself loving someone. It makes you uncomfortable." She looked up at me.

I shook my head. "I don't—"

"No," she said, "I'm not asking you to confirm what I'm saying. I know this to be true. I will not tell you what I see if you don't want me to."

"Please," I said. "Don't."

Her hands moved over mine. "There is something else." She hesitated, then slid her hands up over my wrists and back down again. She looked into my eyes for a long moment. Then she let go of my hands and stood up. "Let me get you some more tea."

She took my cup, refilled it, put it in front of me, and sat down.

"You said there was something else," I said.

"It's not clear," she said. "Shall we explore it?"

"It's about me?"

"Yes."

"I don't want to explore it."

"As you wish." She smiled at me. "You have a photograph, you said?"

"I do." I reached down, unsnapped my briefcase, and took out a picture of Christa. I put it on the table in front of the princess. "I'm looking for this girl."

She looked at the picture. "This is not your daughter," she said.

"No. You can see she looks nothing like me. She's the daughter of my friend. She ran away two years ago. I think she's here, on the island."

Princess Ishewa moved her fingertips over Christa's picture. She gazed up at the ceiling and was silent for a long time. Muted voices came in through the curtained doorway to the shop, and the bells and flutes played softly in the candlelit room. I could smell the melting candle wax and the faint aroma of herbal tea and something else—a musky scent, perhaps the princess's perfume.

When she finally spoke, it was in a soft, faraway whisper, and I had to bend toward her to hear her words.

"I see bright lights," she murmured. "Bursting, fiery lights. Green and red and blue lights, exploding lights, and a single large eye watching them. An eye . . . in the sky. Loud sounds. This girl, she is surrounded by the lights and the sounds. There are other people with her. Much noise, much chaos, many spirits colliding." She looked up at me. "You are there. You—" She stopped abruptly and looked up at me. "That is all," she said.

"Please go on," I said.

She shook her head. "I see no more."

"This is bad?" I said. "What you are seeing?"

She pushed Christa's picture away from her. "Nothing is bad, nothing is good. It is as the gods make it to be. And so we adore it."

"But these lights," I said, "these noises. Are they—?"

"My vision is gone," she said. "It was a glimpse. I can tell you nothing more."

"Chaos," I repeated. "Spirits colliding. A big eye in the sky. I don't like the sound of that."

Princess Ishewa looked up at me and smiled. "But you don't have faith in my gift."

"Well, not really, but . . ."

"Then it means nothing," she said. She tapped Christa's photo. "I have not seen her. I know your mission is a good and important one. I hope you find her."

"Will you keep the picture, let me know if you do see her, or if . . . if you have another vision?"

"I will have no visions without your presence," she said. "But I will keep the picture."

I wrote my name and the Jacksons' phone number on the back of it, then stood up. "What do I owe you?"

"You owe me nothing."

"But surely—"

"I have given you the gift of my vision. A gift does not create a debt. One must not sell the gift the gods have given. In my people's tradition, we give and we accept, we do not buy and sell."

"Then I will give you a gift," I said. I took out my wallet and put five twenty-dollar bills on the table.

She glanced at the money, then came around the table and stood in front of me. She reached up and held my face between her hands. She was standing very close to me, and her musky perfume seemed to fill my brain. "May the gods walk beside you," she whispered.

I covered her hands with mine. "And with you," I said.

And then I got the hell out of there before I started chanting in tongues.

Chapter Nine

J.W.

Evangeline's face was white as bleached flour, and her eyes were wide. She turned as I came toward her and ran back to the house. I caught her at the door. She tried to jerk her arm free from my grasp.

"Let go! We've got to find her!"

"Calm down," I said. "You couldn't have looked through the whole house. Do that now. I'll check the garage. What sort of car does Hale Drummand drive?"

"I don't know! It's something he brought with him. A Chevy or a Ford, maybe. It's blue. Let go of me!"

I let her go and she ran into the house, not bothering to shut the door behind her. I heard her calling for her daughter.

I went up the short flight of steps that led to the open breezeway between the house and the garage. The door leading into the garage was unlocked. I checked it and then went inside. In the far stall was a blue Volkswagen sedan. I looked inside the car, then popped the trunk. Nothing looked out of place.

There was no attic room above the garage, so I went back to the house. The breezeway door to the house was locked, so I went to the still-open front door. As I checked that door, I could hear Evangeline's voice upstairs calling for Janie. I went inside and crossed to the back door. It was locked.

I examined it, then found the basement stairs, flipped a light switch, and went down. I turned on more lights. It was a large basement divided into rooms: a shop with a bench and a collection of power and hand tools, a laundry room, a furnace room, a rec room with a full-size pool table in the middle, storage rooms. I surveyed all of them and looked in every closet and cubbyhole. Nothing. I checked the bulkhead door. It was locked on the inside.

I turned back upstairs, dousing lights as I climbed. On the ground floor I went through every room and looked in every closet. Nothing. I made my way to the second floor and met Evangeline coming down from the attic. She looked ill with worry.

"They're not here. Where can they be? They should be here! I've looked everywhere!"

I'd seen no sign of forced entry at either door or of damage at any of the windows on the ground floor, but I didn't mention that I'd looked for any. "Drummand's car is still in the garage," I said. "He and Janie are probably outside somewhere and they've lost track of time. Come on. We'll find them."

"I'll kill Hale Drummand for this!"

"Let's find him first," I said.

We went out the back door and down the steps on the pond side of the veranda. I looked at the dock and the small boats.

"The canoe's missing," I said. "They've probably gone for a paddle on the pond."

"Damn him! He should be back by now! Hale knows I want her here when I get home!"

I was looking out over the pond. A small wind rippled

its surface. About a quarter of a mile to the east a forested point of land cut off my view of the pond's far end. I saw no sign of human beings. "You're home a little early today," I said. "Have they ever been late before?"

"No, never." She ran her hands over her head, knocking her wig askew. She yanked the wig off and threw it on the ground.

"Let's take the motorboat," I said. "We'll probably meet them heading home."

It was a small boat with a small motor. We put-putted to the east until we rounded the point. There was no sign of a canoe on the water.

I was beginning to feel calm and cold, the way you sometimes do when something bad has happened and there's only so much you can do about it. Time had slowed down; my thoughts and actions seemed to be occurring at about three-quarter speed.

Then I saw the canoe on the shore of the point of land that jutted into the pond. I ran the motorboat alongside it. Evangeline leaped out of the boat and ran into the woods shouting Janie's name before I got the motor turned off.

I went to the canoe and saw no sign of anything being amiss. Two paddles and two life jackets lay inside it, and it was pulled well up onto the shore so there'd be no chance of it floating away.

There was a picnic basket in the bow of the boat. I opened it and found empty soft drink cans and sandwich-size plastic bags along with a partially filled potato chip bag that had been clipped shut with a clothespin. Whatever had delayed Hale Drummand and Janie's return to the house had occurred after lunch.

The footprints on the sandy shore were too confused

for me to make much of them other than that they were all adult size. There were no small ones.

From the woodlands that reached down to the shore, I could hear Evangeline's voice growing fainter as she moved inland, away from the water.

I stood and looked around the pond, wishing that I'd been smart enough to bring my binoculars.

To the east, in the distance, there were two or three houses near the shore. Pond People, surely. Such homes could be found near every pond on the south shore of the island. I turned and looked out at the barrier beach separating the pond from the Atlantic. I saw no boats or people.

Then some movement caught my eye. I looked again and my heart gave a small leap. I could barely hear Evangeline now, and I didn't want to waste time catching up with her and bringing her back, so I got the outboard going and motored across to the barrier beach. The closer I got, the better I felt, for there, growing larger in my vision, was a small girl in a bathing suit watching me approach.

I cut the motor and coasted to the shore, where I pulled the bow up onto the sand.

The girl watched me with wary, pale blue eyes, as if she was preparing to run away. She had Evangeline's blonde hair.

"My name is Jackson," I said. "I work for your mother. You're Janie, aren't you?"

She nodded.

"Your mother is over there," I said, pointing across the pond. "She's looking for you in the woods. She's worried about you. I'll take you to her."

"My mom doesn't want me to go with strangers." A smart kid.

"Good advice," I said. "If you'd rather stay here until we get back, I'll go get your mother and bring her to you."

"Hale told me not to go with anybody but him. He said he'd come back and get me. He told me to lie on the beach and to stay out of the surf until he came. But he's been gone a long time. Where is he?"

She seemed agitated but also vaguely trusting, as if she wanted me to tell her that everything was okay. The trouble was, I had a feeling it wasn't.

"I don't know where he is," I said. "The canoe is over there where your mother is looking. Is there anyone here with you?"

She shook her head.

"Stay right where you are, then. I'll go get your mother."

"Do you drive her car?"

"Yes. I saw you yesterday when I brought her home. Did you see me?"

A nod. "Yes. I don't want to be alone anymore."

"You can come with me if you want."

She thought and made her choice. "I better get my blanket and my water bottle and my sun shade. Hale will be mad if I don't have them."

She went out of sight over a dune and immediately returned carrying the blanket and bottles. We put them in the boat, boarded, and went back across the pond.

As we neared the point, Evangeline came out of the woods and saw us. She ran to the beach and when the boat nosed onto the sand, she waded out, took Janie in her arms, and carried her ashore. Her cheeks were stained from tears and the sleeve of her blouse was torn.

"Oh, Janie! Where have you been? Are you all right?"

Janie waved toward the barrier beach. "I'm fine, Mom. I was right there where we had lunch. I was getting scared, though. I thought Hale had forgotten me. But when Jackson came, I remembered him from yesterday, so I came with him. I think I got some sunburn even though I used sunscreen."

"Oh, dear, I think you're right. Wrap this around you." Evangeline put the girl down and put the blanket over her shoulders.

I sat on my heels, bringing my eyes down to Janie's level. "Tell me if this is what happened: This morning you and Hale decided to go for a ride in the canoe and take a lunch. Is that right?" She nodded. "Was it his idea or yours?" I asked.

"He said it would be fun to have lunch on the beach, so that's where we went. We both paddled. I was in front."

"And you did have lunch. I saw the basket in the canoe. Then what happened?"

"Then we played tag with the waves, but Hale wouldn't let me swim because they were too big, so we swam in the pond. Then we watched birds through his field glasses."

"When did he leave?"

"When we watched the birds. He was watching them and then he said he had to go across the pond but that he'd be back, but he never came back."

"Did he look toward this beach just before he left you?"

"Yes. Then he said I should stay there until he came back, but he didn't come back." Her lower lip began to quiver.

"And you stayed right there and didn't go into the surf. Good girl." I stood up and looked as far as I could into the woods. I saw nothing but trees. "Let's get back to the house," I said to Evangeline. "We'll leave the canoe in case Drummand needs it to come home."

"He'll be looking for another job the next time I see him!" she muttered, jaw clenched.

"Don't make up your mind about that just yet," I advised.

She opened her mouth, then shut it again when she looked at my face.

We all piled into the boat and the sound of the motor kept us from speaking until I tied up at the Carberg house's dock.

"We have to talk," said Evangeline, as we went inside. "You're thinking about something and I want to know what it is."

I didn't stop walking. "Put Janie in the shower and then get some more lotion on that burn of hers. Then put her into something other than a bathing suit and pack yourselves a couple of overnight bags. I'm going to check the map in the truck. We'll talk then."

I didn't wait for her to reply, but went out to the Explorer and from the glove compartment retrieved the island map I'd loaned her the day before. I've lived on the Vineyard for years, but there are many parts of it that I've never seen. I unfolded the map and studied the depiction of the island's south shore to double-check a memory that was dancing around in my brain.

I located the driveway to the Carberg house and, sure enough, there was a parallel road to the east, going from the highway down to the pond on the far side of the point where we'd found the canoe. It was an old lane that had probably originally been used to link the pond and fields, long since overgrown, to the main road.

I hadn't been back in the house for long before Evangeline and Janie came downstairs. I was glad as well as a bit surprised to see that they carried small suitcases because Evangeline wasn't a woman who took orders. She was used to giving them.

"What's this all about?" she snapped.

"Hale Drummand is missing," I said, "and I don't want you two to be alone in this house. Right now I'm going to check out that point of land and I want you with me when I do it. After that, if we can't find someone to stay here with you, I think you should bunk somewhere else for a while, until we can get this situation sorted out."

Her anger went away. She'd been rich and famous long enough to know that those attributes made her and her daughter targets.

"All right. Do you know what's happening? Do you know what happened to Hale or what he's doing?"

"All I have are some guesses. Let's lock this place up and get going."

We did that and I drove out to the highway. Marty, the young cop, had again pulled the detail at the end of the driveway, but I didn't think he had the authority to put a guard at the house, so I just waved as we passed by and took a right toward Edgartown. A quarter of a mile along the highway a narrow, sandy road led off to the south. I took it and followed it, first through oak and pine, then across mostly overgrown onetime fields, then across marshy grasslands, and finally out onto the point of land where the lane hooked left and ended at a small beach.

The pond was visible on both sides of the woods that covered the point. The distant houses I'd seen from the barrier beach were closer now but still well to the east. To the west, over the marsh grasses, the Carberg house was clearly in view.

I parked and we got out.

"Wait for me on the beach," I said. "If you see anybody, sing out."

"All right." Evangeline took Janie's hand and they walked toward the little beach.

I studied the terrain, then made my way back to a clump of trees on the west side of road. There I was not surprised to see fresh tire tracks where a vehicle had pulled off and parked, hidden from view from the Carberg house. There were shoe prints in the dust leading to and from the point of land.

I followed the prints into the woods until I came to a sheltered spot that offered a particularly good view of the house. There I found an empty soft drink can and half a dozen cigarette butts on the ground. The watcher was the careless type. I picked up the can with my handkerchief, put a couple of the butts in with it, then went back to the beach.

"Well?" asked Evangeline.

I told her what I'd seen, then said, "What I think happened is that whoever was watching the house saw Hale and Janie come this way in the canoe and went out to the point to meet them or maybe to intercept them. But Hale didn't land here; he went to the barrier beach instead. Later, when he was bird-watching with his binoculars, he saw somebody on the point, maybe somebody who was watching him and Janie, so he came to see what was going on."

"Who could it have been? What happened when Hale got here?"

"I don't know," I said. But I had a bad feeling. "I'm

going to take you away from here. We'll go to my place first. I can't put you up there because our guest room is already taken, but I have friends who own a big old farmhouse. I'll give them a call. I'm pretty sure they have a couple of empty rooms where you can spend the night. No one will know you're there."

We got into the Explorer and I started driving.

"You're going to a lot of trouble," said Evangeline. She didn't sound happy.

"I'm getting paid to tend to trouble. What do you know about Hale Drummand?"

Fire reappeared in her voice. "I could wring his neck, I know that!"

"That's just your anger talking. How long has he been with you? Where did you find him?"

She took a deep breath and let it out slowly. "When I knew I was coming here, my people in Scotland got in touch with an agency in Boston that handles security matters. Thornberry International. Hale is one of their agents. I needed somebody who was good with children, and until today Hale has done his job very well."

"I know Thornberry. He runs a good outfit. If Drummand works for them, he can be trusted."

When I turned down our sandy driveway, I said, "My wife and kids should be home. My wife is Zee and the kids are Joshua and Diana. You two can stay here while I phone John and Mattie Skye. John teaches at Weststock College. You'll like them."

"I feel like a fugitive."

I tried to lighten the mood: "Well, the witness protection program this ain't, but you'll be comfortable enough."

Zee's Jeep was parked in the yard, but my old Land

Cruiser was not, indicating that Brady had taken it out looking for Christa.

As we got out of the car, my children came running around the corner of the house and skidded to a stop as they took in Janie and her mother.

I introduced everyone to everyone. Janie and Diana were of a size. The children eyed each other.

"How are things in the tree house?" I asked.

Joshua deemed that was a proper question. "Good, Pa. We have lemonade up there. You want to come and drink some with us? We have paper cups and cookies."

"I have to make a telephone call and I want to introduce Mrs. Price to your mother. Maybe Janie would like a look at the tree house."

"You want to see it?" Diana asked Janie.

Janie looked up at her mother then back at Diana. "Okay," she said.

The three children skipped around the house and out of sight.

"A tree house sounds dangerous," said Evangeline.

"They'll be all right. So far nobody's broken any bones falling out of the tree."

"I worry. She's my only child."

"All parents worry. Yours did, too."

"How well I know. And they had reason!" She seemed to loosen up, remembering.

"If you want, I'll go out and cancel the visit."

But she shook her head. "No. Let them go. I'm sure Janie will be all right."

"Come on inside, then."

When Zee and Evangeline met I was struck by the vivid contrast between Zee's dark beauty and Evangeline's pale blonde splendor.

"Zee, this is Ethel Price. Ethel, this is my wife, Zee."

Some feminine evaluations filled the room, and both of them seemed amused by it.

"Very nice to meet you, Ethel," said Zee with a smile. "Jeff and I usually have a cocktail on the balcony about now. Will you join us?"

"I'll take a glass of white wine, if you have it."

"White wine is what the good ladies in the soap operas drink," I said. "You two go up and I'll bring the booze."

They climbed the wooden stairs and I got drinks and snacks, put them on a tray, and carried everything to the balcony. There, Zee and Evangeline were sitting and chatting easily while watching their children play in the tree house in the giant beech at the rear of the yard.

"I'll be back," I said. "I have to make a couple of phone calls."

I used the bedroom phone and called the Skyes. Mattie answered, and I told her what I needed.

Mattie had two college-age daughters, and it took a lot to rattle her. "Evangeline and her daughter here for the night? Sure. But I may have to go buy some smelling salts to revive the twins."

"You're a sweetheart. And I'd just as soon no one knows about this."

"Keeping such a secret might cost the girls a few burst blood vessels, but I think they can manage it for Evangeline's sake. It'll be something like dying heroically for your country.

"Why don't you bring the two of them over right now. I'll have John toss a couple extra burgers on the grill, and we can all size each other up. Maybe Janie would like to take a look at the twins' horses before dark. Girls are usually crazy about horses."

"We'll be there as soon as we finish this round of cocktails."

I hung up and called the number at the bottom of the ID that Jake Spitz had given me. I got an answering machine. I hung up again and called the Edgartown police station. The chief was out, but Kit Goulart, the officer at the desk, gave me a phone number for Jake Spitz. It was the same one I'd just called. I called it again and told the machine that I needed to talk with Jake ASAP.

Then I went up onto the balcony and joined the ladies. They seemed to be hitting it off, as did the children out in the tree house. I was glad.

When our glasses were empty, we rounded up Janie, who was reluctant to abandon her new playmates so soon, and I took her and her mother to the Skyes' place, where Mattie, John, and the twins welcomed Mrs. Price and her daughter to the farm.

"I'll be back in the morning," I said to Evangeline. "You'll be safe here."

I hoped I was right.

When I got home, my rusty Land Cruiser was parked beside Zee's Jeep. I got myself another drink, and followed the sounds of voices and laughter up to the balcony, where I found Brady Coyne having cocktails with my wife.

I shook his hand. "What's new in the lawyer biz?"

"I've had a busy day," he replied.

"Me, too. We can trade tales. You go first."

Chapter Ten

Brady

"You really want to talk business?" I said to J.W.

He shrugged. "I figured you'd want to."

I held up my martini. "In due course."

The Jacksons' balcony looked out at the salt pond and, beyond it, Nantucket Sound. The sky toward the east was darkening and the ocean looked flat and purple. A gang of swallows were chasing mosquitoes around the yard, and a couple of half-grown cottontails were hopping on the lawn, approaching dangerously close to Zee's vegetable garden.

"What's your secret?" I said, holding up my glass. I'm not normally a martini guy, but J.W. made excellent ones.

"Oh, no, you don't," he said. "I tell you, you tell the bartender at the Ritz, next thing you know it won't be a secret."

"I don't know the bartender at the Ritz."

Zee laughed. "He won't even tell me. Says he's going to bequeath the recipe to Joshua. But not Diana. It's a guy thing, he says. Seems to me, everything's a guy thing."

"At least tell me whether you stir or shake."

J.W. shook his head. "Can't say. There's a woman present." He refilled all of our glasses from the pitcher. "You feel like talking about your day?"

"Sure," I said. "I damn near had my fortune told."

"I wouldn't've taken you for a believer," said Zee.

"I'm not," I said. "It's silly. Thing is, I think she was seeing—or hearing, or smelling, or whatever she does—she was seeing something. About me, I mean. It was actually a little spooky. I told her not to tell me. I can't imagine knowing what my fate is, you know?"

Zee laughed. "If you feel that way, it means you *do* believe in it. If you didn't, you wouldn't care if she told you."

"She got you there, pal," said J.W.

I shrugged. "Point is, I *was* interested in what she might conjure up about Christa. I showed her the picture. She saw bright lights and explosions and chaos and a big eye in the sky, or some damn thing, watching it all, and—how did she say it?—and spirits colliding."

"What do you make of that?" said Zee.

"Nothing. Like I said, I don't believe in it. It was . . . interesting, that's all." I held up my half-empty martini glass. "You don't shake a good martini, I know that much. Ice cubes colliding with each other chips them. Melted ice dilutes the vodka. This is definitely not watered down." I arched my eyebrows at J.W.

"Flattery'll get you nowhere," he said.

I handed J.W. Christa's picture. "Don't suppose you've run into her in your travels?"

He frowned at it, closed his eyes for a minute, then shook his head. "I don't know," he said. "There's something familiar about her, but it's probably some face I've seen on TV or something." He squinted at the picture again, then put it down on the table. "The problem, of course, is that lots of people look like lots of other people. I'll keep an eye out for this girl in my travels with the singer."

"And how are the travels with the singer going?" I said.

J.W. rolled his eyes. "You don't want to know."

"Sure I do. It'll give us an excuse to have one more refill." I handed him my glass.

He gave us all refills. Then he told me about his adventures with Evangeline.

When he finished, Zee turned to me and said, "See, Brady, I knew it sounded too good to be true. Tooling around the island in a nice new air-conditioned car. Showing the visiting celebrity the sights. No danger. Cushy work. Easy money. Ha! My instinct was to refuse to let him do it."

"But when you found out it was Evangeline," said J.W., "you changed your tune."

"I should've trusted my instincts," she said. "Always trust your instincts. My mother taught me that."

"Wise woman, your mother," said J.W.

The next morning I woke up with a nervous, acid feeling in my stomach, as if something was going to happen if I didn't do something about it. The fact that I had no idea what might happen or what I should do made the feeling worse. I attributed it to Princess Ishewa and her damn clairvoyance. I never should've gone within a mile of her shop.

I was itchy to get going. I told J.W. my plan for the day, such as it was, and he told me his. Then I climbed into his ancient Land Cruiser, drove down to the harbor in Edgartown, and had breakfast at the Dock Street Café.

On an island with scores of excellent eateries, the Dock Street Café was the one I liked the best. As well as I could determine, they served breakfast all day and night. It seemed to be a gathering place for locals. It was always noisy, with people walking around talking to other people, but if you wanted to prop your newspaper up in front of you and read about the Red Sox, nobody bothered you.

I sat at the counter and had three over-easy eggs on top of corned beef hash, with home fries and wheat toast and a big glass of orange juice. A breakfast intended to get me through the whole day.

When I finished, the waitress took away my dishes, then came back to refill my coffee mug. She looked about twenty. She had brown hair and brown eyes and olive skin and a quick smile. Her name tag said KATE.

"Kate," I said to her, "can I bother you for a minute?"

She glanced around the café. "A minute, I guess."

"I wonder if you've seen this girl." I put Christa's picture on the counter.

Kate glanced at it, narrowed her eyes, then shook her head. "I'm terrible at faces. I might've seen her. She looks like lots of people. I don't know her, I can tell you that."

"Do you go to parties, hang out with the young people down here?"

"Sure."

"If I gave you this picture, would you keep an eye out for her and let me know if you see her?"

She frowned. "Depends."

"On what?"

"On what you want with her."

"If I told you, would you believe me?"

She looked at me for a moment. "Why should I?"

I fished out one of my business cards and handed it to her. "I'm a lawyer."

She smiled. "And that makes you trustworthy?"

"Touché," I said. I tapped Christa's picture. "This girl

ran away two years ago. Her parents want me to find her. Her father's dying, and I hope to talk her into going home to see him."

"Oh, man," she said. "That sucks big-time." She peered at me. "That's the truth?"

"It is," I said. "Honest."

"You're not like a cop or something?"

"No. Her name is Christa Doyle, and she's eighteen years old. She's committed no crime, unless you count breaking her mother's and father's hearts. I just want to talk with her." I wrote Christa's name and the Jacksons' phone number on the back of the picture and pushed it toward her. "Keep this. If you see her, please don't say anything about this to her. Just call me." I hesitated. "There's a reward."

"Oh yeah?"

"Yes," I said. "Five hundred dollars if you spot her and help me find her and I get to talk with her."

"What if I see her but you can't find her and talk to her."

I shook my head. "No deal. You could tell me anything."

She stuck out her lower lip and pretended to pout. "You don't trust me?"

"Five hundred bucks is a lot of money."

At that moment, another waitress came over and said, "Hey, Katie. Let's go, huh?"

Kate took Christa's picture, folded it twice, and shoved it into the pocket of her jeans. "I'll see what I can do," she said. "They're yelling at me."

"Thank you," I said.

I left Kate a big tip and walked out of the Dock Street Café smiling. A reward. Brilliant, Coyne. Offering Kate a reward had come out of my mouth without, as far as I could tell, passing through my brain. But now that I thought about it, it seemed like a good idea. If it led me to Christa, five hundred dollars would be a bargain.

My plan, if you could call it that, was to spend this Monday covering as much of the three easternmost towns on the Vineyard—Edgartown, Oak Bluffs, and Vineyard Haven—as I could, although I wasn't exactly sure what "covering" meant. I figured I'd walk up and down the streets, go into any business establishments that struck me as places that might attract people like Christa, study as many faces as I could, leave her picture with likely people, repeat the reward offer, and see what happened. Putting in the hours. Thrashing around.

If nothing flew out of the bushes today, I'd start prowling around the other parts of the island, and I'd keep prowling and thrashing and looking at faces and talking to people until something happened. The Celebration for Humanity was scheduled for Friday and Saturday nights, and if I hadn't found Christa before then, that would be a good place to look for her. I figured J.W. could get me in.

I spent the rest of the morning in Edgartown. I talked to shop owners, restaurant hostesses, real estate brokers, gas station attendants. I dropped into clothing stores and gift shops and bookstores. In three or four hours, I found nobody who thought they'd seen Christa Doyle.

I left her photo with some people, but I didn't want to paper the island with her face. If Christa saw it, there was the danger that she'd hole up or flee, and then I'd never find her. So I chose carefully—people who I felt reasonably confident would not be indiscreet.

A little after noontime I figured I'd done what I could in Edgartown. Geographically, Oak Bluffs should be my next stop, but I'd already put in some time there, so I headed over to Vineyard Haven.

I spent an hour or so walking around the ferry landing and then began strolling the narrow streets just up the hill, and on one of those streets I spotted a couple of college kids, a boy and a girl, coming out of a tattoo parlor. The girl was as tall as the boy, and she had long, jet-black hair, which she wore in a long braid that dangled down the middle of her back. From behind, I thought it might be Christa.

I crossed the street, looped around ahead of them, crossed back, and started down the sidewalk toward them. As they approached me, I stopped and pretended to look into a shop window. I didn't want Christa to recognize me. Not until I had a plan for approaching her. Finding her was the first step.

Well, this girl wasn't Christa. Right age, right height, right hair color, right complexion. But her face was too round, her mouth was too small, and her nose was wrong.

I don't know why it made me feel good to spot someone who vaguely resembled Christa, but it did. It felt like progress.

That couple had come out of a tattoo parlor. I went in.

Tattoos were no longer the exclusive domain of sailors and bikers and prison convicts. I remembered all the earrings that Christa wore. If she was into body piercing, maybe she was also into tattoos.

The walls of the little shop were lined with colored drawings that were, I assumed, tattoo designs. Many of them were quite elaborate and artistic. There were Indian chiefs in full headdress, a variety of American-flag motifs, bald eagles, cartoon characters, dozens of religious pictures ranging from simple crosses to crosses with Jesus nailed to them. There were animals and fish and reptiles and lizards and butterflies and bugs. There were abstract designs and ancient symbols and alphabets.

A woman was leaning her elbows on the counter. Dark blonde hair cut in a Beatles mop-top, rimless glasses, flowered blouse buttoned primly to the throat. She looked like a fifth-grade schoolteacher—a bit out of place in a tattoo parlor. She had her chin in her hands, and she was smiling at me.

"Are you the artist?" I said to her.

"I'm one of 'em," she said. "I'm Stormy."

"Brady," I said.

"First time?"

"Huh?"

"First tattoo?"

"Oh," I said. "No. I don't think I want a tattoo."

"Window-shopping, huh?"

"Something like that. I didn't even realize tattooing was legal in Massachusetts."

"It's only been a few years," she said. "I used to work in New Hampshire."

"So is business good?"

"Unbelievable. Last few weeks we've had to make appointments for people."

"Actually," I said, "I'm trying to find somebody. I wonder if you might've seen her." I showed her Christa's picture.

She looked at it, then looked up at me. "Why are you looking for this girl?"

I told her about Mike and Neddie Doyle.

Stormy hesitated. "That's the truth, huh?"

"Yes."

"You're a lawyer?"

I nodded.

"She was here," she said.

"Really? You sure?"

"I'm pretty sure. It was, oh, a week ago. I didn't do her, but I was here when she came in. She's the kind of girl you notice."

"Who, um, did her, then?"

"Buster. He's out back with a client now. You can talk to him when he's done if you want."

"I definitely do," I said. "Tell me what you remember about Christa."

Stormy shrugged. "Not much. I noticed her, that's all. She was with a guy, I think. I didn't pay too much attention. I was talking with somebody else, and she was with Buster. You should talk to him."

"I will. How soon will he be available?"

"Hang on." She pushed open a door behind the counter, stuck her head into the doorway, and there was an exchange of voices. Then she closed the door. "He's just finishing up. Another few minutes."

Some other people had come into the shop, and Stormy turned her attention to them. I looked at the tattoo designs on the wall, and five minutes later a man's voice said, "Sir? You wanted to talk to me?"

I turned. Buster was a skinny fiftyish guy with a half-bald head, a gray ponytail, a gold hoop in his left ear, and thick glasses. An old hippie, or maybe an easy rider—or both.

I shook hands with him, and when I did, I noticed the colorful designs tattooed on his fingers and wrists and forearms. They snaked their way up under his shirtsleeves and peeked out at the open throat of his shirt. "Stormy says you might've done a tattoo for a girl about a week ago. Her name is Christa, and I need to find her."

He frowned. "I don't remember the name."

I showed him Christa's picture.

He glanced at it and nodded. "Oh, okay. I do remember her. She wanted an eye."

"An eye?" I said. "The tattoo, you mean?"

"Come on out back, I'll show you."

I followed him into the cramped back room where he kept his tattooing equipment. There was a padded, waist-high table and a couple of chairs. Buster and I sat in the chairs, facing each other.

He took out a sketch pad, drew quickly on it, and handed it to me. It looked like a child's drawing of an eye—just a circle inside an eye-shaped oval with a pupil in the middle and a few abstract lines to suggest a brow and the bridge of a nose.

Princess Ishewa had mentioned an eye in the sky. Christa had an eye tattoo. Hmm. I'm a confirmed skeptic, but I couldn't help wondering if the princess did have some kind of second sight.

"Is there some significance to this?" I said to Buster. "It looks sort of familiar."

"It's some kind of ancient symbol, I think. I've done others like it." He shrugged. "Don't know what it's called. I'm an artist, man. I make pictures. People ask for something, I assume it has significance to them. They ask for it, I draw it."

"Where did she get it done?"

"Right here." He waved his hand around the room.

I smiled. "I meant, what part of her body."

"Ah," he said. "Her left hip." He patted his own skinny hip. "Toward the back."

"Well, as I said, I'm looking for her. No chance you might have an address or phone number or something, is there?"

He reached up to a shelf and brought down the kind of notebook that I used to take lecture notes in when I was in college. "I keep track of all my work," he mumbled. He squinted at the page. "Here it is. Week ago yesterday. Girl said her name was Raven. No address or phone number. I always ask, but I don't require it if they pay cash."

"Raven?"

He shrugged. "I didn't ask for her identification. She looked plenty old enough. Mid-twenties, I'd guess. I just ask their name so we can talk. She said it was Raven."

"But you're sure it's this girl." I pointed at Christa's picture.

"Oh, sure. It was her, all right. Nice kid. Nervous, though."

"What makes you say that?"

"Most people are nervous about their first tattoo. I didn't have the feeling that was it with her, though."

"No?"

"No. She was with a guy. It seemed like something was going on between them."

"Like boyfriend-girlfriend stuff?"

"Could be, but I didn't really get that feeling. It was more like he brought her here to get this done. As if it was his idea and she was doing it for him."

"This guy, did you get his name?"

Buster closed his eyes for a minute. "Sorry." He shook his head. "I guess she might've said his name, but if she did, I don't remember what it was. They didn't talk much. He came back here while I did her. Had to see the whole thing."

"You let people do that?"

"Why not?"

I shrugged. "So she paid cash?"

"Yes. Actually, he did. The guy paid for it. Sixty bucks. That's cheap for a tattoo. This eye. Just a few lines. About as easy as it gets."

"I was hoping you might have a credit-card receipt."

"Sorry."

"You said you've done some of these eye tattoos before?"

"Up until this summer, I don't believe I did more than one or two in my whole career. Lately there's been a little run on 'em, for some reason. I've done six or eight in the past two, three weeks. All on women."

"This same eye?"

"Exactly like this one."

"Young, attractive women?"

Buster frowned at me. "What makes you say that?"

I shrugged. "Just wondering."

"Well, now that I think about it, I'd guess that would be right. Young, attractive women. All on the left hip. Some new fad, I guess."

As I walked back to where I'd parked J.W.'s car down by the ferry landing, I realized that I'd better try to learn the significance of eye tattoos on the left hips of attractive young women.

I sat in the car for a few minutes with the sea breeze blowing through the windows. I'd taken Buster's sketch of Christa's eye tattoo with me. I took it out of my shirt pocket and looked at it. It looked back at me. No words were exchanged.

In about two minutes my mood swung from elated to discouraged. All I'd really learned was that Christa had, indeed, been here on the Vineyard a week ago, and if Alyssa Romano was to be believed, I already knew that.

The fact that she was wearing a small tattoo on a part of her anatomy that would not normally be exposed meant something, I supposed. But it didn't bring me any closer to finding her.

I was thinking maybe I should go hang around the beaches and ogle all the attractive young women wearing bikinis. I should look closely at their, um, hips, and see if an eye was looking back at me. If anyone asked me what I thought I was doing, I'd just say it was lawyer business.

A lawyer getting paid to ogle young women in bikinis? Who wouldn't buy that story?

I looked at my watch. It was a little after three o'clock. That gave me a few hours before martini time on the Jackson balcony—plenty of time to drive around the island and remind myself of the lay of the land. I figured I'd follow the road that skirted the salt ponds on the south side through Edgartown and on out to Chilmark, take a swing around the westernmost tip of the island at Gay Head, then back around the north side through West Tisbury and Tisbury, and complete my circle at the Jacksons' abode.

Call it reconnaissance. If anything struck me as a likely Christa clue, I'd make a note to go back on Tuesday when I had more time to check it out.

Also call it decompression. I hadn't done much relaxing in the past few days. A leisurely summer-afternoon drive around a beautiful island with nobody talking to me, maybe some classical music or quiet jazz or even some good ol' rock and roll on the radio—that's what I needed.

I was on the Edgartown Road in Tisbury heading south when the blue light started flashing in my rearview window.

Chapter Eleven

J.W.

Early the next morning, I phoned the Carberg house hoping that Hale Drummand would be home. No one answered. I'd barely hung up when Jack Spitz finally returned my call of the previous evening

"So much for my ASAP message on your machine," I groused. "I thought you government types were supposed to be servants of us civilians. Some servant."

"I had to go down to Washington," he explained. "I just got back. What's up?"

I told him about Drummand's disappearance and about finding the site from which someone had been watching the Carberg house.

He became immediately serious. "I'll get out to the house and have a look at things. Are the woman and child safe?"

I told him where they were.

"Good," he said. "I remember meeting Professor Skye and his family. They're good people. Try to keep Mrs. Price and the girl with them until we find out what's going on."

"I'm going to see them this morning after breakfast. Then I'll meet you at the Carberg house and show you where I found the soda can and cigarette butts. Maybe your lab guys can learn something from them."

"It would be nice to find Drummand while we're at it."

"Yes, it would." I hung up.

In the kitchen Zee and the kids were digging into blueberry pancakes, and Brady was drinking coffee.

"If you have hopes of sharing these, you'd better sit down and start eating," said Zee, pouring maple syrup over her stack of cakes.

That seemed like good advice, so I followed it. While I ate I announced my plans for the day and got Brady's outline of his.

"We can then exchange gleaned wisdom over cocktails this evening," he concluded.

I gave him an admiring look. "You're the only person I can ever remember saying 'gleaned.' Is that lawyer talk?"

"Lawspeak 101. I aced it." He smiled modestly.

Zee got up and put her dishes in the sink. "Two halfwits usually make one whole wit, but I'm not sure it adds up that high in this case. Well, I'm off to work. I'll drop the kids at camp on my way."

"Ma."

"What, Diana?"

"Can we go to the beach instead?"

"Not today. Your dad and I and Brady all have to work."

"Rats."

"Double rats," agreed Joshua.

But the rats gave me an idea.

After Zee and the children left, Brady, a prodigious coffee drinker, finished a final cup and stood up. "Normally I'd stay here and help do the dishes, but I'm a busy man with places to go, things to do, and people to see. You know what I mean?"

I feigned disgust. "I know lawyers are like cops: You

can never find one when you need one but they surround you when you don't."

"I'll see you tonight." He grinned and breezed out the door.

I often point out to Zee that I have to do everything, and here was more proof. But I couldn't really complain because of our house rule that the person who cooks doesn't have to clean up afterward as long as the food is good, and blueberry pancakes are very good indeed. I did some thinking while I washed and stacked the dishes, then got into the snappy white Explorer and drove to the Skyes' farm.

There, everyone was at breakfast except the twins, who were at that age when rising early never happens unless a ride is leaving for the ski slopes or the beach. I accepted another cup of coffee. If I drank much more of the stuff I'd probably qualify for law school.

"While you're all here in one spot," I began, "I want to make a suggestion. If I was in any position to make it an order, I would."

"You people who don't take orders very well are always anxious to give them," said John, chewing a piece of toast. "What exactly do you have in mind?"

I told them about my conversation with Jake Spitz then said, "What I'd like to have happen is for Ethel and Janie to stay here for another day. They'll be safe from prying eyes and I'll be free to work with Jake and try and find out what's going on."

"Oh, no," said Evangeline, shaking her head. "We couldn't do that. It was asking too much for John and Mattie to put us up last night. We'll go back to the house."

"Of course they can stay with us!" said Mattie. Then

she turned to Evangeline. "It's nice to have a grown-up woman to talk to, and you'll be doing my daughters the biggest favor they could ever imagine. One night with you in the same house was almost heaven. Another one will be paradise! Do stay."

"In another day or so you should be able to go back to your own house," I said. "Meanwhile, I thought you might all go over to East Beach for the day. There won't be any celebs or reporters there, so you can swim and relax like normal human beings." I pointed a finger at rosy Janie. "Except you, of course. You should stay under an umbrella with a lot of sunscreen on."

"Mom, do I have to stay under an umbrella?"

"Well, maybe not all the time."

"If you want company," I said to Janie, "Joshua and Diana are dying to go to the beach."

"Yes!" Janie looked pleased. She was a child who, I suspected, spent a lot of time with adults and was happy at the thought of spending some with people her own age.

"Plenty of room in the Jeep for everybody," said John.

I looked at Evangeline. "Did you pack your bathing suits in those overnight bags?"

She smiled the smile that had caused many a young man's heart to throb. "Amazing, but true. Maybe I have the sight."

"If John wasn't such a prude you could probably all swim in the buff, but professors are notorious puritans."

"Speak for yourself," said Mattie, theatrically ogling her husband then popping a last bite of sausage into her mouth. "Stop at your kids' camp and tell them we'll be coming by for Diana and Joshua. We'll pick up their swimsuits at your place on the way to Chappy and we'll have the cell phone so you can get in touch if you have to."

I rose from my chair. "I'll come by before supper and let you know what's going on, if I get it figured out by then."

Evangeline touched my arm. "I'm worried about Hale."

"Don't let it ruin your day. There's probably a pretty simple explanation for him not showing up. He may be back at the house right now, talking with Jake Spitz."

"I hope so."

I hoped so, too, but I doubted it.

I drove to the Carberg house. Spitz was inside. A small pair of binoculars hung around his neck. Hale Drummand was not in sight.

"How many keys are there to this place?" I asked.

"Three that I know of. One for Drummand, one for Mrs. Price, and one for me. I've been through the house and garage and there's no sign of anything unusual having happened."

"Is there an answering machine?"

"Yes, but there are no messages on it. Let's take a ride over yonder." He gestured toward the point of land thrusting out into the pond to the east. "That's the place where Drummand went missing, isn't it?"

"That's it."

We drove there in the white Ford and I showed him the tire tracks behind the trees and the spot where I'd found the can and cigarette butts. There, he put his binoculars to his eyes and studied the house to the west.

"Good view, but who was here, and why?"

"The benign possibilities include fans who stumbled onto where Evangeline was staying, or paparazzi trying for a scoop."

He grunted. "And on the malignant side, maybe somebody with bad intentions. Kidnapping, maybe, or worse."

"Worse?"

He opened his mouth, hesitated, then said, "Celebrities get stalked all the time and shot often enough to keep guys like Hale Drummand in business. Evangeline is a star with a capital *S*. A guy with the right rifle and scope could do a lot of damage from here and probably be back in Edgartown before the cops showed up." He swept the pond with his binoculars. "If I wasn't so damned short-handed already I'd put a man out here."

"The whole island's short of fuzz right now. Maybe Thornberry can contribute more agents. I imagine Evangeline can afford them."

"Show me where Drummand came ashore."

There was no path leading through the woods, so we followed the beach out to the point, where we found the canoe right where I'd left it.

Spitz again used his glasses to sweep the pond and the barrier beach. "Drummand must have gone somewhere after he landed here, but where?"

"Janie didn't watch him when he paddled across," I said. "She was on the ocean side of the barrier beach. But he saw something or someone that made him want to come over here."

"Friend or enemy?"

"He expected to go back to the little girl. He told her to wait for him."

"Friend, then. Or someone he didn't consider dangerous, at least."

"That's how I see it. But maybe he was wrong."

Spitz frowned at the trees and underbrush. "Let's take a look. You follow the beach on around the point and I'll cut through the woods. Meet you on the other side. Sing out if you cut sign."

He went into the trees, walking a hunter's walk, silent, his eyes roaming ahead of him and to either side.

Mine was the easier job, for if there was a sign to be found, I'd see it in the sand and short beach grass.

But there was nothing to suggest Drummand or anyone else had walked there; I saw only deer tracks and signs of birds and small mammals. I completed my circumnavigation of the point and cut back to the Explorer. I was headed into the woods when Spitz came into view.

"Anything?"

"No." Spitz wiped his brow with a handkerchief. "Let's go through these woods again, keeping about twenty feet apart. We should be able to sweep the area pretty well in a couple of hours."

That roused my curiosity, but I said nothing. Spitz and I searched slowly back to the beach, keeping on paths as parallel as the undergrowth would allow. Then we moved to the west and reversed our course, coming back toward the Explorer. It was hot, sweaty work. We continued the search pattern, moving steadily to the west.

About an hour after we'd begun I came to a patch of disturbed earth and leaves. A faint trail of overturned leaves and broken twigs led to my left where there was a fallen tree. Growing next to its rotting trunk was a low scrub oak. As I nudged my foot through the leaves beneath my feet my sandal hit a chopped-off stump. I kicked the leaves away and saw small, fresh wood chips.

I followed the faint trail to the tree and saw that the oak brush wasn't alive. It was leaning there, its leaves already beginning to wilt. I pushed it aside and saw more disturbed earth. A bloody hand was partially uncovered, thanks to some hungry animal or bird.

I called to Spitz and he came. He looked where I

pointed and pulled a phone from his jacket pocket. When he finished his call and we had nothing to do but wait for the state police, I said, "Drummand wasn't just a Thornberry PI, was he? He was more than that. Otherwise you wouldn't have spent the morning sweating back and forth through the woods looking for him."

Spitz wiped his brow again. He looked unwell, but he was already pulling himself together. "He was one of ours."

"One of yours?" I was only mildly surprised. "What's going on?"

He shook his head, as if to clear it. "I don't know, but it's something big and it has to do with Evangeline."

He hadn't quite gotten himself together yet, so I pushed it. "The FBI doesn't play nursemaid to rock stars, as far as I know, not even the Beatles or the Stones or the Bristol Tars. Not even Evangeline. You got me into this, whatever it is, so level with me."

He willed himself back to an even keel. "I can tell you this much," he said, hedging carefully. "For months now we've been picking up chatter. Bits and pieces and sometimes whole messages. Cell phone calls, e-mail, even telegraph and snail mail, you name it. All very obscure. Some clearly coded. We don't know what's planned, but it's big and it's bad and some of it involves Evangeline and it's going to happen soon if we don't do something about it."

"Are you telling me that Evangeline is some sort of terrorist?"

"No, I'm not telling you that. But her name keeps coming up. We're here right now in part because she's on the island. Drummand was our inside man."

"Well, he must have reported to you," I said impatiently. "What did he tell you?"

"He never reported anything worth reporting. And he won't be telling us anything in the future." Spitz's face had lost its pallor and was back to its normal color. He looked at me very hard. "Evangeline trusts you," he said. "You're going to be our inside man from now on."

Chapter Twelve

Brady

The officer in the cruiser behind me gave his siren a quick, rude squeal, just in case I wasn't aware of the implications of his flashing blue light. I pulled to the side of the road, turned off the ignition, and went rummaging in the glove compartment for J.W.'s registration. I found road maps, expired shellfishing licenses, lollipops, flashlights, and one chewed-up bluefish plug minus its treble hooks, but damned if I could come up with any automobile registration.

Had I been speeding? I didn't think J.W.'s Land Cruiser was even capable of speed-limit speeds. But I hadn't been paying attention.

In my rearview mirror I saw the officer sitting in his cruiser behind me. I assumed he was running the old Toyota's plates. I didn't think I'd done anything wrong. Maybe he was after J.W. for scallop hunting out of season, or sassing some radical environmentalist, or refusing to divulge his martini recipe. J.W.'s crimes were legion.

After a minute or two, the cop opened his door, got out, and approached me. He stopped just behind the car window. "License and registration, please," he said, as expected.

"I'm not J. W. Jackson," I said, "and this isn't my car

and I don't know where the registration is. But I can explain. I wasn't—?"

"Do you have your driver's license, sir?"

"Sure." I fumbled it out of my wallet and handed it to him.

He squinted at it and handed it back to me. "Mr. Coyne, I'd like you to follow me, sir."

"Huh? What's up?"

"There's a state police officer who needs to talk to you."

"Me?"

"Yes, sir. I'll pull out in front of you. Just stay behind me, please."

I nodded. I knew he wouldn't tell me anything, so there was no sense in asking. I was relieved that I'd apparently escaped a speeding ticket.

I followed the cruiser to the state police barracks on Temahigan Avenue in Oak Bluffs. J.W. and I had come here a couple of times in the past. I was ushered into a bare conference room equipped with a rectangular metal table, four metal chairs, two wire-mesh-covered windows high on the wall, and a tin ashtray brimming with old butts.

Pretty soon a chunky, thirtyish woman with a crabby look on her face came in. She wore a mannish outfit—pale blue summer-weight sport jacket, a white button-down shirt, khaki pants, and sturdy black shoes. A manila folder was tucked into her armpit.

She gave me a perfunctory smile. Her teeth were very white against her deeply tanned skin. "I'm Olive Otero," she said. "State cops."

"Brady Coyne," I said. "Boston lawyer."

"I know who you are, Mr. Coyne."

"I know who you are, too, Miz Otero. J. W. Jackson has mentioned you."

"I bet he has. You should watch the company you keep." Olive Otero scowled. "Last time you were down here hanging around with Jackson, if I remember correctly, all kinds of unpleasant things started happening. You two seem to have a knack for stirring things up. If I had my wits about me, I'd ban you from the island and exile him. Between the two of you . . ." She waved her hand in the air. "So what is it this time, Mr. Coyne? Business or pleasure? You fishing for fish or something else? Fish, I hope."

"Business. Sorry."

"Staying with the Jacksons, are you?"

"Yes. You knew that. That's how you knew you'd find me in J.W.'s Land Cruiser. So are you going to ask me a lot of questions you already know the answers to, or can we get to why you had me brought here?"

She gave me a quick, sour smile in which her eyes did not participate. "Certainly." She opened the manila folder and slid out Christa's picture. "You're looking for this girl, right?"

"Come on, ma'am. You know that, too. Kit Goulart had this photo faxed to all the departments on the island."

"I didn't get this out of any fax machine." She arched an eyebrow at me. "I got it off a dead body."

I stared at her. "Who?"

"Anita Montgomery's her name."

I frowned. "I don't think I know anybody named Anita Montgomery."

"No, I expect not. She goes by the name of Princess Ishewa. Works at the Four Winds Trading Post?" She made it a question.

"Jesus." I blew out a breath. "The fortune-teller. I saw her just yesterday. What happened?"

"I'm the cop, Mr. Coyne. Do you mind if I ask the questions?"

"Am I some kind of suspect?"

Olive Otero shook her head.

"Then you ought to be able to tell me what happened."

She shrugged. "Car crash on the Edgartown–West Tisbury road out past the airport. Head-on with a good-sized oak tree. Happened a little after two this morning."

"God," I said. "That's terrible. She was a young, vital woman. Interesting person. Very spiritual. She seemed to have a—a gift of some kind. I liked her. She wanted to tell me my fortune. She—" I stopped and looked at her. "Why are you talking to me about a car accident?"

"I didn't say accident, Mr. Coyne. I said crash. It appears that Ms. Montgomery was run off the road."

"Hit-and-run, huh? Some drunk, you think?"

"Not necessarily."

I looked at her. "You think somebody did it on purpose?"

She nodded. "We think it's very possible. Scrape marks on the driver's side of her car. Tire tracks in the sand at the scene indicate somebody pulled over, stopped and got out, walked over to the crash. Since nobody called it in, we don't figure it was some Good Samaritan. Okay, maybe it was an accident, some drunk, and he stopped to see what he could do, saw she was dead, then panicked and took off, which would make it a hit-and-run homicide. But the other possibility is, he stopped to check her out, make sure she was dead." She hesitated. "Which she was. Broken neck. She was driving an old Ford Pinto. You don't see many of them around anymore. She was wearing her seat belt, but in those old cars, there's no shoulder strap." She snapped her arm down and back as if she were slapping something rubber and it bounced back. "See?"

"Whiplash," I said.

She nodded. "The ME figures she died instantly. Before the fire."

"The car caught fire?"

"Cops who came on the scene managed to haul her out before it exploded."

"But if you're thinking someone did it on purpose," I said, "wanted to kill her—"

"Why?" She gave me another one of her humorless smiles. "That's the question. That's what we're trying to figure out." Olive Otero tapped Christa's picture. "She had this folded in her shirt pocket."

"What do you make of that?"

"I was hoping you could tell me. It's got your name and your friend Jackson's phone number written on the back of it."

"I gave her that picture yesterday when I saw her. Asked her to keep an eye out for the girl, just like I've been asking everybody. I'm trying to find her for her parents."

"Yes," she said. "I know about that. Did Ms. Montgomery give you any idea that she might go looking for her?"

"No. She said she'd never seen her. Is that what you think she was doing last night? Looking for Christa?"

She shrugged. "She's got the picture in her pocket. Must've put it there for some reason, huh?"

I thought for a minute. "She put it in her pants pocket when I gave it to her. So she took it out. To show somebody, maybe, huh? Is that what you're thinking?"

She spread her hands. "Could be. Could be she actually did show it to them. Somebody out toward Gay Head, Chilmark, Menemsha, maybe West Tisbury. Ms. Montgomery had a little place, opposite end of the island in East Chop, that she shared with her business partner. It appears she was heading back home when it happened. Point is, if you've got any idea where she might've been before this happened to her, it would be a big help."

"What did her roommate say?"

Olive Otero smiled. This time her eyes crinkled a little, as if I'd finally said something amusing. "There are some things I'm not going to tell you, Mr. Coyne, okay?"

"Well, obviously the roommate didn't tell you where the princess—Ms. Montgomery, I mean—where she was going, or you wouldn't be asking me." I shrugged. "To answer your question, I have no idea where she might've been. I don't know where Christa is, and the princess told me she didn't recognize her, didn't know anything about her. I showed her the picture, asked her if she could use her, um, powers to tell me anything, and she—" I smacked my palm with my fist. "Jesus. She had some kind of vision. She saw bright lights, heard loud noises."

"Like—"

"Like an explosion," I said. "Like fire. Like a car crash." I blew out a breath. "Princess Ishewa wasn't seeing Christa Doyle's fate. She was seeing her own."

"Me," said Olive Otero, "I don't believe in that crap."

"I didn't think I did, either," I said.

"Well," she said, "it looks like—" At that moment a buzz came from her jacket pocket. She reached in and pulled out a cell phone. "Yeah, Otero," she said, then listened for a minute. "You're sure it's him? . . . Well, shit . . . Right, he's here with me now. We're about done. I'll fill you in." She snapped the miniature telephone shut, dropped it back into her pocket, and stood up. "I gotta go. Probably want to talk to you some more. I can reach you at Jackson's house, right?"

I nodded. "Except when I'm driving around in his car, and you seem to be able to locate me then, too."

Olive Otero walked outside with me, and as I was climbing into the Land Cruiser, she put her hand on my arm and said, "You be careful, now, Mr. Coyne, okay?"

That was a kindly thought, and coming from Olive Otero, it was touching. But it wasn't a particularly comforting thought. I didn't like it when people felt they had to tell me to be careful, even if it was good advice.

I'd been with Officer Otero for about an hour. Still a couple hours before martini time at the Jacksons. I decided to continue with my plan to drive around the island, get the lay of the land. Besides, I needed some time to think, and driving alone had always been a good way for me to do that.

The thought that kept ricocheting around inside my brain, of course, was that if somebody had murdered Princess Ishewa because she was looking for Christa, it was my fault. If I hadn't spotted the Kokopelli on that sign in Oak Bluffs, if I hadn't decided to go into the shop, if I hadn't done something totally out of character for me—visiting a fortune-teller—Princess Ishewa might still be alive.

I hoped to hell that it turned out to be some random, drunken hit-and-run. That was an awful thing to hope for, but for my peace of mind, it was preferable to Olive Otero's other hypothesis.

As I drove, I tried to invent scenarios that would explain committing murder to preserve Christa Doyle's privacy. But I couldn't. It didn't make any sense.

What I couldn't quite get my head around was the princess carrying Christa's picture in her shirt pocket. What was she doing with it? What vision had she seen when she looked at it?

Well, I didn't know. Damn good questions, though.

Guilt would gnaw at me until Princess Ishewa's death was explained. Possibly longer than that. I knew that about myself.

I was driving on the long east-west road on the south side of the island. It cut through pine-and-oak woods, giving an occasional glimpse of one of the ponds off to the left. Here and there long sandy driveways meandered through the trees, and I knew that they led to the estates of the Truly Rich Summer People, with their horse barns and swimming pools and tennis courts and skeet fields.

On the Vineyard there were the year-rounders like the Jacksons, mostly descendants of island fishermen and shipbuilders, folks whose families had owned property there long before it turned to gold, plus off-islanders who'd worked hard all their lives, bought their modest places back when they were affordable, and then retired on the island.

Then there were the Ordinary Summer People, hard-working folks who scraped together enough money to buy cottages and houses and who helped pay their mortgages by renting their places when they weren't around.

There were also the Rich Summer People, who didn't need to scrape for their money and didn't need to rent out their places.

And then there were the Truly Rich Summer People, the filthy, disgustingly rich—the CEOs and Manhattan psychiatrists and State Street law partners and oil tycoons and high-tech moguls and movie stars and bestselling authors and old-money Boston Brahmins, the people who didn't care—didn't even notice—what things cost. They bought up multiacre tracts of land with ocean views and built their mansions and installed their security systems and erected their tall gates and commuted by yacht and entertained presidents and foreign heads of state.

J.W. was acquainted with some of the Truly Rich Summer People. A few were my clients. Even when they wore T-shirts and baggy shorts and rubber flip-flops and neglected to shave and rode around on old bicycles, you'd never mistake them for clam diggers or bartenders or schoolteachers.

I wasn't jealous. Not even a little bit. I never knew a Truly Rich Person who was truly happy.

There were two uniformed men standing at the entrance to the airport, and a little farther on, where the road ran alongside the state forest, a couple of Edgartown cruisers were pulled to the side of the road. Two more uniformed officers were standing there talking to a cluster of young people.

I was getting the impression that Martha's Vineyard was under siege.

Around a bend I came upon what I assumed was the scene of Princess Ishewa's fatal crash. Still another police cruiser plus an unmarked gray sedan were parked there, and the area was fenced in with yellow police-scene tape. I slowed to a crawl and looked. A jagged white scar had been gouged into the trunk of a big oak just off the shoulder of the road, and I could see where deep furrows had been plowed into the sandy earth when the princess's little Pinto slewed off the road and smashed into the tree.

I pulled onto the shoulder and stopped, but a uniformed officer stepped into the road and waved me along.

Well, okay. Fine with me. I was no gawker. I had lots of curiosity, but none of it was morbid.

As I continued my circuit of the island, the accident scene kept playing in my imagination—the princess, tooling down the empty night road in her old Pinto, yawning, maybe, eager to get home to her warm bed, then headlights appearing suddenly in her rearview mirror, the vehicle pulling alongside her, moving fast, apparently in a hurry to pass her, then suddenly swerving, slamming against the side of her car, angling her off the road, and the princess skidding, fighting the wheel, standing on the brakes, out of control now, and then the big oak tree looming square in her headlights . . .

I wondered what kind of visions the fortune-teller had in those last few seconds of her life.

I found I had lost whatever enthusiasm for sleuthing I'd started the day with. My search for Christa Doyle would have to wait till tomorrow. Princess Ishewa was dead. It weighed heavily on my heart.

Chapter Thirteen

J.W.

I looked hard at Spitz. "You want me to be your inside man? Me? I've been on this job for three days and you want me to—?"

He held up a hand that stopped my words. "Evangeline knows you. She agreed to spend last night with the Skyes, so she apparently trusts you. So do I. I don't have time to find somebody else she trusts. I need you until Saturday. After that, she'll be gone and you can go back to your wife and kids."

He'd gotten my attention. "Saturday is five days away. You're saying that this bad thing you've been getting wind of—the end of the world, or whatever—is going to happen in the next five days?"

He frowned. "I didn't say that."

"You haven't said a lot about anything. I'm in a coal mine with no lights. If I'm going to be any good to you, I have to know what's going on and what I'm supposed to be doing."

He brightened slightly. "Does that mean you'll do it? It's important, J.W."

I felt that little tingle you get sometimes just before you do something irrational, but I tried to ignore it. "You talk first and then I'll decide. People are getting killed at a pretty fast pace around here. First that director, Ogden Warner, now Hale Drummand. I don't want Evangeline or Janie or me to be the next corpse. So either talk or don't. I won't go any farther blindfolded."

Spitz stared south as though he could see through the trees to where the restless blue Atlantic was rolling toward us from Hispaniola, far beyond the curve of the earth. While he made up his mind, he put his hands on his hips and in doing so brushed back his jacket and revealed the holstered pistol on his belt.

"You know the old joke about intelligence agencies being oxymorons," he said, making his decision. "One of our problems is that we keep tabs on so many organizations and individuals that we have trouble sorting everything out. We've got people watching foreign terrorist groups, local right-wing militias, neo-Nazis, environmental extremists, militant pacifists, racists of all hues, religious fanatics, you name it.

"We get bad information, good information, rumors, contradictory information, out-and-out lies, hints, whole scenarios, fantasies, slanders, and innuendoes. We have counterintelligence groups sending us fake info. We have agencies that won't cooperate with us or with each other. Our computers and people are working twenty-four hours a day trying to sort the wheat from the chaff."

"Give me the wheat," I said.

He nodded. "Such as it is. Several months ago we began to intercept some cryptic communications that seemed to be early discussions of plans for a major anti-American incident of some sort. Most of the communications seemed to be between people here in the United States, but some were international. Do you know much about terrorism?"

"Only what I read."

"That's enough for you to know that one guy's terrorist is another guy's heroic freedom fighter, so the terrorist you think everybody should hate is actually somebody with a lot of friends who'll hide him and help him if they can."

"Every scumbag has a mother who thinks he's just misunderstood."

"Yeah. And you also know that these guys, whatever you call them, are very interested in symbols. They like to display their own and they like to destroy their enemy's. The nine-eleven incident was an immensely symbolic attack. It used commercial airplanes, one symbol of Western technology and wealth, to attack the World Trade Center towers and the Pentagon, which were symbols of capitalism and American military power. When the towers fell down, Bin Laden was astonished but delighted, and when Americans panicked, he was even happier because it meant that his decadent Western enemies attached the same significance to all those symbols as he did. He'd hit them hard, right where they lived."

I mouthed a truism: "People often attach more significance to symbols than to what they symbolize."

"Exactly. A guy will go into debt to buy an expensive car so he can impress people with his wealth."

"Or invade Grenada to symbolize our resolve to save the world from communism."

"You could make that argument. Anyway, from the beginning we figured that whatever was being planned would have some major symbolic significance to it, and that whoever was planning it probably had associates who'd be on their side and would aid and abet when possible. We worked on dates that might be significant: April nineteenth, the Fourth of July, that sort of thing. We wondered if Boulder Dam might be a target, or maybe Mount Rushmore."

"Somebody might blow Washington's nose with some dynamite?"

"You get the idea. We worked hard but we didn't make a lot of progress until one of our bright young people who's a big fan of Evangeline and thinks the Celebration for Humanity is the most important cultural event since Woodstock noticed that the messages about a possible incident started just after initial plans were made to hold the Celebration."

"Aha, as the detectives say." In the distance I could hear the sound of cars coming down the sandy road.

"Aha, indeed," said Spitz, looking toward the sound. "With that new bird in our cage, we may have begun to crack the code in the messages, and we think the incident involves someone who will be at the Celebration. Have you heard enough to take the job?"

"Is Evangeline the somebody?"

"Her name has been mentioned a lot."

My mouth seemed to speak of its own accord. "I guess I'll take the job, then."

"Good. You can begin by going out to our car and bringing the police back this way. I'll wait for them." He looked somberly down at the hand sticking out of the sandy earth.

I got out to the road just as the state police cruiser, an Edgartown cruiser, and the sheriff's SUV came into view. Dom Agganis led a collection of police, and Dr. Feeney, the local ME, over to where I stood.

Dom shook his head. "What is it about you and bodies? Are you part vulture or something?"

"Almost," I said. "I'm working for the government, so you could say I'm a scavenger. Come on. I'll take you to the scene of the crime and you can talk to my boss."

"Spitz is your boss?"

"Only temporarily."

Back in the woods, I waited while Spitz talked, photographs were snapped, Feeney carefully uncovered the corpse, and tape went up around the site. When that was done, Spitz came to me.

"I'll get a ride with these guys. You take the car and go find Evangeline. Stay with her. Talk with her. Find out if she knows something. Call me this evening."

"Will I get you or your answering machine?"

"You'll get me. Try to talk Evangeline into staying with the Skyes for at least another night."

"I already did that."

"Good. Keep your eyes open for a tail, in case somebody thinks he can find her by following you."

On my way to the Explorer I paused at the site where the watcher had spied on the Carberg house. The house was about a thousand yards away, I guessed. Not a hard shot for a good sniper.

I went on to the car and drove to Katama. There I deflated my tires down to sixteen pounds of pressure, got into four-wheel drive, and headed east over the barrier beach to Chappaquiddick.

For most of the summer the beach had been closed to SUV traffic, as part of the Fish and Wildlife Department's futile effort to protect piping plovers. Since piping plover chicks and eggs were destroyed by skunks, gulls, and other predators rather than by SUVs, the policy of banning cars made no sense at all. But car banning was dogma to the Fish and Wildlife people, who, like the pope, claimed infallibility on certain matters. Maddening.

To my right were parked Jeeps and bathers playing in the Atlantic surf, and to my left was Katama Bay. There were small sailboats on the bay, and through the narrows at its north end I could see the white buildings of Edgartown. Above me the August sun blazed in a pale blue sky. It was a lovely scene that gave no hint of the violence I'd left behind me, for nature is always innocent.

It cost me the price of a beach sticker to get onto East Beach, but I figured I'd get my money back from Spitz as a business expense. Maybe if I cooked my books I could make some money on the deal. Nah! I was no Arthur Andersen.

I found the Skyes and their guests on the beach just south of Cape Pogue. John was having a try at catching fish, but his gear was too heavy for bonito and there are few bluefish near the shore in August. Still, like most fishermen, he made his casts anyway, since fishing and catching fish are two different games and the former is far more important than the latter.

The three children, Janie well smeared with sunscreen, were playing at the edge of the water, and the women, Mattie and Evangeline, were seated on blankets under a large umbrella. Evangeline, I immediately noticed, wore a bikini bathing suit and wore it very well. I took off my shirt, wrapped it around my pistol, and stuck the shirt under my arm.

"Well, hello," said Mattie as I strolled up. "I didn't expect to see you here. I thought you were working."

"I am working." I put down my shirt, took off my Tevas, and unrolled my beach towel. "On Martha's Vineyard," I explained to Evangeline, "going to the beach is as much work as a lot of people ever do."

"It's a tough job, but you're the man for it," said Mattie, reaching for a picnic basket. "Would you like a beer? I know it's not noon here, but it is somewhere."

"I think I'll take a walk first." I looked at Evangeline. "You two want to come along? It will do worlds for my reputation if I'm seen with two of the three most beautiful women on the East Coast."

"No thanks," said Mattie, who like Evangeline had seen my eyes. "John's had a chance to sit with us and he's abandoned us for fishing. You'll probably be just as faithless. I'm staying right here so my heart won't be broken twice in one day."

"I'll go," said Evangeline, flowing up from her blanket. Then she paused and looked toward the children.

"I'll keep an eye on them," said Mattie.

I left the Tevas on my towel, but carried my rolled-up shirt. "Come along, Mrs. Price. I'll show you where the old lighthouse used to stand before the cliff wore away."

She was golden in the late-morning sun. We walked north toward the point under the cliff. I told her about my morning. When I was through we were standing near a broken brick wall that had once been part of the lighthouse's foundation, before the tower had been picked up by a helicopter and moved inland from the crumbling cliff.

"Do you know anything about this business?" I asked.

Instead of answering she asked, "Is Hale Drummand really dead?"

"Yes. Do you know anything about this business, this incident the FBI has been trying to prevent?"

"No, nothing." She turned abruptly back. "I don't want Janie back there alone." She started down the beach.

I caught up with her. “Janie’s fine. Nobody knows where she is. Or where you are. I want it to stay that way. That’s why I want you to stay longer with John and Mattie. You’ll be safe.”

“If I’m there, they’ll be in danger, too. I can’t put them in harm’s way.”

“Why do you think you’re in danger?”

She made an angry gesture. “People like me are always in danger. From fans and freaks of all kinds. Everywhere we go. It’s the price we pay for being who we are and doing what we do.”

“It seems a high one.”

“Too high,” she snapped. “I’m tired of it!” Then she became almost wistful. “I’ve been thinking of retiring after this concert or maybe after a farewell tour. I have plenty of money. I don’t have to work this way any longer. I’d like to spend time with Janie. I’d like a normal life like John and Mattie’s or yours and Zee’s.”

“If nobody knows you’re with John and Mattie, they’ll be in no danger and neither will you.”

Her anger came back. “I can’t hide. I have to rehearse more than once with Flurge and the Bristol Tars. I have to make sure the lights and sound system are the way I want.”

I walked beside her. “Stay with John and Mattie at least for the time being. When it’s time to rehearse, I’ll take you where you want to go when you want to go there. Nobody not directly involved will know where you came from. We can get whatever you need from the Carberg house. You can wear one of your fancy wigs when we go out.”

She said nothing for several paces, then nodded and turned toward me. When she did I saw the tattoo on her left hip and realized that by some quirk I’d been on her right side ever since arriving at the beach.

"All right," she said. "If John and Mattie will have us, we'll be glad to stay. But they have to let me pay for our food, at least."

"You can fight that out with them. The twins will think they've died and gone to heaven. This fall, when they go back to Weststock and tell their friends that they lived with Evangeline for almost a week, they'll be the envy of every kid at the college."

She smiled ironically. "I remember when I felt that way about some superstars. It was before I knew what the life was really like."

"I've seen your tattoo before," I said. "What is it?"

Her smile went away and she tugged her bikini bottom down an inch or so, but it was too small to cover the tattoo.

Her voice became cool. "It's called the Eye of Horus. When I got it I thought tattoos were romantic. I should have it removed."

"Not many people will see it and most of them will be polite enough not to mention it."

"You mentioned it."

"I'm not as mannerly as some. Besides, I noticed the hip first. I'm a leg man and you have the second-best hips I've seen lately. Zee has you beat, but not by much."

"Do you always ogle women?"

"Only the ones worth ogling. When did you get the tattoo?"

"A few years ago. I'd rather forget that it happened."

"It's forgotten," I lied. "And I'll forsake ogling you, too, if you want," I lied again.

But she suddenly relaxed and laughed. "Ogle away, but don't expect much in return. My heart's in the highlands."

"Is it now? Does its object wear a kilt?"

"Both genders wear skirts in Scotland. Didn't you know that?"

I felt a smile grow on my face.

By the time I got home that night we were almost friends.

I was having a martini on the balcony and telling Zee about my day, except for the ogling part, when I heard my old Land Cruiser rattling down the driveway. Brady Coyne parked and got out. We waved to him. He fixed himself a drink and joined us.

"Long day?" I said as he eased into a deck chair.

"You don't know the half," said Brady.

Chapter Fourteen

Brady

By the time I got to the Jacksons' house, the sun was low over America and shadows were beginning to seep out from under the trees. J.W. and Zee were on the balcony sipping their evening martinis and watching the barn swallows and purple martins chase moths.

"Long day?" said J.W.

"You don't know the half," I said. I poured a martini for myself, spread some bluefish pâté on a cracker, and slumped into a chair. "You waited supper for me," I said. "You didn't need to. But thanks." I gobbled the cracker. I realized I hadn't eaten since breakfast.

"We knew you'd be delayed," said Zee. "Olive Otera called, looking for you. I told her you were rattling around in J.W.'s Land Cruiser. Figured she'd catch up with you. What'd you do this time?"

I summarized my conversation with Olive Otera, and when I finished, J.W. shook his head. "Corpses all over our blessed isle. Something bad is brewing." He told me about the FBI's suspicions and the possibility of terrorist activity on the Vineyard.

"But who'd kill some innocent fortune-teller?" I said.

"Maybe she saw into somebody's future. Saw them do something before they did it."

"Well," I said, "I can tell you this: I don't feel good about it. According to your friend Olive Otera, Princess Ishewa's death might be my fault. And it makes me worry about Christa Doyle, too. I talked to someone today who saw her."

"Yeah?" said J.W. "Who?"

I told him about my conversation with Buster, the tattoo artist. I took his sketch of Christa's tattoo out of my shirt pocket, unfolded it, and spread it on the table. "This is what he drew on her hip. Buster said he's done several of these eyes recently. All on young, pretty women, all on the left hip."

"Ha," said J.W.

"Ha?" I said.

"Evangeline's got one just like that," he said. "It's on her left hip, too. She told me she got it done a few years ago. Didn't seem too eager to talk about it."

Zee was peering at the picture. "It's the Eye of Horus," she said.

"Horace?" I said.

Zee smiled. "Horus." She pronounced it carefully for me. "He's Egyptian. The falcon god. According to the legend, Horus lost his left eye in battle, and his wife restored it. This symbol represents protection from evil. Strength. Healing. Making whole. It was a powerful symbol for the ancient Egyptians. It's all over the tombs."

"So Evangeline got one," I said, "and some scandal sheet got a picture of her in a bikini, and now every teenybopper in America has got to get their very own Eye of Horus tattooed on their left hip. Buster, the tattoo guy, said he figured it was the latest fad."

"Yeah, maybe," said J.W. doubtfully. He got up and poured more chilled vodka into our martini glasses.

When he sat down, I said, "When she was in Oregon, Christa was living in some kind of commune. You got any communes on this island?"

"Lots of college kids live together in those rented houses," Zee said, "and from what I hear, they share everything, including their drugs and their bodily fluids."

"From each according to his ability, to each according to his needs," said J.W. "The late great Karl Marx." He hesitated. "Is an ashram a commune?"

"Technically," I said, "I would think not. Why?"

He told me about Alain Duval, the spiritual guru. "This guy, from what I can tell, attracts women like flies to a cow flop. Young women. Young, pretty women. Evangeline knows him."

"And she's got a tattoo like Christa's," I said. "What about all these young, pretty ashram women? Do they all sport Eye of Horus tattoos on their left hips?"

He shrugged. "Alas, I've had few opportunities to scrutinize uncovered hips, though it doesn't sound like unpleasant work."

"You managed a peek at Evangeline's hips," said Zee. "How were they?"

"Second-best I've ever seen," said J.W. with a straight face.

"I think I'd better pay this Duval guy a visit," I said.

J.W. shook his head. "You won't get past the guards."

"Wanna bet?"

"Be smart, Coyne. My impression is, Duval is not somebody you want for an enemy."

"Neither am I," I said. "Tell me what to expect."

"Well," said J.W., "he keeps his compound buttoned tight. Guards everywhere."

"As if he were hiding something?"

"As if he placed a high value on his privacy. Not unusual around here." J.W. squinted at the sky for a moment, then said, "You got one of those pictures of Christa handy?"

I went over to my briefcase where I'd dropped it on the balcony, slid out one of Christa's photos, and handed it to him. He studied it for a minute. "I thought she might've looked familiar when you showed it to me before," he said. "I still think so." He tapped the picture. "I think I saw her at Duval's."

"You sure?"

"Nope. Not sure. This girl I saw, I didn't get much of a look at her face." He glanced at Zee. "She was, um, wearing a bikini."

Zee laughed. "You old goat."

"You didn't notice her left hip?" I said.

J.W. closed his eyes for a moment. "Nope. She was facing the other way. Saw her right hip. Didn't notice any tattoo." He opened his eyes. "I'm not sure it was her. Like I said—"

"You weren't looking at her face," finished Zee.

"Look," I said. "My mission here is pretty straightforward. I just need to tell Christa about her father and see if I can persuade her to go home before he dies. So why don't I just go to that ashram place and knock on the door and tell whoever answers that I want to talk to her? What's wrong with that?"

"Worth a try, I guess," said J.W. doubtfully.

"You think they'll refuse me?"

He shrugged. "Wouldn't be surprised."

"Well, if they do, I'll think of something else."

"I don't like the sound of that," said J.W. He leaned forward and put his hand on my arm. "Listen to me, old boy. I've got my hands full trying to babysit the singer. I don't need to be worrying about you."

"Oh, don't worry about me," I said.

"What I'm trying to say is, if you end up thinking about doing something stupid, at least wait for me."

"Oh, great," said Zee. "The two of you doing something stupid together. Terrific. Let's double the stupidity quotient."

J.W. looked at me. "Promise me, Coyne."

"I've made too damn many promises lately," I said. "But I will consider your generous offer."

He shrugged. "Consider it seriously." He picked up the martini pitcher, peered inside, and said, "Empty. Must be time for dinner."

Linguine with shrimp, clams, and scallops and a light, garlicky olive-oil-and-wine sauce. Crusty Portuguese bread. Greens from Zee's garden. A local microbrew to wash it down. I proclaimed it delish, beating J.W. to the punch.

I was sopping up the remnants of sauce with my last piece of bread when J.W. said, "Hey, Brady. Whaddya say. Let's go fishin'."

I looked up at him. "Really?"

He looked at Zee. "Okay with you?"

"Sure," she said. "Next time it's my turn."

"I didn't bring any gear," I said.

"I've got plenty," said J.W., "if you don't mind surf rods."

I grinned. "I don't mind at all."

He glanced at his watch. "Tide turns in a couple hours. I'd love to be out at the gut at Cape Pogue about then." He shook his head. "Can't do it, though. That'd end up being an all-nighter. When I was younger I could fish all night and work all day and do it for a week. No more. What do you say to a few hours of casting off State Beach?"

"Let's go," I said. "A little salt air will clean out my head."

We clamped four of J.W.'s surf-casting rods, already rigged with plugs, on the rod rack of the old Land Cruiser I'd been driving, and ten minutes later we were standing in a sandy pullover beside the beach looking easterly. The flat water reflected the purple evening sky. Not a breeze stirred, and the wavelets lapped softly at the sand.

"Well," said J.W., "we've got the place to ourselves. That's probably a bad sign. When everyone else is fishing in other places, I always figure they know something I don't know."

"I don't care," I said. "It'll be good just to throw a plug and think simple fishing thoughts for a while."

I took off my shoes and socks and left them in the car. Then I grabbed a rod armed with a top-water popper and went down to the beach. I heaved the plug way out there, and the monofilament line caught the fading light from the sky. It looked like the faint trail of a skyrocket arcing out toward the horizon and then falling softly onto the water.

I reeled in the plug with a series of sharp tugs, and way the hell out there it kicked up a fuss on the water. I prefer top-water fishing, especially when surf casting. I like to see what's going on. When there are bluefish around, you can see them coming, splashing and slashing at the plug, whacking it and sometimes throwing it into the air, and the trick is to try to ignore them and keep reeling until you feel one of them hook itself.

Well, J.W. said not to expect blues. It was still a couple of weeks too early for them to show up in Vineyard waters. But he'd heard that the false albacore and bonito had started to appear, and there were always stripers.

And so I worked my way along the beach, moving to my right, casting and walking, up to my ankles in the cool water, the wet sand scrunching between my toes, the night air damp on my arms. After a while, thoughts of Christa Doyle and Princess Ishewa and Eye of Horus tattoos receded as the deserted beach and the dark, mysterious ocean and the rhythms of casting and reeling filled my head.

The buzz of civilization had faded to a subaudible hum. Out there where I couldn't quite see it, my cup-faced plug was making plooping sounds as I reeled it in. Overhead the sky was a bowl of stars reflecting on the water.

When I thought to look back toward the Land Cruiser, I realized I'd walked a long way. I couldn't see J.W.'s silhouette on the edge of the water. I'd assumed he would follow along behind me. But apparently he didn't want to fish water I'd already covered so he'd headed down the beach in the other direction.

Fishing together didn't mean actually being together. At its best, fishing is a private occupation, and J.W. understood that the same way I did. We didn't need to talk and make jokes while we fished. We both liked the solitude of the beach at night. We were fishing together even when we were a mile apart.

After a while, I figured it was time to head back to the car. I cast my way along the beach, moving to my left now, heaving out the plug, taking a few steps as I reeled it in, casting again, chugging the plug across the water. By now I had lost that anticipation I always start with, that keyed-up expectation that any moment something would hit my lure. It was plain that the fish hadn't come out to play along State Beach tonight.

I was just a hundred yards or so from where we'd parked when I heard a shout. It sounded like J.W. He must've hooked a fish.

He shouted again. I reeled in and began jogging along the wet sand in his direction. If he'd hooked a fish that was big enough to yell about, I wanted to see it.

I was nearly back to our parking place when I heard the roar of an engine and the squeal of tires, and an instant later headlights zipped by, moving fast along the road that paralleled the beach.

I found J.W. standing beside his Land Cruiser clenching and unclenching his fists.

"What happened?" I said.

"Bastards," he muttered. "They were gonna steal our rods."

The two spare rods were still clamped in the rod rack on the roof of the Land Cruiser. "You got here in the nick of time, then," I said.

"Something bit off my plug," he said. "So I came back for another one. Otherwise they would've gotten them. One of these rods is Zee's favorite. She'd've killed me. There were three of 'em. One was nosing around our rods, and two were in the front seat of their getaway car. I yelled and they took off." He shook his head. "Damn off-islanders. No local would think of swiping somebody's surf rod."

"Did you get a look at them? What about the vehicle?"

"I couldn't see what color it was or anything. Too dark. Some kind of SUV, is all I could tell you. Spewed up a helluva lot of sand getting out of here." He hesitated. "When he jumped in the back, the dome light went on, and I caught a glimpse of two in the front." He shrugged. "I couldn't tell you what any of them looked like. My impression is they were young guys. College age, I'd say."

I put my rod in its rack, then leaned against the fender of the Land Cruiser. "You sure they were after the rods?"

He turned and glared at me. "What the hell else would they be after?"

"Calm down," I said. "They didn't get anything."

"Doesn't matter. It's the principle of it. We never lock our cars down here. Never worry about our rods or anything. None of us. We go out at night, we leave the house unlocked. It's how we live on the Vineyard. Even the Summer People understand that. But this particular summer . . ." He blew out a breath and slouched against the car beside me. "It makes me mad, that's all."

"Supposing," I said, "they weren't surf-rod thieves."

"So they're looking for beer in the backseat. What's the difference?"

"I've been driving this car around the island for the past two days," I said, "spreading the word that I'm looking for Christa Doyle, talking to people who end up crashing into oak trees. And you, the owner of this unique and easily identified vehicle, you've been witness to two murders. Something's going on around here, and you—and for all we know, I—are in the middle of it."

J.W. was silent for a minute. Then he said, "You're right. It could be something like that."

"On the other hand," I said, "you scared them off. How dangerous could they be?"

"Don't be naive," he growled. "Just because they fled doesn't mean they were scared."

I glanced at my watch. It was a little before eleven. "You sleepy?" I said.

"I'm too pissed to be sleepy. Why?"

"How about showing me where that Duval guy hangs out."

"The ashram?" He narrowed his eyes at me. "I told you not to do something stupid without me."

"I won't do anything stupid. And if you haven't noticed, I *am* with you."

"I got a feeling our definitions of stupid might not be the same." He shrugged. "What the hell. It's over in West Tisbury. Hop in."

We headed up-island. I tried to memorize J.W.'s route, but he seemed to take some shortcuts, and in the darkness I lost my sense of direction. But fifteen or twenty minutes later, when we passed the entrance to the Fairchild place, where an old client used to live, I knew where we were.

J.W. took a right onto a two-lane paved road. "This is Indian Hill Road," he said.

"Got it," I said.

He went slowly, and a minute later he stopped and said, "See that little sign?"

"The one that says EXETER?"

"Do you see any other signs?"

"I see that one."

"That driveway goes over a hill and down toward the water and ends at Duval's place."

"I don't see any guards," I said.

"Don't mean they ain't there."

J.W. executed a three-point turn, a neat trick on the narrow roadway in the lumbering old Land Cruiser, and twenty minutes later we pulled into his driveway.

"Lucky me," he said, "I get to crawl into bed with the best hips on the island."

"Me," I said, "I think I'll call Evie, if you don't mind me using your phone."

"Just behave yourself," he said.

Evie answered with that familiar mumbly little hum in her throat. "Mmm, hi, swee'ie."

"How'd you know it was me? Or do you call everybody sweetie?"

"I got that caller ID thingie, remember?"

"Wake you up?"

"Kinda. It's okay."

"I just wanted to hear your voice."

"And what did you want my voice to say?"

"It doesn't have to say anything particular. I just wanted to hear it."

"So how's it going?" she said. "Find that girl yet?"

"Getting warm, I think. I don't want to talk about it."

"Well, okay."

We were silent for a minute.

"So," said Evie, "what *do* you want to talk about?"

"I don't want to talk," I said. "I just wanted to—to connect."

"Connect, huh?" She chuckled.

"There you go, talking dirty."

"The telephone is a poor substitute for the real thing."

"That's what I've been thinking," I said.

"Well, I miss you," she said. "G'night, then."

I hung up the phone, smiled into the darkness, and fell asleep instantly.

Chapter Fifteen

J.W.

On Tuesday morning I had the Eye of Horus on my mind. Across the breakfast table from me Diana the huntress swallowed her mouthful of cereal. "Pa?"

"What?"

"Can Janie come and spend the day with us? She likes the tree house a lot and Ma's got the day off, so we can play here first then go to the beach again. Can she?" She looked at me with Zee's large, dark eyes.

"You have to ask your mother. I have to work and she's the one who'll be at home with you guys." I looked at Zee, who was sitting beside Brady having coffee with her bagel.

"She already said to ask you," said Diana.

Ah, the old parental irresponsibility ploy.

Zee smiled at me.

"Well," I said, looking back at Diana, "you tell her that it's fine with me."

"Ma."

"What, Diana?"

"Pa says it's fine with him."

"That means it's fine with both of us."

"Oh, good!" Diana and Joshua exchanged satisfied glances.

"But now we have to find out if it's fine with Janie and her mother," said Zee. "They may have other plans."

"Can I telephone her and find out?" asked Joshua, pushing away his empty cereal bowl.

"Yes. Talk with her mother, too, and tell her that your father and I will be glad to have Janie come over for the day."

I finished my coffee as he climbed off his chair. "And tell Mrs. Price that I'm on my way over there right now. If Janie gets permission to come here, I'll bring her back with me."

"Your day is starting early," said Zee, flicking her eyes at the wall clock.

"Man works from dawn to setting sun." I carried my breakfast dishes to the sink, kissed Zee, and pointed a forefinger at Brady. "Try to stay out of trouble," I said.

He placed a hand upon his chest. "Who? Me? Get in trouble? Unimaginable. I'm a lawyer. Lawyers are the epitome of morality." He gave Zee a lascivious look and put a long arm around her shoulders. "Well, I can't see any reason for you to delay your departure, J.W. And don't rush home."

I got into the Explorer and drove to the Skyes' farm. It was going to be a warm day. The pale dome of the August sky was without a cloud and the morning sun was already hot. No one seemed to be following me.

Janie met me at the door. "Mom says I can go!"

"Good. Take your bathing suit and don't forget your sunscreen. You still look pretty pink to me."

She led me into the house and left me at the breakfast table with the elder Skyes and her mother, while she headed for her room to collect her gear.

"You're sure this isn't an imposition?" asked golden-haired Evangeline, and I thought again that she was one of those women who, like Zee, Ayesha, and Helen, would be beautiful all of her life.

"It's my kids' idea, so they should be fine together," I said, "and looking after one more won't bother Zee a bit."

"Well," she said, "it's very convenient for me today because I want to pick up some things at the house, then track down Flurge and some other people and arrange a rehearsal time. If we're going to have half the world watching us on Saturday night, we'd better have some idea about what we're doing."

"Your limo awaits, madam."

The three of us drove to chez Jackson, where the children melded and disappeared around the corner of the house toward the big beech tree.

"You're sure we're not exploiting you?" asked Evangeline.

"I'm sure," said Zee. "I figure they'll wear themselves out by noon, and then we'll head to East Beach for lunch. If you two are free before midafternoon, come and join us. I'll make sure Janie doesn't overdo it in the sun."

I put my arms around Zee and gave her a kiss and then whispered in her ear, "I don't think you'll need them but keep your cell phone and your pistol handy."

She leaned back and frowned thoughtfully up at me. "I love you, too, Jefferson. Have a careful day."

"I will."

Evangeline, in her dark wig and glasses, thanked Zee again and we drove away.

No car began tailing us when we came out onto the highway. No helicopter beat its blades above the road.

"The house first," said Evangeline. "Then we'll find Flurge."

I was driving toward Vineyard Haven. When I got to Airport Road I took a left.

"We need to talk," I said. "Three people have died in the last couple of days and that's a lot of coincidence. I think you're in the middle of it all, somehow."

"What do you mean?"

"I mean that Hale Drummand was killed by somebody watching your house. I mean that Ogden Warner was director of the Celebration and an ex-friend of yours. I mean that a woman who died in a supposed accident yesterday had been talking with a friend of mine who's looking for a girl down here who has a tattoo of the Eye of Horus on her left hip, just like you do. Three deaths, and there's a shadow on every corpse that looks like yours."

She hadn't gotten where she was by being fragile. She stared ahead through the windshield saying nothing while she thought.

"I'm not a killer," she said finally. Her voice was icy.

"I believe you, but somehow you're in every picture I can paint. Tell me about the tattoo."

She thought some more, then came to some agreement with herself. "Alain Duval has his women do that. There are laws against branding, but none against tattoos. It's his mark. I got mine a long time ago, when I was pretty young. I've kept it as a reminder not to put myself in anyone's hands like that again."

"Are you suggesting that he'd actually have branded you if he thought he could get away with it?"

"He joked about it, and I suspect that some of his girls would have allowed it. They'd have seen it as a sign of undying love and devotion between them." Her voice became colder. "Some people are born to be slaves. It took me time to realize I wasn't one of them, but when I finally saw things as they were, I left him."

"But two days ago you went back and apologized for not saying good-bye."

She nodded. "I don't like sneaks and I don't like cowards, but I felt like both after I left him because I waited until he was out of the country on one of his so-called spiritual journeys to India and the Middle East to do it. By apologizing I got clean. Does that make any sense to you? No matter. I've felt better ever since."

"Do your fans, your girl fans in particular, know about the tattoo? Do they get themselves the same tattoo because you have one?"

She gave me a quick, ironic glance. "A lot of people think they know more about me than they actually do. The tattoo is a private penance. I was careless when I let you see it. It's never gotten into the media."

"It won't get in because of me." I gave her what I hoped was a reassuring glance.

We came to the Edgartown–West Tisbury road and I turned left. When we passed the driveway down which Joe Callahan, the now ex-president of the United States, used to drive to his vacation cottage, I pointed it out.

"He's a fan," she said, seemingly pleased. "I hear he and the family are coming to the Celebration."

"I don't think the current prez is planning to attend."

"He prefers country-and-western and bluegrass, I think."

Prez and I agreed about one thing, at least. I said, "Tell me again about Ogden Warner. I know you and he were close once."

"I cut my first record when I was fifteen. It made number one on the charts. It was just called *Evangeline.* Maybe you remember it."

"Sounds familiar," I lied.

"Sure it does. I saw your tapes when I was at your house. All C-and-W and classical stuff. I saw that inscribed picture of you and the Callahans on the wall, too."

"You have sharp eyes. Tell me about Warner."

"This will probably raise your eyebrows. I met him at the Temple of Light in California. He was already a Follower and I was a new convert."

My brows did rise. "Warner was a Follower?"

She nodded. "In those days a lot of people in Hollywood were Followers. Alain was all the rage. Guru of the rich and famous, idol of boys and girls who thought themselves spiritual but misunderstood. I should know. I was one of them. I had a ton of money and I was famous but something spiritual was lacking. Alain seemed to offer it. Of course with him, body and soul were the same, so he traded one for the other, at least with the girls. Ogden swept me away first, but it wasn't long before Alain offered more. It was sort of like going from an apostle to the messiah himself, if that makes any sense."

"I can see how it could happen."

"Then, just about the time that I went to Alain, maybe because I went, Ogden left the temple. From then on he bad-mouthed Alain every chance he got. He couldn't stand anything associated with the temple and made no bones about it."

A reformed drunk is often the most strident and unforgiving teetotaler. "Born-again people are pretty common," I said, turning into her driveway and flashing my nifty FBI ID card at the young cop guarding the entrance before driving on.

"Looking back," said Evangeline in a musing voice, "I think Ogden left at the high point of Alain's popularity. By the time I left Alain a year later, he'd definitely begun to be less fashionable, and that decline has continued."

"According to what I hear he still has plenty of influence."

"He's still a power but he doesn't have the prestige he had before. He's beginning to preach the vengeance of God upon sinners along with his meditations on love and the oneness of all things. This Celebration is important to him. He's been pushing it from the beginning. If his PR people work it right, he could be back on top again."

"Once again the spiritual leader of democracy and the arts?"

"I don't know if he actually thinks of himself as God's Chosen One or if he's just playing the role."

"Leaders don't have to believe what they say, they just have to have followers who believe it."

"He's still got plenty of those!"

We came to the courtyard in front of the Carberg house. I saw nothing unusual. I turned the Explorer so it was facing the driveway.

"Can you drive?" I asked.

"Of course I can drive."

I stepped out of the car. "Give me your house keys, then slide over here into the driver's seat. I'm going to check things out before you go in. If something happens to me, I want you to get out of here in a hurry. Understood?"

She wasn't naive. "Got it," she said. She handed me the house keys and slid behind the steering wheel.

I walked around the house and garage, then went inside and entered every room. Nothing. No sign of anyone having been there recently. The garage looked the same as before. The boats by the pier looked the same. I studied the point of land where the watcher had smoked his or her cigarettes but could see nothing unusual. Then I went out through the front door and called Evangeline inside.

She was very efficient as she collected clothing and other items and packed them into suitcases. When the suitcases were full she opened a closet and brought out a guitar case. For my benefit she opened it and revealed a Space Age instrument that looked nothing at all like my old Martin.

"I'm not quite Jimi Hendrix," she said, "but I can actually play this thing."

"Very impressive."

"I should make you come to the concert. Maybe I won't pay you unless you do!"

"I understand that tickets are impossible to get."

"Not for me. I'll be giving some VIP seats to the Skyes and to you and Zee."

"Maybe I can scalp mine. Then I won't need my wages."

"You're a musical snob, J.W."

No one had ever called me that before.

"I liked the Eagles. Does that count?"

"No. Everybody liked the Eagles."

"All right, all right," I said. "I'll come to your danged concert. Are we through here?"

"I'm through. But now I have to talk with Flurge. He and the Tars have taken over a B and B in West Tisbury." She got out her cell phone.

While she talked I looked some more at the point of land where the watcher had watched. When she hung up, she told me that Flurge had agreed to meet her at the stage, so we drove there.

The field was as filled with busy folk as it had been on my last visit. A new director had been flown in from Hollywood, Harry and Frank Dyer were at work with their sound system, and the fireworks people were still tinkering. Added to the scene were several uniformed police officers. I suspected that there were also some in plainclothes and wondered if any progress was being made in solving the murder of Ogden Warner.

A man about my age with longer than average hair met Evangeline as we walked toward the stage. She introduced him as Ian Bell, aka Flurge.

"A nickname I got when I was younger," he explained.

"I've tried to forget the nicknames I had," I said.

"You might resurrect one if you ever go into show business," said Flurge. "The wackier the better."

"Come on," said Evangeline, "let's talk business."

They walked up onto the stage and ducked behind a giant curtain that had not been there on my last trip to the site.

While they were gone I surveyed the scene. Most of the people looked absolutely normal. Maybe show biz was like any other biz, with ordinary people doing most of the jobs and a few stars getting all of the publicity.

Zee had once made a brief appearance on the silver screen and had since been assured by a good many Hollywood types that she was born for the camera. She'd liked most of the motion picture people she'd met, but wasn't interested in being one of them. Me, neither. Of course, I hadn't been offered the opportunity.

Jake Spitz appeared at my side.

"Anybody find out who kacked Ogden Warner?" I asked.

"Not yet, but it had to be somebody with entrance to the grounds."

"That should limit the suspect list to only a few hundred. You check out the fireworks guys? If you're right about somebody having a plan to do something big and bad here, they'd be on the top of my checklist because they make a living from explosions."

"We've triple-vetted the pyrotechnic people," said Spitz, "and they're as pure as the Virgin Mary. Unlike some people I know."

"Don't look at me," I said. "I work for the FBI. I'm untainted in body and mind just like J. Edgar Hoover."

"Call me if you need me." He walked away.

In time Evangeline reappeared, gave Flurge a friendly good-bye-for-now peck on the cheek, and joined me. I looked at my watch. "If we leave right now, we can probably get a table at the Newes," I said. "Good beer and bar food. The pubbiest pub on the island."

"I'm starving. Let's go." We walked to the Explorer under the hot sun, and Evangeline donned the day's wig.

The Newes From America is the best pub in Edgartown, but if you get there before noon you can usually find a table. I ordered the large Red Tail Ale and was pleased when Evangeline did the same. Ah, an honest, beer-drinking woman, just like Zee. She ordered fish and chips and I ordered fried calamari. Two good choices. Both delish. By the time we were finished, the place was full.

"Your tab," I said when the bill arrived. "You've got the big bucks and I'm just a hired hand."

"Oh, no, you don't. I'm a lady. Gents pay when they take ladies to lunch."

I dug out my wallet. "No wonder the rich get richer while the poor get poorer. What next, Mrs. Midas?"

"Give me a plan. And don't make such a fuss over paying the bill. I'll tack it on to your fee."

"How about joining our children on the beach?"

"Excellent."

I drove to the Skyes' farm, then to my house, then, in our bathing suits, we drove to East Beach, where we found Zee and the children right about where I thought they'd be.

I studied Janie's face when she came running to hug her mother, telling her she just had to get into the water right away because it was wonderful and the sun was so hot.

"I think there's room for you here on the blanket," said Zee as I walked her way.

There was, and I lay down in the bright, warm sunlight.

We alternated swimming and lying in the sun, and a time came when Evangeline and I were both in the water at the same time. She was laughing and splashing like a little girl. I moved close to her and said, "You forgot to tell me one important thing."

"What's that?"

"That Alain Duval is Janie's father. She's got those pale blue eyes of his, and when you know what you're looking for, you can see his bone structure in her face."

She said nothing at all, but her laughter stopped.

"It's important," I said, "because if he's the kind of man you say he is, the people who were watching your house and who probably killed Hale Drummand might have been working for him. They might be planning to snatch Janie."

Chapter Sixteen

Brady

I woke up before the sun. Outside the window of the Jacksons' guest room, the sky had that pewtery look it gets before a cloudless summer morning dawns.

I lay there for a few minutes. My mind was whirling with scenarios and possibilities, and when I decided I wasn't going to go back to sleep, I slid out of bed and got dressed.

When I wandered into the kitchen, the electric coffeepot had already been turned on. J.W. was a notoriously early riser, and I figured he'd headed off to the store to pick up his morning *Globe.* So I poured myself a mug of coffee and took it up to the balcony, where I could watch the sky grow lighter.

It promised to be another pretty Vineyard day. The birds were chirping and swarming around Zee's feeders, and off toward the horizon a brisk breeze was blowing whitecaps on the ocean. My feet were propped up on the railing and my coffee mug sat on my chest. I'd awakened with Mike and Neddie Doyle on my mind. I'd been debating whether to call them and report that I thought I was getting close to finding Christa. It would make them happy, I thought. It might give Mike a few good days.

But it would be cruel to get their hopes up prematurely.

Perhaps I should wait until I had something more substantial to report than the word of a tattoo artist and J.W.'s uncertain memory.

A few minutes later I heard a car pull into the yard, and then J.W. came out onto the balcony with a newspaper tucked under his arm.

"You're up early," he said.

I shrugged. "Places to go, people to see."

He gazed off toward the sea. "I've been thinking," he said.

"Bad habit," I said, "thinking."

"I can't help it," he said. "It's a curse." He sat beside me. "I've been thinking that you should stay away from Alain Duval until I can go with you."

"That would undoubtedly be prudent," I said.

"Well, good."

I shook my head. "Prudence was never my strong suit."

"Just wait till I get home tonight," he said. "We'll go there together. Why don't you spend a quiet day here, read my books, drink my beer, find a golf match or something on my television, have a nap, just relax? That's what you're supposed to do on the Vineyard in August."

"That would be prudent, all right."

He put his hand on my arm. "That Duval," he said. "He comes across as this holy man. But he's got these bodyguards all around him. They're all big and tough and quick and utterly loyal. Duval calls them Simon Peters. I don't think they'd hesitate to cut off somebody's ear."

"You trying to scare me?"

"Why, sure," said J.W. "So what do you say?"

I shrugged. "I say okay."

"Okay, meaning you'll wait for me?"

"Okay, meaning maybe you scared me. But you know

me. I'm not much good at lying around watching golf on TV when there's something I need to do. I'm even worse at patience than I am at prudence."

"You telling me you're going to ignore my excellent advice?" he said.

I nodded. "I'm going to that ashram today, and I'm going to do whatever needs to be done to talk to Christa. If I'm not back here by martini time and you haven't heard from me, call the cops."

He looked at me for a minute, then shrugged. "Zee made me do it. She worries about you. I told her you'd ignore me, but she insisted." He stood up. "Being careful is a good idea, you know."

"I may be impatient and imprudent, but I'm not stupid."

"There are those who'd debate that," said J.W. "Here. I assume you want the sports page."

I had a bagel with the family at the kitchen table, then retreated to the balcony to get the hell out of everybody's way. That's where I spent the morning, drinking coffee and reading J.W.'s newspaper and thinking about what I should do and how I should do it. Cars drove in and out of the driveway. At one point Zee brought Evangeline up to meet me, and I decided I agreed with J.W.: She was as beautiful in person as she was in the magazines. But Zee had her beat.

After a while Zee and the kids and Evangeline and her daughter all headed off to the beach.

By then I figured I'd thought about as hard and long as I was capable of, so I went to the guest room and changed into my Coop's Bait and Tackle T-shirt, a pair of walking shorts, and sneakers. I found a Red Sox cap in J.W.'s front closet. It was an old one, predating the kind with the adjustable plastic band in back, but it fit just fine. It was faded and sweat-stained—or maybe that was bluefish blood. I suspected it was J.W.'s favorite fishing cap. I hoped he wouldn't mind.

My little tape recorder wasn't much bigger than a pack of cigarettes. I put a fresh tape in it, checked to see that the batteries were working, and slid it into my pants pocket. Then I looped my binoculars around my neck and checked myself in the mirror.

Brady Coyne, Boston barrister, your basic island tourist, a pale-skinned, middle-aged, bird-watching Summer Person. Innocence personified.

I found a travel mug in the kitchen cabinet, filled it up, switched off the coffeepot, grabbed my briefcase, and went out to the old Land Cruiser. It was around noontime.

I didn't even try to retrace the cross-island maze of back roads J.W. had driven the previous night, and with all the midday traffic clogging the main roads I was familiar with, it took nearly three-quarters of an hour to drive from the Jacksons' house in Edgartown to Indian Hill Road in West Tisbury.

I crept past the end of the driveway marked by the sign that read EXETER. I saw no sentry, no gate—nothing to indicate that anything unusual lay over the hill at the other end.

I continued along Indian Hill Road, with its NO TRESPASSING signs tacked to tree trunks every fifty feet or so, and a couple hundred yards along it crested and abruptly ended. I pulled over, got out, and scanned the area with my binoculars. A quarter of a mile away, beyond a stand of low-growing pine and scrub oak, I glimpsed a cluster of white buildings.

Behind the buildings, a wide lawn sloped down to Vineyard Sound. A dozen or so people were at the beach. My binoculars weren't powerful enough to make out their faces, but I could see that four men wearing long pants and skintight black T-shirts and dark glasses were spaced out along the beach with their backs to the ocean. They stood at parade rest looking watchful. The rest of the frolicking beachgoers were women in skimpy bathing suits. If one of them was Christa Doyle, I couldn't tell, but they all looked young and vital.

I went back to the car, turned around, and headed back the way I'd come. I went slowly. I was looking for a turnoff where I could leave the car, walk through the woods and meadows to the edge of the ocean, and then follow it back to the beach behind Duval's place—Brady Coyne, the innocent Summer Person, bumbling along with his bird-watching binoculars, hoping to spy on piping plovers and oyster catchers . . . and to see whether one of the bikini-clad maidens was Christa.

But Indian Hill Road was lined with KEEP OUT signs, and I found no inconspicuous place to leave the Land Cruiser. The last thing I needed was to get arrested for trespassing.

So much for Plan A.

Well, Plan B was more my style anyway.

So when I came to the driveway marked with the EXETER sign, I turned into it and started up the hill. I'd gone barely thirty yards when a man stepped out of the woods and stood in front of the Land Cruiser with his arms folded across his chest. He appeared to be in his mid-twenties. He was wearing dark pants, a dark T-shirt, and dark sunglasses. He had a crew cut, just like the men on the beach. He wasn't particularly tall, but he had the broad chest and bulky shoulders and thick arms of a prizefighter. I saw no evidence that he was armed, although his body looked like a lethal weapon, and his expression suggested that he wouldn't hesitate to use it.

I stopped the Land Cruiser, and an instant later another man, dressed the same as the first one and equally bulked up, appeared at my window. "Sir?" he said. "Do you have business here?"

"Yes," I said. "I'm here to see Mr. Duval."

"Is he expecting you?"

"I don't know. He might be."

This answer didn't seem to faze the man. "Your name, sir?"

"Brady Coyne. I'm a lawyer."

Usually when I tell people I'm a lawyer, they react. People don't like lawyers on principle, and even though I'm an uncommonly affable lawyer, some people don't like me. Folks with something to feel guilty about are especially leery of lawyers. Folks who have trouble love lawyers until they get the bill. Nobody's neutral.

But as far as I could tell, this guy had no feelings about my profession whatsoever. He just looked at me through his dark glasses and said, "What is your business with Mr. Duval, sir?"

"I'm here to talk to Christa Doyle."

I watched his face closely, but Christa's name aroused no reaction from the guy. "Please give me your car keys," he said.

I did.

He pocketed them, then went over to the other guy, who had remained standing about ten feet from my front bumper with his arms folded. The two of them conferred for a minute, and then the one with my car keys took a cell phone from his pocket, pecked out a number, and held it to his ear.

The conversation lasted about thirty seconds. Then he came back to the car and opened my door. "Push over, please," he said. "I'll drive."

I climbed over the console to the passenger seat, and he got in behind the wheel and turned on the ignition. The other guard stepped aside, and we went chugging to the top of the low hill and down the other side.

The layout was pretty much as J.W. had described it—a large, rambling, low-slung house with several ells built onto it, a garage that would house a couple of B-52s with room to spare, a wide, manicured lawn that sloped all the way down to the beach, well-tended gardens, curving fieldstone pathways. The place offered a spectacular view of Vineyard Sound and, out toward the horizon, the Elizabeth Islands.

My escort stopped in the paved parking area outside the garage. There were four other vehicles parked there—two identical dark green Range Rovers with tinted windows, a mint yellow Porsche, vintage 1975, I guessed, and a funky neon pink beach buggy on fat, oversize tires.

He took the keys from the ignition and pocketed them. "Stay there for a minute," he said. He got out of the car, came around to my side, and opened the door. "All right. Step out, now, please."

I stepped out.

"Face the vehicle and put your hands on the roof."

I did, and he patted me down. When he felt my tape recorder, he reached gingerly into the pocket of my shorts, took it out, and slid it into his own pocket.

"Follow me, please."

I followed him into the house. It was quite grand. The

front foyer opened into a front-to-back room with floor-to-ceiling windows on the back wall looking out to the ocean. This room was bigger than my whole apartment back in Boston. A rectangular oak conference table sat on an earth-colored rug in the middle of the room, and about two dozen straight-backed wooden chairs were pushed in around it. The walls were lined with bookcases, and matching stone fireplaces faced each other on the left and right walls. Here and there along the walls were little pedestal tables with abstract sculptures perched atop them.

The guard touched my elbow. "This way, please." He steered me to a doorway just inside the foyer, opened the door, and held it for me. "Wait in here, please."

I went into the room. The door closed behind me, and I heard the click of the lock.

This room was small and square and furnished with a leather sofa, two matching leather chairs, a low table holding a couple of potted plants, and a television set. There was just one window, which looked out to the driveway. I tried to open it. It wouldn't budge.

A small video camera was mounted in the corner where two walls met the ceiling. It had a little red light that was winking on and off like an eye.

Okay, so I was a prisoner.

I sat on a chair and tried to look casual and relaxed, on the assumption that I was being watched.

Forty-three minutes later by my watch I heard the latch click, and then the door opened. The same guy who had brought me here held the door, and a fortyish man stepped in. He wore sandals, white pants, a white shirt, a white jacket, and a friendly smile.

"Mr. Coyne," he said, "welcome to my humble retreat."

His voice was deep and hypnotic. It reminded me of James Earl Jones's. "I trust Simon Peter was cordial?"

Simon Peter had closed the door behind him. I assumed he was waiting on the other side.

"Aside from frisking me, taking my tape recorder and car keys, and locking me up here, yes, he was quite cordial. Although I was beginning to get thirsty."

When he smiled, his blue eyes crinkled. "My apologies for our negligent hospitality, as well as any inconvenience we may have caused you. It is unfortunate that we must take such precautions. I'm sure you understand."

"No problem," I said.

He held out his hand. "My name is Alain Duval. It is good to meet you."

I took his hand. His skin was soft and smooth, but his grip was firm. "Brady Coyne."

He gestured to one of the chairs. "Sit, please."

I sat.

Duval tapped on the door, and it opened. He whispered something to Simon Peter, and then the door closed.

He came over and sat in the leather chair beside me. "Now, Mr. Coyne, is there some way I can be of assistance to you?"

"I need to talk with Christa Doyle," I said. "I believe she's here."

"Christa Doyle?" He frowned. "No, I don't know any Christa Doyle."

"She's eighteen. Black hair, dark eyes. She has an Eye of Horus tattoo on her left hip."

He shrugged. I detected no trace of reaction to any of this in his expression. "I'm very sorry. I'm afraid I can't help you."

At that moment there was a soft tap on the door, and

then it opened and the guard came in. He had a tray bearing a pitcher of iced tea and two tall glasses.

"Put it there, please," said Duval, gesturing to the table with the potted plants.

Simon Peter set down the tray, left the room, and closed the door behind him.

Duval poured two glasses full of the iced tea. He picked one of them up and took a sip.

I did the same.

"Sweet enough?" he said.

I nodded. "Hits the spot."

"Now," he said, "was there something else I might help you with?"

"She might be called Raven," I said.

He looked at me with what seemed to be genuine concern. "The Doyle woman?"

I nodded.

"Raven, hmm?"

"Yes."

He shook his head. "I am truly sorry, Mr. Coyne. I have devoted my life to helping people. I wish I could help you."

"Her father is dying, you see," I said. "He has just a short time, and he's desperate to reconcile with Christa."

"They are estranged, then?"

"Christa left home over two years ago."

"And you thought you'd find her here?"

I shrugged. "I did, yes."

He leaned forward and looked at me with intense interest. "And why did you think that, Mr. Coyne?"

Because J.W. saw her here, I thought. *Because Christa and Evangeline both have Eye of Horus tattoos on their left hips.*

Nope. I wasn't giving away anything for free.

"Well, to tell you the truth," I said, trying very hard to appear as if I were in fact telling the truth, "it was pretty much a wild stab in the dark. I heard there were some young people staying here, so I thought I'd give it a shot." I spread my hands and smiled. "Worth a try, huh?"

"I sympathize with your quest," said Duval. "I shall pray for your success." He stood up. "Unless there's something else?"

I shook my head. "No, that's it. Guess I'll just keep banging around. I'm pretty sure she's somewhere here on the Vineyard. If you should hear anything, maybe you'd give me a call? I've got a photo of Christa in the car. I'll write a phone number on the back of it where I can be reached."

He smiled. "Of course. It would please me to help. You can give the photo to Simon Peter."

"Thanks a lot," I said. "That would be great."

Duval tapped on the door, and Simon Peter opened it immediately.

"Please escort Mr. Coyne to his vehicle," Duval said. "He has a photograph for us. Please deliver it to me."

Simon Peter dipped his head, then gestured for me to follow him.

As I left the room, Alain Duval said, "God be with you," in that rumbling James Earl Jones voice of his.

"I really appreciate it," I said. "Thanks a million."

Simon Peter gave me back my car keys and tape recorder, and when I got to the Land Cruiser, I saw my binoculars and briefcase sitting on the front seat. I'd left them in back. So they'd searched the car. No surprise.

I wrote J.W.'s phone number and my name on the back of a photocopy of Christa's picture and gave it to Simon Peter. Then I lifted my hand to him and drove up the driveway.

When I looked back, he was standing by the garage with his arms folded, watching me.

I turned left at the end of the driveway and again followed Indian Hill Road to where it ended at the top of the hill. Then I turned around and retraced my route.

I drove very slowly, and a few hundred yards past the EXETER sign heading back to the main road, I spotted what I'd missed earlier—a break in the stone wall that paralleled the road. There appeared to be an old, rutted cart path angling into the woods. It was overgrown with waist-high weeds and clusters of saplings. Here, I thought, I could pull the solid, old four-wheel-drive Land Cruiser far enough off the road to hide it from traffic on Indian Hill Road.

But not now. Now they'd be watching for me.

I didn't think for a minute that Alain Duval had bought my bumbling bull-in-a-china-shop routine, any more than I'd bought his sympathetic holiness. Maybe it was second sight of some kind on my part, but I felt with absolute certainty that the great white guru with the mesmerizing voice knew exactly where Christa Doyle was hiding.

The question was: Why wouldn't he let me talk to her?

Chapter Seventeen

J.W.

Evangeline and I stood there knee-deep in the ocean, and I saw the truth in her eyes. I had been right: Alain Duval was Janie's father. The warm August water suddenly seemed too cold for her. She shivered, turned, and thrashed toward shore. But I was in front of her.

"Get out of my way!" As intended, her whisper slapped against my ears but didn't reach shore.

"I'll get out of your way," I said in my own low, tight voice. "I'll get out of your life, if that's what you want. You can find yourself another flunky to keep the wolves away."

She paused and flashed a look at Janie, whose laughter was mixed with that of my children.

"But if I stay," I continued, "you've got to level with me. I won't play this game any longer unless you do. This is your only chance. You won't get another one from me. I can't afford the risk. Too many people are already dead."

She was an excellent actress. She reached down and brought up her hands full of water and emptied them over her head as she laughed for the audience onshore.

"All right," she said. "I'll tell you whatever I can. You can sell your story to the tabloids and make a fortune when this is over."

"I'm not a story seller. Does Duval know that he's Janie's father?"

"I was going to tell him when you took me to him. I thought he deserved to know, but at the last second I couldn't."

"I thought there was more to that visit than just an apology for leaving him."

"You were right. But he can count months and I'm in the news every time I sneeze, so he's probably guessed she's his daughter. God knows the tabloids and magazines have speculated enough about who fathered her, and he's on their list of suspects."

"Do I need to know the names of the other contenders they've considered?"

"I think Prince Charles and our beloved former president Joe Callahan are two of the names you might recognize."

"That probably helped sell some papers."

"My groundskeepers tell me that for several weeks there've been more people than usual asking questions in Cragmoor village, but there are always reporters and paparazzi doing that. A couple of them tried to get into the local clinic this spring when Janie fell off her pony and lost some skin from her arm."

"Did they succeed?"

"One of them stole her riding gloves before the security people got them out the door. Maybe they auctioned them off. I don't know what a pair of Janie's bloody gloves would go for on the fan market."

An idea occurred to me: "Alain Duval might have been willing to shell out quite a bit for a good DNA sample."

Her actress's smile went away. "My God! I never thought of that!"

I raised a hand to calm her. "He doesn't know where she is. This little island is a pretty big place when you're looking for one small girl."

"I've got to get her home to Scotland! I can protect her there!"

I felt sorry for her, but like Margaret I may have been mourning for myself. "That's what castles are built for," I said gently, "but you won't be able to get her there today. Listen. She and Diana are hitting it off pretty well. Let Janie sleep over with Diana tonight. Duval will never think of looking for her at our place. You can make plans to ship her home tomorrow, if that's still what you want to do."

"I don't know . . ."

"While you were looking at the photographs on our wall, did you notice the pistol shooting trophies on our mantel? Those belong to Zee. She's what people out West used to call a heller with a gun. No kidnappers will come through our door while Zee's there. And I'm like Scarlett O'Hara: I can shoot pretty well if I don't have to shoot too far. I think Janie will be quite safe. We'd better go ashore. People will start to talk."

"All right," said Evangeline as we sloshed toward the beach, "we'll do it your way. I can take Janie home first thing tomorrow."

We reached shore and Evangeline lay down on her beach towel beside Zee. "Your husband has persuaded me to let my daughter sleep over with Diana, but I know enough about these kinds of plans to clear them with the wives and mothers first."

"I think Diana and Joshua would love it," said Zee with a smile, "so consider it a done deal. That is, of course, if the children approve."

The children approved.

"In that case," I said to Zee, toweling myself dry, "I'll leave Mrs. Price and Janie to ride home with you while I attend to some other business with what's left of the afternoon. You have those items I mentioned earlier, I presume."

Zee patted her canvas beach bag. "Of course. Wasn't it Mrs. Swiss Family Robinson who had a bag with absolutely everything in it that you'd ever need to survive on a desert island? I'm just like her."

I blew her a kiss, got into the white Explorer, and drove away down the beach. When I was out of her sight I stopped and called Jake Spitz.

Jake turned out to be at the Edgartown police station, coordinating security and murder investigations with the state and island cops, so I drove there. The station was surrounded by parked cruisers and other cop cars. I parked behind the firehouse next door and walked back.

The chief's office was crowded with uniformed and plainclothes police. The first one who saw me was Olive Otero, who immediately got up to close the door but was stopped by the long arm of Dom Agganis.

Olive bent and scowled at me from under that arm. "We don't need you here, Jackson. This is a professional meeting."

"Mind your manners," I said. "You're forgetting that my taxes pay your salary."

I have no idea why Olive and I rub each other wrong, but the poet had gotten our feelings down pat when he wrote:

> I do not love thee, Doctor Fell.
> The reason why I cannot tell;

But this alone I know full well:
I do not love thee, Doctor Fell.

"All right, you two, knock it off." Dom put Olive back in her chair and stepped between us. "What brings you here, J.W.?"

"I'm looking for my boss."

Jake Spitz said, "What's up?"

"I want to know more about Hale Drummand."

All eyes and ears turned toward me. Spitz, being FBI, naturally didn't want to share information with the others until he was sure they needed to know. A lot of police officers and organizations are like that, much to the benefit of criminals who otherwise would have shorter careers.

"Let's step into the next office," said Jake.

It was empty, and Jake shut its door behind us. "What about Drummand?"

"Was he ever stationed on the West Coast?"

"Why do you ask?"

"Jake, did you ever notice that you answer questions with other questions?"

He smiled. "Yeah. It's a professional thing. I get paid to ask but I don't get paid to answer. Why do you want to know about Hale Drummand?"

"It's my turn to answer a question with another one. Did you know that Alain Duval is the father of Evangeline's daughter, Janie?"

"I've heard that rumor along with some others. Is it true?"

"Yes, and I think he knows it, although Evangeline never told him. Tell me something: Has the FBI ever investigated Duval's organization?"

"We investigate a lot of oganizations," said Spitz tonelessly.

"Was Drummand involved in that investigation?"

"Maybe."

I liked him but not enough to spend all afternoon trying to get him to talk to me. "Come on, Jake, I'm not wired. Nobody is going to hear what you say. Besides, I'm working for you, remember? Was Drummand involved or not?"

"Why do you want to know?"

"Because if Duval knows that Janie is his kid, he may want her back, and if he does he may be the guy whose spies were watching Evangeline's house, and because Drummand went over there and now he's dead."

"That's two 'ifs' and one fact. Keep going if you've got anyplace to go."

"Drummand was a trained agent and he was armed, but he didn't hesitate to go across to the point, where he got himself killed by whoever was over there. How did that happen?"

"You tell me."

"I don't have to tell you, Jake. You already know. He went over there because he saw somebody he recognized and apparently trusted enough to let down his guard. If he was involved in the investigation of Duval's organization, he may have made a friend or two with some of Duval's people. It wouldn't be the first time a cop befriended a criminal he's investigating. Well, was he involved in that earlier investigation or not?"

Spitz gave some thought to what he'd say, then nodded. "I guess it doesn't matter now, because Hale's dead, but I don't want this going any further. You understand?"

"I don't work for NBC."

"Okay, then. Hale infiltrated the Followers of Light. He was just the kind of guy Duval liked to have as a Simon Peter. You know what a Simon Peter is?"

"I do."

"Hale was a marine when he was a kid and he still looked the part. And he could act slightly wacko when he needed to. He became a Follower after passing himself off as a religious militant in need of a leader and an organization. Hale was inside the ashram for almost a year before they started to look at him funny and we took him out for his own safety."

"Was he in real danger?"

"He thought he might be, so we took him out before anything could really happen. The point is that while he was a Follower he hung out with some of the Simon Peters and made friends of one or two."

"Are they here on the island?"

Spitz frowned. "There are Simon Peters here, but I don't know if any of them were Hale's pals."

"How did Drummand die?"

"Actually, probably pretty painlessly. Somebody caved in the back of his head and then cut his throat. He turned his back on somebody."

"Did he still have his piece?"

"Right on his belt, as if he was meeting someone he knew and trusted. Smart of whoever did him in to leave the gun. If it had been taken and we found it later, it could tie the thief to the killing."

"What do you think of my theory?"

"It's a theory. I don't have a better one. Knowing that Duval is the girl's father gives it more credence than some of the others we're kicking around. You have any more questions?"

"No. Do you?"

"A lot, but none you can answer."

"What happened to the Duval investigation?"

"Lots of smoke but not enough fire to bring charges. Unofficially, Duval is making a lot of money and has a lot of ambition for a man of purely spiritual interests."

"Are there any men with purely spiritual interests these days?"

"Only you and me, J.W."

Chapter Eighteen

Brady

I didn't have a chance to talk to J.W. privately until after the sun had gone down and Zee and Evangeline were putting the kids to bed.

We were sitting out on the balcony. I was sipping coffee, and J.W. had a beer in his hand. I told him about my visit to Alain Duval's estate and my conversation with the guy. "I'm sure he was lying," I said. "I'd bet a million bucks that Christa is there."

J.W. nodded. "Me, too. The more I think about it, I'm sure I saw her. So what do you want to do?"

"I want to go back there. I've got to get ahold of Christa and tell her about her father."

J.W. gazed up to the star-filled sky. "Duval," he said slowly, "is Janie's father. We think he knows it and will try to snatch her."

"So that's why she's here? You're hiding her from Duval?"

"Yep."

I slapped my forehead. "Oh, this is great. I gave him one of those pictures of Christa. Wrote your phone number on the back of it."

He turned to me. "You *what*?"

"I'm sorry," I said.

J.W. gazed off toward the ocean, which was a glimmery

silver line on the horizon. "It doesn't matter," he said after a minute.

"Of course it does," I said. "Now you and I and Evangeline and Janie and Christa, we're all neatly connected for him. Everything leads him here."

"You've already papered the damn island with Christa's picture and your name and my phone number," he said. "And he knows about me and Evangeline. I doubt this was any news to anybody."

"You're trying to make me feel better."

He shrugged.

"J.W.," I said, "what the hell is going on?"

"I haven't put it together," he said. "But here's one thing I do know. I know there are more damn cops and FBI agents on this island than any concert would justify, no matter who was performing and who was planning to attend. When the president and his family used to come here on their vacations, there were nowhere near as many law-enforcement types around."

"Meaning what?"

"Meaning that after nine-eleven everything gets extra attention." He shook his head. "Jake Spitz admitted that they're worried about terrorists. And we've had three murders in the past few days that we know of. Your fortuneteller. Ogden Warner. Hale Drummand. It's hard to see how all that is explained by Alain Duval wanting to snatch his daughter from Evangeline, or by his wanting to keep Christa Doyle from knowing that her father's dying."

"It all comes back to Duval," I said.

"Yes," he said, "it seems to." He stood up. "Let's go fishing."

"Fishing? Hell, the fishing was lousy last night. You got a secret spot?"

He rolled his eyes. "We're gonna go spy on Duval. For Zee's sake, let's just say we're going fishing."

I grinned. "You don't dare tell her what you're doing? Afraid she won't let you go?"

"I just don't want to worry her, dummy."

Twenty minutes later we were pulling out of J.W.'s driveway in the old Land Cruiser with a bundle of rods clamped on the roof rack. I held a thermos of coffee and my binoculars on my lap. We were wearing blue jeans, dark Windbreakers, dark caps, and sneakers such as we might wear for an evening of surf casting—or for skulking through the woods.

J.W., as usual, followed a maze of back roads, and when we turned onto Indian Hill Road, I told him to go slow. When I spotted the break in the stone wall, I pointed. He turned into it, and with all the considerable four-wheel-drive power of the big Land Cruiser, he plowed through the weeds and saplings and tucked the truck behind a stand of pine trees.

We got out, walked back to the road, and looked at where we'd gone in.

J.W. shook his head. "Tire marks," he said. "Bent-over weeds. Broken saplings."

"It's dark," I said. "Who'll be looking?"

"Yeah, I guess. Can't see the car, anyway. As long as we get out of here before daylight . . ."

"If we don't," I said, "we're in deep shit anyway."

"Valid point."

"Look," I said. "Why don't you get in the car and drive home? I can do this alone. No sense both of us getting in trouble."

"Yeah," he said. "Fat chance."

"No, really," I said.

He laughed. "I go back without you, Zee'll never forgive me. Let's see what we can see."

The sky was an inverted bowlful of stars with a half-moon rising on the horizon to light our way, and we crept through the woods easily. After about ten minutes, we came to the top of a rise, and below us in the silvery night light lay the rambling white building with its sweep of lawn. Orange lights glowed from the windows, and floodlights lit the perimeter. Sounds of guitar music and singing voices filtered up to us.

"Gimme them binocs," hissed J.W.

I handed him my binoculars.

He scanned the area. "Looks like a party. I see some people sitting on the lawn. A couple of Simon Peters at the front of the house. A couple out back. Others, probably, that I can't see."

"Gimme a look."

He handed me the binoculars. I scanned the rear lawn. There were about a dozen people, most of them clad all in white, sitting cross-legged in a circle. One of them was playing a guitar. The others were singing. Gospel music, it sounded like. I was too far away and the light was too dim to distinguish their faces. I scanned them slowly. One of them made me pause. She had straight black hair. Her face was shadowy, but in my imagination, at least, she looked like Christa.

I panned the rest of the area with the glasses. Outside the circle, beyond the glow of the floodlights, stood a couple of shadowy, watchful figures dressed in black. Simon Peters. I moved the binoculars over the beach, but it was too dark and distant to see if anybody was there.

"I don't see the great guru," I whispered to J.W.

"Me, neither."

"I think one of those people sitting on the lawn is Christa. Let's try to get closer."

"Then what?"

"I don't know," I said. "We'll figure it out when we get there."

"My kind of plan," said J.W. "I'll go first. You stay right behind me."

We worked our way down the slope. We stayed low and skulked from tree to tree until we got near the front of the house, where we ran out of woods. We stopped about twenty yards from the side of the garage, just beyond the reach of the floodlights, and crouched behind a stand of rhododendrons.

J.W., who was right in front of me, held up his hand, then pointed. I looked. A black-clad Simon Peter appeared from the back of the house and came straight toward us, strolling along the edge of the lawn. His head kept darting from side to side. He stopped on the other side of the shrubs from where we were hiding. I could have reached out and untied his shoe.

A minute later another Simon Peter came over and stood beside him. "Gimme a light," he said.

A lighter snapped and flickered, and I could see two faces bent to it with cigarettes in their mouths. One of them was the guy who'd stopped me in the driveway.

"You believe this shit?" said one of them.

The other one laughed. "Jesus loves us. Sure he does."

After a minute, they both wandered away.

J.W. jerked his thumb off to the right, and we crept along the edge of the bushes until we could see the back of the house. I lifted the binoculars to my eyes, swept them around the half-circle of young people singing on the lawn, and this time I was positive: One of the women was Christa Doyle. She was singing her heart out, the picture of evangelical ecstasy.

Sitting close beside her was a guy who, unlike the others, was dressed in Simon Peter black. He was not a kid—early thirties, I guessed. He wore glasses, and his hair was in a ponytail. He had his arm slung possessively around Christa's shoulders. She was leaning against him, and as I watched, she tilted her face up and he kissed her sweetly.

I touched J.W.'s shoulder and pointed. "That's Christa," I whispered.

He nodded and held out his hand. I gave him the binoculars.

He put them to his eyes, and a moment later I saw his shoulders tense. "I'll be damned," he muttered.

"What do you see?" I hissed.

He was peering intensely through the binoculars. I started to edge up beside him . . . and that's when the night suddenly went black.

In the movies when a bad guy hits a good guy on the head, the good guy remains unconscious for as long as it suits the filmmaker's purpose. Sometimes for hours. Then, when the time is right for the story to work, our hero wakes up clearheaded and ready to go kickboxing.

In real life, a sharp blow to the head causes a momentary blackness, accompanied by exploding lights behind the eyes and a sense of falling through space. It lasts only a few seconds, and when it's over, the victim is left with a crashing headache, dizziness, disorientation, and a queasy feeling in the stomach.

Get hit any harder and you'd at least have a severe concussion, and more likely a skull fracture and bleeding in the brain.

I woke up with my face pressed into the dirt. Yes, there was the dizziness, the queasy feeling, the sharp pain in my head. I tried to focus the disorientation away. I figured I'd been out for less than a minute.

Someone was kneeling on the small of my back. My arms were pulled behind me, and my wrists were bound together.

When I lifted my head, I saw a man wrestling J.W. to his feet.

Then someone grabbed me around the throat and hauled me to my feet, too. I staggered against the sudden dizziness. Then an even queasier feeling came bubbling up in my throat. I swallowed it back.

We were shoved and prodded toward the house, and I stumbled along, concentrating on the ground, which seemed to be rising and falling and swirling beneath me.

A door opened. We went into the garage. It was dimly lit. There were three or four vehicles in there. Then we came to another door. It opened, too, and J.W. and I were shoved inside. We both landed hard on the cement floor. Then came the click of a solid lock.

I lay there with my cheek on the cool concrete and my eyes closed. I took deep breaths and waited for the dizziness to pass.

After a minute, J.W. said, "Hey? You okay?"

"I guess so. You?"

"They are professionals," he said. "They know just where and just how hard to hit you. It's an art."

I pushed myself into a sitting position with my back against the wall and looked around. The room was lit by a row of big fluorescent bulbs in the plaster ceiling. They were so bright they hurt my eyes. Concrete floor and walls, no windows.

J.W. wormed his way over beside me. "Feels like duct tape around my wrists," he said. "See if you can get me loose."

He pushed his back against mine, and after a few minutes I managed to pry loose the end of the tape and pull it off his wrists. Then he undid me.

"Thanks," I said. "You know—"

"Shh," said J.W. He rolled his eyes toward the corner of the room. I glanced up. There was a small video camera with its red light winking at us.

"Well, old buddy," I said for the benefit of the microphone that I assumed was connected to the camera, "sorry about that. Mr. Duval was quite hospitable this afternoon. Guess I've about worn out my welcome."

"Now what're we gonna do?" said J.W. "I'm scared."

I had to look at him twice to see the anger that glittered in his eyes. J.W. was playacting. He had never been scared in his life.

I took his cue. "It's all my fault," I said. "I'm sorry. I just wanted to see if Christa was here. I promised her father—"

"I told you it was a stupid idea," he said. "But, no. Not you. Not the smart lawyer. Can't mind his own business. Gotta go snooping around where he doesn't belong."

"I'll explain it to Mr. Duval. He seems like a good guy. He'll understand."

"We were trespassing," he said. "They're probably calling the police. That's just what I need. I don't know why I ever listen to you. You always get me in trouble."

I had to restrain myself from smiling at J.W.'s overacting. "I said I was sorry, dammit," I said, maybe overacting a bit myself. "What more do you want?"

"I want to go home. You, you can stay here and rot for all I care."

"Thanks a lot," I said, and I turned away from him.

A few minutes later the door opened. One Simon Peter stayed in the doorway, and another one came into the room. He held a large, square, automatic pistol, which he pointed at J.W. "You," he said. "Come."

J.W. pushed himself to his feet, glared at me, then went out the door. The guy with the gun followed him. Then the door shut and the latch clicked.

Sometime later I heard the tumblers click in the lock. Then the door opened. A Simon Peter stood in the doorway and beckoned to somebody outside.

Then Christa Doyle stepped into my little cell.

"Christa," I said.

"Hello, Uncle Brady." She was wearing loose-fitting white pants and a white T-shirt and sandals, an outfit very similar to Alain Duval's.

I took a step toward her, but she backed away.

"Are you okay?" I said.

"I am wonderful," she said. "How are you?"

"They hit me on the head and locked me in this room," I said. "Otherwise I'm okay."

She smiled. It was pretty clear that what I'd said hadn't registered. "I understand you wanted to talk to me?" she said.

"That's why I'm here," I said. "I have important news for you."

Her eyes had a glazed look. Drugs, I guessed. Or maybe it was just the glory of the True Light. "Yes?" she said.

"Christa," I said, "it's about your father. He's very sick."

She continued to smile at me. It didn't look like much was going on behind those glassy eyes.

"He's dying," I said. "He hasn't got much more time. He wants desperately to see you. So does your mother."

She gave me a little shrug and continued to smile.

"Did you understand what I said?"

"Those people are not my parents anymore," she said. "I have a new family now. I am surrounded by love. Please tell them."

"Christa," I said, "listen to me. I don't know how much you remember—"

At that moment the Simon Peter came back into the room. "Okay," he said. "That's it." He put his arm around Christa's shoulders and steered her out of my cell.

She smiled at me over her shoulder as she left.

"He loves you," I called after her. "He just wants to kiss his little girl good-bye before he dies."

Then the door slammed and the lock clicked.

I tried the doorknob. It wouldn't turn, of course. I sat on the floor. I hadn't handled that very well.

Now what?

Now I would wait. For what, I had no way of knowing.

I leaned back against the wall. My head hurt. I closed my eyes. After a while, I guess I dozed off.

I woke up abruptly. My cell was dark, and there was no hum of electricity and machinery. It was utterly and absolutely silent. The absence of sound was deafening.

I stood up and groped my way to the door. I tried the knob. To my surprise, it turned. As I opened the door, J.W.'s voice whispered next to my ear, "Hey, there you are. Come on. Quick!"

I led J.W. into the garage. A single light, apparently lit by an emergency generator, cast the big space in a dim glow. We edged around a big SUV, and as we did I noticed a long dented streak along its side where the paint had been scraped off.

I touched J.W.'s arm and pointed.

He nodded, then jerked his head for me to follow him.

There was a side door. J.W. opened it a crack and peered out. Then he beckoned to me.

We darted out, sprinted across the narrow side lawn, and dove for the bushes.

There were men's voices, and from the back we could see flashlights playing around the house. They were moving randomly, and they didn't seem to be in any hurry.

"No reason for them to think we got out," J.W. said in my ear. "Far as they know, we're still locked in our little cells."

"How *did* we get out?"

"Me," he said, "I cleverly broke out. You, you opened the door and walked out."

"Somebody unlocked my door," I said.

"And somebody must've hit the power supply," said J.W., "because all the lights went out."

"I figured that was you."

"Nope," he said.

"So what happened? Who cut the power?"

"How the hell do I know? Come on. We've got to move. They'll be checking up on us."

"Christa," I said. "It had to be Christa."

Chapter Nineteen

J.W.

When the very large Simon Peter with the very large pistol silently took me out of the room where Brady and I had been locked together, he had simply placed me in another one alone.

I suspected that we'd been split up so we could be questioned separately as Duval and the Simon Peters tried to figure out what we were really up to. Someone would therefore soon be coming to see me. I felt both alarmed and claustrophobic.

I was glad I'd left my .38 under the seat of the Land Cruiser. As the NRA likes to point out, it's better to have a gun when you don't need one than to need one when you don't have one. However, if I'd had the old pistol with me when I'd gotten slugged, it surely would have been found and taken, so I was perhaps better off by having left it in the truck. I was sorry, though, that my pocketknife had been removed.

I tried the door handle. Locked. Moon and starlight came into my room through a window, but it was barred and looked out at dark woods where I could see nothing at all. The floor and walls were stone. On the bright side, I was still alive, my hands were free, and my head was beginning to clear up. And maybe the person who had been monitoring Brady and me actually believed that I was mad at him. If so, it was an edge that might come in handy sometime, somehow.

I circled the walls. They were quite sound. Maybe if I found a rusty nail I could work on the mortar and, like the Count of Monte Cristo, escape in ten or twenty years. I didn't think I had that much time. I found a light switch near the door and flicked it. No light. I looked up and saw that there was no bulb in the socket that hung on a single cord from a rafter.

I studied the roof. If I couldn't get out horizontally, maybe I could vertically. The roof rose to a peak above ancient-looking crossbeams that supported a small loft. I jumped and caught a beam and pulled myself up into the dark loft. It was harder than it would have been ten years earlier.

From the loft I could see that the roof boards were old and dry and I felt a small hope flicker in the midst of my anger and fear. I got close to the stone wall, bent my knees, and put my back against one of the boards. I straightened my knees and heaved up.

The board held, but a nail squeaked. I tried again. Something popped and it seemed that the board moved a bit. Progress, perhaps. Many a task on Martha's Vineyard has been accomplished by brute strength and stupidity. I had plenty of the latter, but did I have enough of the former?

I bent again, put my hands on my knees, and straightened once more, pushing hard with both arms and legs. More squeaks and pops. The board was definitely looser. I rested, then repeated my attacks. A few minutes later I could see stars through a gap where the board had lifted away from the stone wall.

Two more heaves and there was a clatter of falling shingles as the board tore free. I felt a rush of joy as I pulled myself up and out onto the roof.

There I filled my lungs with fresh air while I squatted and listened. Had anyone heard the sounds of the falling shingles? Across a sweep of lawn I could see figures moving about the main house. To my right was the garage, where Brady must still be imprisoned in a side room. I eased down the roof and dropped to the ground.

So far, so good. As I peered around the corner of the stone building, the lights in the main house suddenly went out. A moment later a dark figure materialized near the garage and disappeared inside. A woman, certainly.

Lanterns and flashlights began to wink around the main house, but the garage was still in darkness. I went that way, then suddenly flattened against the wall as someone emerged from the building and ran silently toward the moving lights.

Mysteriouser and mysteriouser. I sidled over to the door, listened and heard nothing, then slipped inside. The garage was dimly lit by some sort of emergency light, and on the far side was the door behind which Brady and I had first been jailed. I was almost there when it opened and Brady stepped out.

There was another door on the side of the garage nearest the woods. "Hey, there you are. Come on," I said, pointing. "Quick!"

He never hesitated but instead led the way. We passed parked cars, and he pointed to a big SUV with a serious new dent in its side. Then we were outside and moving fast through the trees away from the compound.

We hadn't gotten far when Brady asked the logical question: "How *did* we get out?"

I told him of my exit through the roof and of the dark figure I'd seen.

"Christa," he said. "It had to be Christa."

I didn't have breath enough to trot and talk at the same time, so I concentrated on getting away from the compound as quickly and quietly as possible. In the pale moonlight we were able to avoid running into trees but not to keep from being whipped by branches and undergrowth. I saw no lights behind us and heard no sounds of pursuit but I expected both before long.

We were both huffing and puffing, a sad commentary on early middle age. It occurred to me that maybe I should cut down on my beer consumption. Nah.

As we approached the Land Cruiser, Brady touched my arm and put his mouth near my ear. "Listen," he whispered. "If I was a Simon Peter and I caught a couple a guys sneaking around where they didn't belong, I'd wonder where they came from and send somebody out to find their car to see if there were more of them."

A wise thought. Our truck was out of sight, but there were only so many places we could have hidden it, and the Simon Peters probably knew the territory well enough to find it now that they had cause to go looking.

So we moved very carefully, with many pauses for watching and listening, as we got closer to the old Toyota.

The Simon Peter on watch was not so careful. He lit a cigarette.

He was on the driver's side of the truck in the dark shade of a large oak tree. If anyone tried to get into the driver's seat, the Simon Peter would be a very short pistol shot away.

We watched and listened for a minute, but saw and

heard nothing to suggest that our smoker had a compatriot.

It was my turn to whisper in Brady's ear: "We may not have much time before there'll be people on our tail, so I'm going to circle around to the passenger side. In about five minutes you get twenty yards or so behind that guy and make a lot of noise and do some cussing. When I hear you I'm going to get to the truck, open the passenger side door, and snag my pistol and flashlight."

"Forget it," hissed Brady. "When you open the door, the inside light will go on and he'll see you!"

"That inside light hasn't worked in five years!" I said, and before he could argue more I moved away through the woods, making a circle around the truck. I'm no Lew Wetzel or Abraham Mahsimba, but I was quiet enough not to attract the attention of the tobacco-addicted Simon Peter.

I'd just gotten myself positioned opposite him when Brady snapped some branches and uttered a few imaginative oaths, which he immediately pretended to smother. Something moved in the shadow of the oak, and I ran fast across the moonlit sand to the side of the Land Cruiser. I crouched, eased the door open, and stretched a long arm under the seat. The comforting butt of the old .38 slid into my hand. Another grope and I had my five-cell flashlight in my other hand.

Under the oak the Simon Peter had snuffed his cigarette and was speaking quietly into what I guessed must be a cell phone. I couldn't make out his words but I imagined he was calling for reinforcements. Beyond him, Brady continued to thrash around like a man who had fallen into brambles.

I took a deep breath, stood up, and put the beam of my

flashlight under the oak tree. A black-clad Simon Peter whirled toward me, a pistol in one hand, a cell phone in the other.

"Police officers!" I shouted. "Put down your weapon and raise your hands!"

He hesitated, squinting into the light.

"Drop it or I'll drop you!" I shouted. "Sanchez! If he makes a break your way and I miss him, you shoot the son of a bitch! You other men do the same if you have to!"

"I got him in my sights, Sarge!" shouted Brady.

The Simon Peter hesitated a moment longer, then dropped his pistol and raised his hands. His face wore an angry, worried expression.

"Get over here and spread 'em," I snapped in my best Boston PD voice. "I'm damned sure you know the routine!"

The Simon Peter came to the truck, put his hands on the hood, and spread his legs. I walked around behind him and kicked his legs farther back. "Don't try to be smart," I said.

As I relieved him of his phone and patted him down, Brady came out of the woods. I gave him the flashlight and said, "Keep him covered and keep this in his eyes, Sanchez."

I found no other weapons, but my boy did have a wallet identifying him as George Muldoon. George was from L.A. and belonged to the VFW and the NRA. He had his own set of handcuffs. Convenient. I backed him against a small tree and used the cuffs to secure his hands around its trunk.

"That should hold him for a while, boys," I said to my imaginary band of officers. "Now let's get after the rest of them. Sanchez, you and I will get the truck out of here. Come on!"

Brady and I slipped into our seats and left George Muldoon to darkness and deep thought.

"His pals are on their way," I said. "It would be interesting to listen to what they have to say to each other."

"I'm more interested in getting Christa away from that bunch," said Brady, as we drove away.

"Was Christa the dark-haired girl on the far side of the fire?"

"Yes. It must have been her who unlocked my door."

"I couldn't tell you that, but I can tell you this: If the girl at the fire was Christa, she was warbling away with Frank Dyer, and the two of them looked pretty cozy."

"Frank Dyer," said Brady. "Isn't he the assistant soundman? That doesn't make any sense. Christa got herself an Eye of Horus tattoo. That's Duval's mark."

"Maybe Duval's got a new tootsie and passed Christa on to Dyer."

Brady was silent for a moment, then said, "Are you sure that was Dyer?"

"Is the pope Polish?" I glanced at him. "What am I missing here?"

He told me: "The guy I saw sitting and singing beside Christa was wearing Simon Peter gear. Dyer's a soundman. What's he doing in a security uniform?"

What, indeed? Dyer's uniform hadn't registered before, but now the memory came back sharp and clear. Frank Dyer a Simon Peter? Was he a sheep in wolf's clothing or a wolf in sheep's clothing?

I'd been glancing periodically at my rearview window as I drove, but no lights had appeared behind us and I finally began to relax.

"I want your take on this," I said to Brady, "but before

we talk about it, let's get our fishing story straight in case Zee asks us about it."

"Easy," said Brady. "We fished South Beach as far as Metcalf's Hole and got nothing. She'll believe that without any trouble because we're famous for spending lots of time not catching lots of fish."

"Ah, it's good to know a lawyer when you need a convincing lie. Okay, that's our fishing story. Now, tell me about your adventures after they split us up."

He recounted everything in exact detail. Another lawyer trick.

"Okay then," I said. "Now you can explain to me exactly what the hell is going on."

"The bad part," Brady began, "is that we're dealing with people who hit us over the head and tied us up and threw us into locked rooms. All that's illegal as hell, but the Simon Peters don't seem to care.

"If they aren't afraid of the law, it means they don't expect to pay any penalties for their nasty practices. And that means one of three things: They planned to get rid of us, or they planned to persuade us not to bring charges—by threats or bribes or both—or they figured we couldn't prove anything even though we brought charges.

"The good part is that I know that Christa's alive and I know where she is. I also know, or at least I think I know, that she helped me escape from that room, so however much she may have tied herself to the Followers of the Light, she still hasn't totally untied herself from me and, I hope, her parents.

"Another good thing is that we got out of there intact, and another bad thing is that they know who we are in case they want to come after us.

"As for what's going on, I'm still in the dark. You have any brainstorms?"

I flicked another glance at the rearview mirror. Still no lights behind us. "No big ones," I said, "but I've been wondering why Duval has the kind of security he's got. He might need protectors but he shouldn't need goons."

"We already know he's not as spiritual as the Followers think he is," said Brady, "but I agree that the Simon Peters seem to be more muscle than he ought to need."

"And not just muscle. Guns, too. That's not very New Age."

"Is it New Age for him to try to kidnap his daughter?"

"Maybe not, but that's personal. This is professional. There's a difference."

"You have to admit that somebody at the ashram is very interested in keeping strangers away," said Brady. "And what do you make of that dent we saw in that big SUV?"

"I don't know, but I do know that tomorrow I'm going to check out Frank Dyer. If Jake Spitz won't help me, I have another source."

"If your source can also tell me how to get Christa back to her parents, I want to meet him."

"How about chloroform and a fast car?"

"I'm an officer of the court," said Brady loftily. "Officers of the court aren't allowed to chloroform girls and spirit them away." He paused. "You got any chloroform, by any chance?"

"I'm afraid not."

"You're all talk, J.W. All talk and no action. Well, as Scarlett said, tomorrow is another day. We'd better use it well."

Chapter Twenty

Brady

After we turned off Indian Hill Road, J.W. followed a lot of back roads and switchbacks, and a couple times after taking a sharp curve he pulled quickly to the side of the road and turned off the headlights. He wanted to make sure nobody was following us, he said, and when I asked him what he'd do if somebody was, he said he'd drive straight to state police headquarters in Oak Bluffs, jam on his brakes in the middle of Temahigan Avenue, and hope for a rear-end collision.

Nothing short of a Mack truck, he said, could run his lumbering old Land Cruiser off the road.

After a while it became clear that we were not being followed. That seemed to disappoint J.W., who always welcomed an excuse for a little derring-do.

It was well after midnight by the time we got back to the house. Aside from the soft yellow glow of a night-light in the kitchen, the Jackson residence was dark. I was glad that Zee had already gone to bed. It meant that I didn't have to participate in our fishing lie.

A goose egg throbbed on my head, and a jittery brew of adrenaline and anger and fear was pumping through my arteries. It didn't look like I was going to fall asleep anytime soon. So I whispered good-night to J.W., found a beer in his refrigerator, and took it out onto the balcony. From up there, the Vineyard was moonlit and quiet and altogether peaceful, the way it must have looked to the seagoing wanderers who discovered it more than three hundred years ago.

Now what? After that brief, frustrating encounter with glassy-eyed Christa, I'd been mentally preparing to go back to America and tell Mike and Neddie that I'd delivered their message to their daughter, that she was alive, at least, if not necessarily well, but that I doubted they'd see her before Mike died.

But then all the lights had gone out and I'd found my cell door unlocked and we'd escaped, and I was pretty much convinced that Christa had arranged for those things to happen. If she had, it meant there was more going on behind those glazed eyes than she was letting on. Maybe she wasn't simply a brainwashed victim of Alain Duval's charisma—or the tranquilizers he was feeding her, or some combination of both.

Maybe Christa Doyle was Duval's unwilling prisoner, being guarded by those bulky Simon Peters the way J.W. and I had been—and by the Simon Peter named Frank Dyer in particular, it seemed.

I wondered if each of Duval's so-called Followers had a personal full-time Simon Peter to guard her, or if Christa was special.

If she was being held against her will, I figured my job was to spring her and take her home, personal bodyguard or not.

To do that, I needed a good plan. And to make a good plan—as opposed to my usual half-assed plans, such as the one that had gotten me and J.W. whacked on the head and locked up—I needed more information. To get useful information, I needed to know what questions to ask.

By the time my beer bottle was empty, I didn't exactly have a plan. But I'd figured out some of those questions.

It was a start.

I woke up late, and when I wandered into the kitchen, Zee and the kids had already left and J.W. was heading for the door.

"Sleep well?" he said.

"No. You?"

He smiled. "I had Zee to curl up with."

"How'd she swallow your lie?"

"I didn't have to lie. When I crawled in next to her, she sort of mumbled, 'Catch anything?' And I said, 'Nothing. Didn't have a hit, either of us.' And that was the truth." He lifted his hand. "Evangeline's waiting at the Skyes' farmhouse, and I'm running late, so I'm outta here. Stay out of trouble, at least until I can join you. I don't want to miss any of the fun."

I got to the tattoo parlor in Vineyard Haven around ten-thirty. A hand-lettered sign on the door said they opened at eleven. So I got some coffee to go from the deli on the corner and took it to a bench across the street. At five minutes before eleven, Buster, the tattoo artist, arrived. He unlocked the door and went in. I went in two minutes later.

The front room was empty. I called, "Hey, Buster. You here?"

A minute later his head poked out of the curtained doorway. "We're not open yet. Gimme five minutes."

"I need to talk to you," I said.

He blinked at me, then smiled. "Oh, yeah. I remember you." He came into the front room. "What's up?"

"I want to pick your brain some more."

"About that tattoo I did for that girl? The eye?" He shrugged. "I think you picked clean what little is left of my poor old brain the other day. Sorry." He turned and shuffled some papers on the counter.

I took out my wallet. "I'll pay you for your time."

He turned back to me, frowned at me for a moment, then waved the back of his hand at me. "Money? Shit, I'm making more money than I know what to do with as it is. Put that away and have a seat." He gestured at a chair, and we both sat down.

"I know you're looking for that girl," he said. "I ain't seen her since you were here before. I'm guessing you haven't caught up to her."

I shrugged noncommittally. "I wanted to ask you about the guy who was with her."

"I didn't pay much attention to him, man."

"Did she call him Frank?" I said.

"Maybe." He squeezed his eyes shut for a minute, then shrugged. "Could be. Yeah. Now that you say it, that sounds right. The girl might've called him Frank."

"What did he look like?"

Buster smiled. "You know, she was awfully cute, and there she was, laying there on my table with her pants down around her knees and her pretty young butt sticking up for me to draw a picture on . . . and I'm supposed to be noticing the guy?"

"Try, will you?"

"Okay, okay," he muttered. "The guy. Frank. Grouchy bastard, I remember that. I like to talk with folks when I work, but this guy, he didn't want to talk. Seemed like he was in a big hurry. He was in charge. He's the one who gave me that eye picture, told me where he wanted me to draw it. Like she was a piece of meat, like he owned her. She didn't say three words the whole time."

"What did he look like?" I repeated.

"Oh, right." Buster frowned. "Well, okay, um, glasses, long hair in a ponytail. Older than her, I'm pretty sure of that." He shrugged.

This, I thought, had to be Frank Dyer, the guy I'd seen last night snuggling with Christa while they sang about how much they loved the Lord and He loved them.

"So this Frank was the one who wanted the Eye of Horus tattoo?"

Buster nodded.

"Did either of them say anything about its significance?"

He shrugged. "I don't, ah . . . wait. One of 'em—the guy, I think it was, that Frank—he said something about a commitment. In my business we talk about what we call the tattoo commitment. You know, how a tattoo is permanent and getting one commits you to something that's going to be with you for the rest of your life, and how there are two kinds of people—those who have tattoos and those who don't. I remember the girl didn't seem very enthusiastic about her tattoo, and that Frank guy talking about a commitment."

"Like it was a commitment to him?" I said.

"Nah. More like a commitment to God or something. It sounded like the two of 'em had been through it all before. Frank, there, he was not very patient with her. Basically told her to lie still so I could do it, get it over with. When I finished, she didn't even glance at my little work of art. Just climbed down from the table, hiked up her drawers, and walked out."

"Get it over with?" I repeated.

"The guy, like I said, he was in a big hurry. It was like getting the girl her tattoo was some chore on a list of things he wanted to get done." He shrugged. "For most people, getting a tattoo is a big deal. Not these two. She didn't seem to care one way or the other, and the guy, he just wanted to get it done."

"What about the girl's mood? You said she didn't care. Did she seem . . . normal?"

Buster shrugged. "She was real passive, I remember that. Did what the guy told her to do. Didn't have much interest in her tattoo one way or the other. Didn't react to the needle at all."

"Could she have been on something?"

"On something?" He smiled. "Like some kind of, um, controlled substance, you mean?"

"I mean drugs," I said.

Buster fixed me with a sincere look. "People come in here drunk, stoned, I turn 'em away. I don't want anybody waking up the next morning wondering where that spider on their tit came from."

"I wasn't accusing you of anything."

He shrugged. "Kinda sounded like it."

"So Christa . . . ?"

"She could've had a glass of wine, popped a red-and-white, taken a toke for courage," he said. "But she knew what she was doing. Hell, half the people on the Vineyard pop Prozac, and the other half are alcoholics. If I turned away every customer who uses chemicals, I'd be broke in a week."

"What about him? Frank?"

"He was as sober as you are right now," he said.

"Last time I was here," I said, "you mentioned that

you'd done a number of Eye of Horus tattoos. All on youngish women, you said. Were these women usually accompanied by a guy like this one was?"

He nodded. "As I remember it, yes. But it's really not something you pay much attention to. I bet three-quarters of the women who come in for their first tattoos have guys with them."

Just then the door opened and three young people—two girls and one boy—came in. They all looked to be in their late teens, early twenties. They started looking at the tattoo designs on the walls.

I turned to Buster. "Looks like you've got some business. I appreciate your time."

He nodded. "If I see your girl, I'll let you know."

"I'd appreciate it."

I'd gone about a mile along the road to Oak Bluffs before I was certain that the big green Range Rover in my rearview mirror was following me. It had fallen in behind me shortly after I'd pulled out of the municipal lot in Vineyard Haven, and it stayed with me as I weaved through some side streets, and it didn't seem to be making much of an effort to avoid being spotted.

I'd seen a couple of green Range Rovers parked in Alain Duval's driveway and a couple more in his garage. It wasn't much of a stretch to deduce that the one on my tail was one of them.

And then I understood why they hadn't come after me and J.W. last night after we'd made our daring escape from Duval's place. It was a small island. There weren't that many places to hide. Sooner or later, if they tried hard enough, they'd find you.

And now they'd found me, and they were flaunting it. I

was supposed to feel intimidated. Or frightened. Their message, I supposed, was: Back off.

Well, I had a message for them.

I continued into Oak Bluffs, drove directly to Temahigan Avenue, and stopped in front of the state police headquarters. I got out of the Land Cruiser in time to watch the green Range Rover drive slowly past.

I was tempted to flip whoever was sitting behind those tinted windows a middle-fingered salute, but I rejected the idea as immature. I thought about crooking my finger and beckoning them toward me. *Bring it on, baby. Let's see what you've got.*

That wouldn't be particularly grown-up, either.

So I put my hands on my hips and just watched them go. I assumed they'd report to Duval that the guy who they'd captured the night before had gone to the cops. That ought to give them something to chew on.

After the Range Rover passed out of sight, I leaned against J.W.'s Land Cruiser and tried to think about it. I didn't get very far, but one thing seemed pretty clear: This wasn't just about Christa Doyle.

I went inside. As I'd hoped, Olive Otero was on duty.

She was sitting behind a desk staring at her computer. When she saw me, she rolled her eyes at the ceiling, then said, "Mr. Coyne. Now what?"

"I know you and J. W. Jackson don't hit it off," I said. "But I'm not J.W. I come in peace."

She stifled a smile. "Okay, fair enough." She gestured at the chair across the desk from her. "What can I do for you?"

I sat down. "You can exchange information with me."

"I don't exchange information," she said. "I gather it. What have you got for me?"

"I assume you're still working on the Princess Ishewa case."

"Anita Montgomery," she said. "Yes."

"I can tell you where the car that forced her off the road is hiding."

She narrowed her eyes at me. "You sure of that?"

"Sure? No. But I'd bet a lot of money on it. I'd bet that if you checked this car you'd find paint from the princess's car on it. It's got a long dent on the passenger side, and he's keeping it hidden in his garage."

"Who's he?"

"If I tell you, will you tell me what you know about him?"

"Probably not."

I held up my hands and shrugged.

"Mr. Coyne," she said, "you're a lawyer, so I shouldn't have to remind you that withholding information about a crime is itself a crime."

"I am an officer of the court," I said. "I know my duty."

"If that were true, you wouldn't try to bargain with me."

"I just want to know what's going on around here," I said lamely.

"I'll tell you what I'm at liberty to tell you," she said. "That's all I can do."

"There must have been paint scrapings on the princess's old Pinto," I said. "Your lab can analyze them and determine what kind of car ran her off the road. I bet that paint was green. I bet your forensics people have told you it came from a Range Rover."

Olive Otero looked at me without expression.

"Okay," I said. "You win. Alain Duval. That green Range Rover is in his garage."

Olive Otero stared at me for a moment. "You're telling me that Alain Duval drove Ms. Montgomery off the road with the intention of killing her?"

"He or one of his henchmen."

"Why would he do that?"

"I don't know. But I believe it has something to do with Christa Doyle."

She narrowed her eyes. "That's the girl you're looking for."

"That's the girl I've found," I said. "She's being held prisoner at Duval's place in West Tisbury."

"Prisoner?"

I shrugged. "They let me talk to her. She seems to be drugged, or brainwashed, or both. Anyway, when I was there, I saw a green Range Rover in the garage. It's got a big long dent on its side."

She smiled. "What else have you got for me?"

"What else? Isn't that enough?"

"I wish it were," she said. "How about a motive? How about an eyewitness? How about something I can take to a judge that will convince him to issue a warrant to enter that garage? Come on, Mr. Coyne. You know how it works."

"You must have some idea about motive," I said. "We both know something's cooking here on the island. People are being killed. Duval has this army of tough guys around him. They drive green Range Rovers like the one in his garage with the dented side. One of them followed me over here just now. That setup of Duval's doesn't look like any spiritual commune to me."

"What *does* it look like to you?"

I shook my head. "That's what I hoped you could tell me."

"Well," she said, "I can't. But I can give you some advice."

"What?" I said. I was pretty sure I knew what was coming.

"Leave the police work to the police," she said, "and we'll leave the lawyer work to the lawyers."

"If J.W. or I get killed," I said, "it's on your head."

"If one of you guys gets killed," she said, "it's because you didn't mind your own business."

"Check out Duval, Ms. Otero."

"I appreciate your help," she said. "Please deliver my message to your friend Jackson." She lifted her hand. "Have a good day." She turned her attention to her computer.

"While you're at it," I said, "you should check out Frank Dyer, too."

Her eyes didn't leave her computer monitor. "We check out everybody," she said. "Good-bye, Mr. Coyne."

Chapter Twenty-one

J.W.

Zee had Wednesday off. The sky was bright and there was a soft wind from the southwest so it wasn't hard for the kids to persuade her to take them and Janie for a day's sail on the *Shirley J.*, our eighteen-foot Herreshoff catboat. I couldn't think of a safer place for Janie to be, and a phone call to Evangeline procured permission for her daughter to share the adventure. Evangeline also informed me that she had to be at the stage site for a morning rehearsal with Flurge and the Bristol Tars.

I helped prepare a proper picnic basket for the sailors, approved Zee's plan to sail first up to Oak Bluffs, then back into Cape Pogue Pond, where she'd anchor at the south end so they could have lunch and the kids could explore a beach they usually didn't get to.

"Some of you get to play while the rest of us have to work," I observed as Zee climbed behind the wheel of her little Jeep.

She kissed me and said, "Your pitiful tale moves me greatly. Notice my tears of sympathy for your sad plight."

She and the children drove away and I went back inside for a last cup of coffee before starting my day.

While I sipped I ran things through my mind, trying to winnow the wheat from the chaff. It seemed clear that

Duval was an important character in the odd and dangerous drama in which I'd gotten myself involved. But now soundman Frank Dyer had emerged as perhaps more than a bit player and I still didn't have a grasp of the plot or its author, if such existed. When patterns begin to emerge amid nature's random incidents and actions, it's not unwise to guess that Man, the eternal planner and schemer, is at work. So I brooded about the living and the dead.

I was ready to go pick up Evangeline when Brady, looking none too rested, made an appearance.

"Sleep well?" I asked.

"No."

Red-eyed Brady was pouring his first cup of coffee as I went out the door.

John and Mattie Skye were finishing breakfast with Evangeline when I got to the farm. Evangeline glanced at her watch, and rose fluidly out of her chair.

"Perfect timing. I'm meeting Flurge and the Tars in half an hour."

She started to collect her dishes, but Mattie waved her away. "None of that. Go rehearse so we'll see you at your best Saturday night."

"Ah," I said, "I presume that means that you Skyes have gotten your hands on some of those priceless Celebration tickets?"

"Not yet," said Evangeline, "but I'll pick them up today. And I'll also get a couple for you and Zee."

"At last I'll be able to say I've listened to music that's younger than I am."

"It'll be good for you to listen to something besides opera and bluegrass," said Mattie. "The twins keep John and me musically up-to-date whether we like it or not."

"Do you really dislike modern music as much as you say?" Evangeline asked as we drove away from the farm.

"I just don't listen to much of it. I don't go to the movies much either. Modern entertainment seems mostly aimed at teenagers with lots of money to spend. I haven't been a teenager for a long time, and even when I was I didn't like pop music very much."

"Stuffy even in youth, eh?"

We both laughed.

At the entrance to the long driveway leading to the stage area I flashed my FBI card at a cop I didn't know and he allowed us to enter the hallowed ground.

The stage curtain had been pulled shut and some, but far from all, of the preparation activities seemed to have lessened.

Large speakers now completely surrounded the field so the audience wouldn't miss any of the sounds from the stage. Several film and television camera stations had been set up. The sound truck had been moved behind the stage so as not to block the view of paying patrons. Two long rows of low chairs had been set directly in front of the stage, to give the VIPs more comfortable seating than would be enjoyed by the rest of the fans, who would be seated on blankets on the ground in informal Vineyard style.

I parked and we got out. Evangeline nodded toward the stage. "We'll rehearse behind the curtain. If we don't have any problems, it should take about an hour and a half. Otherwise it may take longer. I'll come back here when we're through and you can take me somewhere I haven't been."

I was very conscious of the charisma that had induced several million people to shell out even more millions of dollars to buy her records and films and to see her perform.

"Do I need to guard your body while you're onstage?" I asked.

"I think I'll be all right there." She smiled

"In that case, I'll see you afterwards."

There were cables snaking across the ground leading to lights, speakers, and other apparatus. People who seemed to know what they were doing were moving here and there, installing, checking, and double-checking gear and wires.

I circumnavigated the stage and behind it found mobile dressing rooms and even more cables and gear. At a good distance behind the dressing rooms sat the pyrotechnics truck. The grand-finale fireworks would apparently be launched from that area.

If the size and complexity of the preparations were an indication of things to come, the Celebration for Humanity was clearly going to be a Very Big Deal.

I walked to the sound truck. The door was open and inside I saw Harry the soundman, wearing earphones, busy at his switches. From somewhere I heard muffled voices and recognized one as being Evangeline's. She was talking with someone about choreography, and I realized that her voice was being picked up by one of the onstage mikes.

Harry saw me, frowned at the intrusion, then brightened. He took off his earphones and stepped out of the truck. "You're Vangie's driver, right? Johnson, isn't it?"

"Jackson."

"I almost got it right. That's not bad for me. Well, it won't be long now. A little fine-tuning and we're all set."

"Nervous?"

"Nervous? Nah. Well, a little, maybe. Everything is working fine but things can always go wrong. Don't expect any problems, though. We'll test everything full-blast later today, just to make sure."

"Where's your helper? What's his name? Frank Dwyer?"

"You're as bad as me, by God! Frank *Dyer,* that's his name. He's out there checking the speakers. You'll find him if you look for him."

"How's he working out?"

"Fine, just fine. Lucky to have him. He knows his stuff and he's a real worker. Set up the speakers all by his lonesome. Didn't need any help at all. Nice fellah. Cute girlfriend, too. Makes me wish I was thirty years younger."

I wondered if my ears actually perked up. "Where'd you meet his girlfriend?"

"Right here. He brought her by so she could see what kind of work he does. Pretty girl. Didn't say much. Stoned, maybe. Frank talked me into letting her sit here with him during the show and watch it on our TV. Why not? We ain't got a lot of space but we can fit her in okay. Be an education for her."

"Local girl?" I almost held my breath.

"Never asked."

"What was her name?"

"Raven, like the bird. People give their kids odd names these days."

"Dark-haired girl about yay tall?" I held out my hand, indicating height.

"Yeah. You know her?"

"I may have seen her someplace. So, how did Frank get this gig? You mentioned your original guy was in an accident."

He shrugged. "Frank had just got through with a job and figured that on a big show like this one a guy like him could probably find some work that paid real money. I quizzed him and knew right away that he knew his stuff. No regrets at all. The guy is good." He looked past me. "There he is now, over yonder at that speaker." He lifted a hand and waved.

I turned and saw Frank Dyer looking at us across the field. After a moment he returned Harry's wave and went back to work at the speaker.

"Where was he working before?" I asked.

Harry thought. "Local place called the Hot Tin Roof. Over at the airport, I think he said. We don't talk about much but our work here. And speaking of work, I better get back to doing mine. Say hi to Vangie for me."

I said I would and he stepped back into the truck and donned his earphones. I turned and looked for Frank Dyer, but he had moved out of sight.

I walked around the field and never found Dyer, but I did find Jake Spitz.

"What are you doing here?" I asked. "Why aren't you at the beach like the sensible people?"

"Eternal vigilance is my calling," he replied. "I'm just wandering around trying to figure out if there's any way we can make this place more secure."

"Let me add to your worries. What do you know about a guy named Frank Dyer?"

Spitz tilted his head and looked at me. "Who's Frank Dyer?"

"I think you've answered my question. Always nice to talk to a servant of the people. I'll be on my way."

"Wait," said Spitz. "Who's Frank Dyer?"

I waved toward the sound truck. "He's the assistant soundman. His name must be on your list of people working here."

He produced a small electronic device, punched a few buttons, and peered at a tiny screen. "He's an electrician. That's all it says here. What about him?"

"I think he's also a Simon Peter."

He raised an eyebrow. "What makes you think so?"

I wasn't anxious to tell him about sneaking into the ashram and getting myself knocked in the head for my troubles, so I combined two truths to create the falsehood I needed.

"I took Evangeline to see Duval up at his compound. I saw Frank Dyer there, wearing the uniform, but I didn't attach any significance to it until yesterday."

Spitz's worried eyes met mine. "You take care of Mrs. Price and her daughter and I'll check up on Dyer. You have anything else I should know about?"

"Nothing."

He turned and walked away.

Back at the Explorer I had only a short wait before Evangeline appeared and climbed in beside me. She handed me an envelope. "Here. Two passes that will get you and Zee in both nights if you want to come. Ringside seats. I don't want to hear any talk about scalping them."

I thought one night would probably be plenty.

"Thanks," I said, sticking the envelope into a pocket. "Was the rehearsal a success?"

She showed me the famous smile. "Flurge and I have worked together before. We won't have any problems. Well, what do you have in mind for me for the rest of the day?"

"I thought I'd take you with me while I talk with a man I know."

"Oh? What man is that?"

"His name is Joe Begay. He was my sergeant during my

very short career as a soldier. You'll find him interesting, I think."

"Let's go, then. I'm always interested in meeting interesting men. You can tell me about him on the way."

"You won't learn much," I said, but I told her what I knew as I drove to Aquinnah. Begay had been born and raised near Second Mesa in Arizona. He claimed he was part Hopi, part Navajo, and part whoever else had traveled through those arid lands. I'd met him in a faraway war just in time to have an enemy mortarman drop rounds on our patrol, sending those of us who survived to hospitals. Twenty years later he'd married a Wampanoag girl and had supposedly retired to the Vineyard.

During those twenty years he'd worked for some group he never identified doing jobs he never described in places he never named. Since he still went away for a few days from time to time, it was my guess that he still worked for someone, but I never asked him any who, where, why, or what.

"Which," I said to Evangeline, "is probably the reason we're friends."

"Fascinating," she replied. "And why are we visiting him today?"

"To ask him to get me information about Frank Dyer. Joe Begay has a lot of contacts."

"Frank Dyer?" she said, perplexed. "Isn't he the man working with Harry? Why do you want to know about an assistant soundman?"

"Maybe for no good reason, but he's got me curious because I've started tripping over him wherever I walk. You can listen in when I make my pitch to Joe. Both of you may think I'm out of my gourd."

"I'm much too sweet to tell you you're out of your gourd, even if I think so."

"I should have you give lessons to Zee."

Joe Begay and his family lived in a small house not far from the beach, north of the famous multicolored clay cliffs. When I pulled into his yard, Joe was sitting on the porch smoking a self-rolled cigarette and drinking a beer. It looked like a good way of life.

Evangeline, in dark glasses and a brunette wig, followed me to the house. Joe watched us with sleepy eyes and rose smoothly from his rocking chair.

"Joe, meet Ethel Price. Mrs. Price, meet Joe Begay."

They exchanged handshakes, slightly ironic smiles, and murmurs about the great pleasure the meeting was giving them.

"I do believe we have met before, Mrs. Price," said Begay, "but on that occasion your hair was blonde and you were not wearing shades."

"I believe you are correct, Mr. Begay."

"It was a rather large gathering in Edinburgh Castle. I was the one without a kilt."

"Surely you were wearing something, Mr. Begay."

"A bit more than you were, as I remember. You were providing entertainment for the ladies and gentlemen. It was the high point of the evening."

"It was one of those political alliance gatherings, wasn't it? Ministers and generals of a United Europe celebrating themselves?"

"Indeed. And now I find you here with J. W. Jackson."

"And I find you here, far from Edinburgh."

"Everyone has to be somewhere." He glanced at the sun. "It's past noon in Scotland. May I offer you a beer?"

"You may."

He waved us to chairs on the porch and disappeared into the house.

"More evidence of a small world," I said.

"I'd forgotten his name but I remember the size of his chest."

Begay returned with beers for all. We sipped. Delish. There is nothing as good as a cool beer on a warm day. Well, maybe a cold beer on a hot day.

"Now," said Begay to me, "you don't have any fishing rods with you, so you want something. What is it?"

"Anything you can tell me about a man named Frank Dyer. He's in his thirties, I'd guess. He's an electrician who's working as a soundman setting up the Celebration for Humanity. He's also a Simon Peter. Simon Peters are the security people for Alain Duval. You know who Duval is?"

Begay nodded but said nothing.

I went on until I'd told him all I knew or had been told about Duval, the Simon Peters, and Dyer. "Lately, everywhere I look I see Dyer," I concluded. "I'd like to know whether I should worry about him more or stop worrying altogether."

Begay sat for a few silent moments, then got up. "There's more beer in the fridge," he said. "I have to make some phone calls." He went into the house.

"You were right," said Evangeline. "He is an interesting man."

"Married, too."

"I saw the ring, Mr. Jackson."

"To one of Zee's best friends. Their daughter's about the same age as yours. Another beer?"

"Please."

We were finishing our second beers when Begay came out of the house. "The wheels are turning," he said to me. Then he looked at Evangeline. "Would you two care to stay for lunch? Afterward we can take a walk under the cliffs."

"How charming of you," said Evangeline. "We're delighted to accept, aren't we, J.W.?"

"Delighted," I said. "Absolutely delighted."

Later, while we walked under the cliffs and Begay explained their origin and significance, I was thinking thoughts having nothing to do with multicolored clay.

Chapter Twenty-two

Brady

After I left Olive Otera at the state police headquarters, I had a tuna sandwich and a mug of coffee at an outdoor cafeteria in Oak Bluffs and tried to figure out how I could pry Christa Doyle away from Alain Duval's compound.

Trying to break in again seemed like a bad plan. My best hope was to catch her when she was away from the place. I was beginning to suspect that she might come willingly.

My other hope was that the police would decide to bust up Duval's cozy little family. Olive Otero had hinted they might do that if they could connect Princess Ishewa's death to that dented Range Rover. The problem was, the police, unlike citizens such as J.W. and I, needed what they called probable cause to enter private places to search for evidence of a crime. All J.W. and I needed was probable suspicion . . . or improbable cause.

It was a breezy, cloudless day on the Vineyard, and from my table at the cafeteria I had a good view of the harbor. It was studded with watercraft. Sailboats skittered around like water bugs. Fishing boats threw big wakes behind them as they headed off for whatever secret spots they had in mind.

I lingered at my table after my sandwich was gone, sipping coffee in an effort to give my system a boost. I hadn't slept much the previous night, and already, at a little after one in the afternoon, it was catching up with me.

After a while, the caffeine did its job. I paid my bill and headed for the Four Winds Trading Post, where, a few days earlier, I'd had a fateful encounter with Anita Montgomery, aka Princess Ishewa. I wanted to talk to the princess's business partner.

But when I got there, I found the inside of the shop dark and a sign in the window that said CLOSED.

I pondered that. It seemed that the blonde woman who worked there had decided that mourning the death of her partner was more important than selling Native American wares to Vineyard tourists. Good for her.

Next to the Four Winds Trading Post was a shop that sold women's clothing. A bookshop was on the other side. I went into the bookshop. It was narrow and cramped, and a dozen or so shoppers were wandering around, picking up books, thumbing through them, putting them back. Bluesy music was playing softly from hidden speakers. Stevie Ray Vaughan, if I wasn't mistaken.

A teenage girl sat behind the counter. She was twirling a strand of hair with her index finger and reading a magazine.

I went up to her and cleared my throat.

She looked up. "Help you?"

I jerked my head in the direction of the Four Winds Trading Post next door. "Any idea why the Indian shop is closed?"

The girl closed the magazine on her lap. "One of the owners died," she said.

"Anita Montgomery," I said. "I heard about it."

She nodded. "You knew her?"

"Yes. I was hoping to pay my respects to her partner."

"Viv," said the girl.

"Viv . . . ?"

"Vivienne Boyer. I hear she's pretty broken up. Awful accident. The police are investigating it. I guess they think it was a hit-and-run. They won't even let Viv arrange a funeral. They need to keep Anita's body or something. She was a pretty cool lady. Everybody's awfully sad about it."

"Any idea when they plan to reopen the shop?"

"I hear they might not," said the girl. "They didn't make much money anyway." She looked past my shoulder and smiled. "Can I help you, ma'am?"

I turned. An elderly woman stood behind me holding a book.

I thanked the girl, left the shop, and headed down the street. I found a pay phone inside the doorway to a restaurant. I remembered Olive Otero mentioning that Anita Montgomery shared a house in East Chop with her partner. The bookshop girl had given me Vivienne Boyer's name, and the Information operator gave me her phone number. I dialed it.

It rang five times before the answering machine clicked on. "It's Viv and Anita," came a cheerful woman's voice—Vivienne's, if I remembered correctly. "We're not home, but if you leave your name and number after the beep we promise to get back to you." Then, sure enough, came the beep.

I started to hang up, then thought better of it. "My name is Brady Coyne," I said. "I need to talk with Ms. Boyer. It's about what happened to—"

"I'm here." The voice was the same one that had recorded the message.

"Ms. Boyer?"

"It's Viv, yes. You're the lawyer who gave me that girl's picture. You had a session with Anita the day before she . . ."

"That's right," I said.

"What do you want?"

"I was hoping we could talk. About what happened."

"Why?"

"I feel . . . responsible. The princess had a picture of Christa Doyle, like the one I gave you. She had it in her pocket when . . . when she had her accident. I can't help feeling there was a connection."

Vivienne was silent for so long that I thought we'd lost our connection. Then she said, "I'm sure there was." She paused again, then said, "Mr. Coyne, would you like to come over?"

"I wouldn't want to intrude."

"I'm inviting you to my house. It wouldn't be intruding."

"I'd like that very much," I said.

She gave me directions, and fifteen minutes later I pulled into a sandy driveway beside a little square bungalow with an open front porch at the end of a winding road. A narrow rectangle of lawn in front needed mowing, but roses and annuals bloomed profusely in the gardens. Goldfinches and chickadees flitted in and out of half a dozen bird feeders hanging from the fruit trees bordering the yard.

When I got out of J.W.'s Land Cruiser, the front door of the house opened and Vivienne Boyer stepped out onto the porch. Her gray-streaked blonde hair was piled on top of her head, and she wore a shapeless ankle-length cotton dress. She looked older than I remembered. Grief will do that to a person.

She stood there with her arms folded across her chest, watching me, neither smiling nor frowning.

I went to the foot of the steps that led up onto the porch. "Are you sure this is okay?" I said.

She nodded. "Please. Let's sit out here."

There were two wooden rocking chairs on the porch. I took one of them.

"Something to drink?" she said.

I waved my hand. "That's not necessary."

"Let's have some iced tea," she said. She went inside, and a few minutes later she was back with two tall glasses and a pitcher.

She poured the glasses full and handed one to me. "I've been thinking about you," she said.

"Me?"

"Anita was very disturbed by your session. I've rarely seen her so affected."

"Did she say why?"

Vivienne shook her head. She was gazing out into her front yard. "After you left, she just mooned around the shop. It wasn't like her. I guess I got a little impatient with her. Finally I told her if she didn't want to work, she might as well go home. I didn't make the connection until . . . until afterward."

"What connection?"

"The connection between her session with you and what happened to her."

I sipped my tea and waited.

"Anita had a gift," said Vivienne after a minute. "She really did. I never understood it, but sometimes she was downright spooky. I could be thinking about somebody she didn't even know, and she'd tell me all about that person. She always knew what I wanted, or what was making me unhappy, things she had no way of knowing, things I didn't even consciously know sometimes. She could tell me the dreams I had at night or things that happened to me when we weren't together. She could tell me what was bothering me before I figured it out myself." She reached over and put her hand on my arm. "It wasn't you. It was the picture of the girl. When I came home that afternoon, I found Anita sitting at the kitchen table. She had that picture in front of her, and she was touching it with her fingertips and crying. I asked her to tell me what was wrong. She kept saying it was too awful."

"She mentioned an explosion to me," I said.

"Yes," said Vivienne. "Explosions and death. That's what she said to me."

"Her accident," I said. "She foresaw her own death."

Vivienne shook her head. "That's not how it worked. She couldn't see into the future, predict events. It wasn't like that. What she could do was, she could get into people's minds. She saw the images they saw, heard the noises and voices they heard, smelled what they smelled. All of it."

"I'm sure I had no thoughts or images of explosions when I was with her," I said.

"No. It was the girl. She got it from the picture."

"So from Christa's picture," I said, "Anita got images of explosions and death. As if those things were in Christa's mind?"

She nodded. "That's how it worked for her. It doesn't mean Christa was consciously thinking such thoughts. But it means those thoughts were there, in her mind somewhere."

"Just from a picture?"

She shrugged. "Anita could do that."

"So that evening . . . ?"

"Oh, the police asked me about it a hundred times in a hundred different ways. Where did she go? What was her purpose? Who was she going to see?" Vivienne smiled quickly. "The police had no interest in Anita's gift. I told them about that girl's picture, the images Anita got from them. Explosions and death and a big eye in the sky."

"That eye," I said. "She mentioned that to me. Christa has an Eye of Horus tattoo on her hip. Could that be what she saw?"

Vivienne nodded. "I bet it was. The police, though, being police, they insisted there had to be a more rational explanation for what Anita did." She shrugged. "If there was, I don't know it. Rationality doesn't account for Anita's gift. I'm sure the police thought I was lying to them."

"You don't know where she went, then?"

She shook her head. "I've gone over that afternoon a million times. She never gave a hint. After supper, she just said there was something she had to do, and she got into that beat-up old Pinto of hers, and . . ." She brushed her hand across her eyes. "And I never saw her again."

"I'm very sorry," I said lamely.

"Now I don't know what I'm going to do. The shop, this house, my . . . my whole life. Everything was all about us. Anita and me. I feel like my heart has been ripped out of my chest."

I took a sip of iced tea. "The police are saying it wasn't an accident."

"I know," she said. "I find that hard to believe. There wasn't a gentler, sweeter person on earth than Anita."

"But if she really saw something . . ."

"Yes. And if she confronted somebody about it." She narrowed her eyes at me. "If we knew who that somebody was, we'd know who killed her, wouldn't we?"

"Not Christa," I said. "She wouldn't kill anybody."

But, I thought, *Alain Duval or one of his loyal Simon Peters might.*

There were no cars in the driveway at the Jackson house when I got there. I saw the perfect opportunity for an afternoon nap, and I seized it.

I slept fitfully, vaguely aware of the hiss of the breeze in the trees outside my window and the constant barking of some distant dog, and when cars drove into the driveway, I heard them without really waking.

Sometime later when J.W. banged on my door, I was in the middle of a very pleasant trout-fishing dream.

"Martini time," he said. "Interested?"

"I'm more interested in coffee."

"I'll put some on. Dinner's in an hour."

I took a quick shower, got dressed, poured a mugful of coffee in the kitchen, and took it out to the balcony, where Zee and J.W. were sipping martinis and watching the birds.

"Feeling better?" said Zee.

I slouched into an empty chair. "Ask me after I finish my coffee."

She put her empty glass on the table and stood up. "I'll do better than that. I'm off to the kitchen. Be grouchy with J.W. to your heart's content."

"I'm sorry," I grumbled.

She came over and kissed the back of my neck. "Don't worry about it. I'm used to crabby men."

After Zee left, J.W. said, "Any adventures today?"

I told him about my visits with Buster, the tattoo artist, and Olive Otero and Vivienne Boyer.

"You've been busy," he said.

"I'm not sure it adds up to anything."

"So the fortune-teller got images of explosions and death from Christa's picture?"

I nodded. "That's Vivienne's conclusion."

"You buy it?"

I shrugged. "Buy it or not, if Princess Ishewa believed it and pursued it and it got her killed, it means there's a connection between her death and Christa."

"Christa Doyle didn't kill anybody," said J.W.

"I don't think she did, either," I said. "But somebody did."

He looked at me. "You thinking what I'm thinking?"

"I'm thinking about Frank Dyer."

"Me, too," he said. "What're you doing tonight?"

"I'll tell you what I'm not doing. I'm not getting whacked on the head and thrown into a locked room. How about you?"

"I'm hoping to get together with a friend of mine named Joe Begay. He's trying to get some information about Dyer for me."

"Yeah?" I said. "Can I come?"

"That's why I mentioned it. I figure you've got an equal stake in this . . . whatever it is that's going on. Dyer brought Christa Doyle to work with him the other day."

"At the site of the Celebration?"

He nodded. "Dyer's in charge of setting up the speakers. Guy named Harry told me that Christa's going to be there backstage during the performance."

"That's my chance right there," I said. "That's when I can help her escape."

"Assuming she wants to escape."

"I assume she does. That's why she helped us last night."

"Assuming it was she who helped us."

I looked at him. "I assume that, too. Now I've just got to find a way to get into the damn Celebration."

J.W. grinned. “Me, I’ve got tickets.”

“How many?”

He held up two fingers. “Me and Zee.”

“Can you get me one?” I said.

“Sure you wouldn’t rather try to sneak in?”

“I’m sure. Last time I tried to sneak in somewhere I ended up with a splitting headache.”

“Well,” said J.W., “let me see what I can do. I happen to be on friendly terms with the headline performer.”

The telephone rang somewhere inside the house, and a minute later Zee came out to the balcony and handed a portable phone to J.W.

“Who is it?” he said.

“Joe Begay. When you’re done, dinner’s ready.”

J.W. put the phone to his ear. “Any luck?” He listened for a minute, then said, “Okay. Brady Coyne will be with me. . . . Right. He’s a lawyer.” He listened for a minute, then a smile spread over his face. “No, don’t worry. He’s nothing like those lawyers. We’ll be there around eight.”

Chapter Twenty-three

J.W.

I drove the old Land Cruiser, and on the way to Aquinnah I told Brady what I knew about Joe Begay.

"Who do you think he works for?" asked Brady, when I finished. He shook out a cigarette and dug for a lighter.

"I've often wondered but never asked. He says he's retired."

"All right, who do you think he doesn't work for?"

"I have no idea, but he knows a lot of people. Still, I'm surprised that he got back to me this fast."

"Maybe he picked up some chatter when he asked about Dyer and what he heard made him decide to speed things up."

"Or maybe Dyer was just easy to trace."

"Or maybe both."

"Do you think that maybe we're using too many 'maybes' in this conversation?"

Brady looked out his window. "Maybe," he said.

The road behind us was empty of cars. Above us the night sky was darkening, disdaining all that man is, all mere complexities, the fury and the mire of human veins.

Toni Begay met us at the door and gave me a kiss. "Joe's reading bedtime stories to the kids. He'll be out in a minute. Come in."

I introduced Brady to her and her to him. "Toni runs a tourist shop up on the cliffs," I said. "What makes it different from some other shops is that most of her Native American stuff is actually made by Native Americans instead of Koreans and Chinese."

"J.W. is a bit behind the nominal times," said Toni to Brady. "In this house and in my shop we're in a post–Native American period. We've decided to be Indians again, and to sell Indian crafts. Joe says Native Americans are any people born in America. He's not high on political correctness."

"Hear, hear," said Brady. "Me neither."

Joe appeared and shook Brady's hand. "You're not wearing a tie. You sure you're a lawyer?"

"My clients sometimes wonder," said Brady. "No doubt about you, though. You look like an Indian's supposed to look."

"I thought the same thing the first time I saw him!" said Toni with a smile.

Joe Begay was tall, with wide shoulders and not much in the way of hips. His hair was black as ebony. He looked at me. "I don't remember what I thought the first time I saw you."

"Just another seventeen-year-old wannabe warrior you had to try to keep alive, probably."

Begay nodded. "Probably something like that." He waved us toward the door. "Let's go outside where I can smoke while I tell you about Frank Dyer."

We sat on the porch, where Begay rolled a cigarette and lit up. In my marijuana days I had learned to roll a good joint, so I recognized Begay's work as first-class.

"I'll give you the shorthand version," said Begay. "Dyer is a California boy. Grew up near L.A. Average kid from a middle-of-the-road family. Dad was a Korean vet; mom stayed home with Frank and his sisters. Good student, played high school football, patriotic, idealistic. Went to a community college and majored in electronics."

Begay blew a smoke ring. It floated into the darkness. "Nothing unusual so far. Now it gets more interesting. He met a girl, got jilted, joined the army to forget her, trained in Special Forces, attended the Gulf War. Saw a lot of dead people, including civilians. Lost idealism and patriotism.

"Came home, tried religion. Didn't take. Hung out with militia types for a while. Joined Followers of the Light just about the time your boss Evangeline was Duval's main squeeze. Made the grade as a Simon Peter. Earns outside money as an electrician and soundman for local shows. Came east and got work on the Celebration set."

He stopped talking.

I looked at him. "That's it?"

"That's the short version. What else do you want to know?"

"How about what he did during the Gulf War," said Brady.

"Cleared mines, among other things. He didn't get them all, of course. He saw some kids get blown apart. They were herding goats, according to the report I got. Did you know that there are still a lot of land mines in Zimbabwe, left over from when it was Rhodesia and the whites lolutionaries? Thirty years later people and elephants are still getting their legs blown off every now and then."

Nature is violent, but only man is vile.

"Why did Dyer become a Follower of the Light?" I asked. "Did he decide to try religion again?"

"I don't know. Could be, I guess. Duval offers enlightenment and sex mixed together. After what he saw in Kuwait and Iraq, maybe that's just what Dyer wants."

"While you're guessing," said Brady, "why do you think Duval has so many toughs working for him as Simon Peters? Why does he need guys like that?"

Begay snubbed out his cigarette. "J.W. didn't ask me about Duval, he asked me about Dyer. Right now I know the same things about Duval that everybody knows or thinks he knows: He's charismatic, he preaches a religion that lets him and his people have lots of sex and call it a spiritual experience, he plays poor but lives rich, and he's one of the people behind this Celebration for Humanity. You want more, I'll look for it, but I doubt if there's much that the tabloids haven't dug up already."

"I think there's a good chance he's going to try to get his hands on his daughter," I said, and told him who she was.

"You and her mother didn't mention the girl this morning," said Begay, "but if he does try that, he won't be the first father who snatches his own kid." He paused. "I doubt if he's going to do it, though."

I tried to think his thoughts, but failed. "Why not?"

"Because he lives in this country and he's a very public person. Usually when parents kidnap their own children they take them to another country or they try to disappear in their own. They change names and dye the kid's hair. If Duval kidnaps the girl, he can't hide. Ergo, I don't think he'd kidnap her. I think it's more likely he'd try to get legal rights to share custody of her." He looked at Brady. "You'd know more about that than I would."

"It wouldn't be easy," said Brady. "He and her mother were never married, and he'd have to prove he's her father and that the girl would be better off having a closer relationship with him. And that's just for starters."

"Well, something's going on," I said. "Drummand is dead, and whoever killed him had his reasons."

Begay straightened in his chair. He projected a regal calm. "There's a lot you haven't mentioned to me, J.W. Who's Drummand?"

I told him what I knew and what I thought about what had happened to Drummand.

When I finished, he was silent for a while, then said, "If Duval planned to kidnap his daughter, an overzealous Simon Peter might have killed Drummand to get the girl for his boss. But I can't see Duval planning any such thing."

"Maybe Duval isn't interested in kidnapping the girl," said Brady thoughtfully. "Maybe somebody else is." We looked at him and he returned our stares. "Why do people get kidnapped?" he asked rhetorically.

"For starters, there's sex, revenge, political pull, or money," I said. "Evangeline is worth millions and she'd exchange it all for Janie."

Begay nodded. "If somebody is after the girl, he knows who her mother is, and maybe who her father is, and he knows one or both of them will pay through the nose to get her back. Could be that Drummand got in the way and got himself killed. Makes sense to me. But who's the kidnapper?"

"A Simon Peter," said Brady. "Drummand made friends with some of them when he infiltrated the Followers out in California. One of those friends told him his shoelace was untied and when Drummand looked down, the guy hit him with a rock."

"More likely several Simon Peters," I said. "There were a lot of footprints on the shore where Drummand beached his canoe. They were made by more than one man."

"Where's the girl now?" asked Begay.

"At my place," I said. "Overnighting with Diana. Nobody knows she's there. She's safe enough." But my words brought me worry even as I spoke them.

"I'm not sure how much or little people know," said Brady. "Earlier today someone was tailing me in a green Land Rover like I saw up at Duval's place. I lost the tail by stopping at the state police station. I had the impression whoever it was could find me anytime they wanted."

Begay frowned and stood up. "I think you two had better go home right now."

Brady and I didn't argue, but headed for the Land Cruiser. Above us the sky was full of stars, but below, on the island, it was black as the pit. My headlights lanced through the darkness as I drove fast toward Edgartown.

"Did anyone follow you again after you left the station?" I asked.

"Not that I saw."

But it was possible that he hadn't seen what was really there. Maybe there were several cars involved, both in front and in back of him. The green Land Rovers could have been only a feint while the real trackers were in other cars, keeping in touch by phone and taking turns at following my old Land Cruiser. If you have the manpower, it isn't too hard to tail people, especially if they don't know they're being tailed.

Had the tailers seen Brady turn down my driveway? Had they looked at the name on my mailbox? Had they speculated? Had they watched Brady and me drive away to visit Joe Begay? Had they waited until they were sure we were really gone, and then . . . ?

For the first time in my life I wished the island's narrow, winding roads were autobahns. I put the pedal closer to the floor. Beside me, Brady said not a word, but raised an arm and gripped the handle above his door.

My headlights split the night, and the dark shapes of trees on either side of the road fled away behind us.

Chapter Twenty-four

Brady

I never realized that a Land Cruiser could be handled like a sports car, or that J.W. could drive like Mario Andretti in his prime . . . or so it seemed as we sped through the dark night over the narrow, twisting back roads of Martha's Vineyard.

"You trying to get us killed?" I said when we slewed around a sandy curve, barely missing a mailbox.

"I know what I'm doing," he grunted. "Your job is to hang on and shut up."

"We hit a tree or get stopped by the cops, we're going to be a while getting home."

"You didn't hear the shut-up part?"

So I shut up, and it seemed to me J.W. stomped a little harder on the gas pedal.

As we approached the long, sandy driveway that led to his house, he slowed way down and doused his headlights. We crept along by the ambient light of the stars, and when we were still about fifty yards from the end of the driveway, he pulled to the side and shut off the engine.

"We go afoot from here," he whispered.

So we got out and shut the car doors carefully and began skulking along the side of the road.

We turned down his driveway, and when we came to the last bend, we saw that every light in the Jackson house was blazing, and the floodlights on the corners were bathing the front and side yards in bright white light. Zee's little red Jeep and the spiffy white Ford Explorer sat right where they had been sitting when we left for Joe Begay's house. Nothing struck me as amiss.

"That's not like Zee," whispered J.W. "She never leaves on lights she's not using. She'd rather light a candle than waste electricity." He pointed. "I'll go around that way, come at it from the back. You wait a couple minutes, then sneak around to the front. Keep in the shadows. See what you can see, listen for what you can hear, and don't do anything dumb."

I nodded, and in ten seconds J.W. had disappeared in the shadows.

I waited until I figured J.W. had reached the rear of the house, then began slipping through the shadows beside the road until I was crouching behind a tree alongside the driveway. I stopped there and listened.

I heard nothing but crickets.

I waited another minute, then darted from the tree to the shadow of the Jeep. I knelt there . . . and then, from the direction of the screen porch, I heard a sharp click. I recognized that click. It was the unmistakable click of a cartridge being jacked into the chamber of an automatic pistol.

"Hey!" Zee's shout was a sudden explosion in the silence. "You, there, by the car. I see you. Come out of there with your hands on top of your head, goddamn it, or I will blow you away. I am a crack shot, and if you don't believe me, you've got five seconds to find out."

"Zee," I shouted. "It's me. It's Brady. For God's sake, don't shoot me."

There was a pause. "You don't sound like Brady," she said.

"My voice is high because I'm trying not to pee my pants," I said. "My hands are on my head. I'm stepping out now. Please don't point that thing at me."

I stepped into the light and stood there with my hands on top of my head.

I couldn't see her, but from the porch came the sound of Zee chuckling. "Okay, you can put your hands down," she said. "You look silly. Come on up and have a beer."

I went onto the porch. Zee was sitting in a chair against the inside wall. She had a big .45 automatic on her lap and a little smile on her face.

"What are you *doing*?" I said. "You could've killed me."

"No," she said, "what are *you* doing, sneaking around in the shadows?"

"We were worried—"

At that moment, J.W. stepped onto the porch from the inside door. "Is everybody okay?" he said.

"I about had a heart attack," I said.

J.W. ignored me. He went over and hugged Zee. "What's with the forty-five?"

Zee looked at both of us. "First there were those phone calls," she said. "Then there was a car with its headlights turned off. So I got my gun and turned on all the lights. I've been sitting here for about an hour. Nothing happened. Everything's okay. I guess I was overreacting. Boy, it's good to see you guys. You should've seen Brady, though. His eyes were as big as dinner plates."

"I know you're a sharpshooter," I said. "I know what a forty-five hollow point does to a man."

"Honey," said Zee to J.W., "why don't you fetch us all a beer?"

J.W. nodded. He was back in a minute with three cold bottles. I drained half of mine in one long, delicious slug.

"Okay," said J.W. to Zee. "Now tell me about the car with its headlights turned off."

"The kids were all tucked in," she said. "It had just gotten dark. I was inside reading and I heard a car coming down the driveway. I thought maybe it was you guys coming back, so I got up and looked out. It was coming toward the house real slow, and its headlights were turned off. That spooked me."

"As it should," said J.W.

"So I turned on the floodlights and got my gun, and when I looked again, the car had turned around and was leaving." She shrugged. "I guess it was just somebody who made a wrong turn."

"Why would they shut off their headlights?" he said.

"I don't know. It sure spooked me. Anyway, they never came back. Probably if it hadn't been for those phone calls—"

"What phone calls?" said J.W.

She shrugged. "Hang-ups. Three of them, about fifteen minutes apart. All before that car came by."

"They didn't say anything?"

"No. I answered, said hello, and there was a pause on the other end, as if they realized my voice was the wrong person, like they had the wrong number, and then they hung up."

"Did you hear anything in the background?" I said. "Voices, music, traffic?"

Zee frowned. "No, I don't think so."

"Where's your phone?"

She picked up a portable phone from the table beside her. "I kept it here with me."

"Gimme," I said.

She handed me the phone. I dialed *-6-9, which is supposed to give you the number from which the last incoming call was made. The mechanical voice said: "The number you are trying to call cannot be reached by this method. Please hang up and try again."

I looked at Zee and J.W. and shook my head. "Pay phone or eight hundred number or cellular or blocked."

"Whatever," said Zee. "There was somebody there. I could sense somebody on the other end."

J.W. sipped his beer and looked thoughtful. "I'm glad you had the gun," he said after a minute. "I'm glad you're a sharpshooter. I'm sorry we weren't here."

She shrugged. "I'm sure it was nothing. But those calls and that car, together like that, and what's been happening . . ."

"You handled it well," he said.

"I'm glad you didn't shoot me," I added.

Sometime in the middle of the night J.W. barged into my bedroom, turned on the lights, and shook me awake. "It's for you," he said, handing me the telephone.

I put it to my ear and said hello.

"Uncle Brady?" She was whispering.

"Christa?" I said. "Where are you?"

"I only got a minute. Please. I want to go home."

"Good. I'll come get you. Are you—?"

"Not now." She paused. "I might have to hang up quickly. I called before but couldn't talk. I stole a cell phone. I'll have to put it back. The only time is the second night of the Celebration. Can you be there?"

"Yes," I said.

"I'll be at the sound truck right after the finale. Can you?"

"I'll find you," I said. "But what about—?"

At that moment, she disconnected.

J.W. had remained standing there beside my bed. "Well?" he said.

"It was Christa," I said. "She's ready to go home. She wants me to rescue her after the finale."

He cocked his head and looked at me. "You trust her?"

"What do you mean?"

"I mean," he said, "it could be some kind of trap."

"I don't see that I've got any choice but to trust her," I said.

He nodded. "Valid point."

"So I'm going to try to rescue her," I said. "Wanna help?"

"You bet," he said.

The next morning after breakfast J.W. came out onto the balcony while I was having my second mug of coffee. He perched on the railing and looked at me. "You gonna tell her parents?"

I shook my head. "I want to wait till it's done. We do it right after the finale."

"Yeah? How?"

"She's going to be at the sound truck," I said, "and one, or preferably both of us, have got to be there. There will be fireworks and everybody singing and celebrating humanity. Nobody will be paying attention. I figure the only thing standing in our way will be Frank Dyer. You handle him, and I'll snatch Christa, and we'll scoot the hell out of there before anybody notices."

J.W. rolled his eyes. "You got a plan, all right."

"What? You don't think you can handle Dyer?"

"That," he said, "will be the least of our problems."

"What am I missing?" I said.

"You're missing about a dozen and a half other Simon Peters, not to mention Alain Duval. If Christa's a prisoner at that place, she's got lots of keepers."

I looked up at the sky for a minute. "I wonder . . ."

J.W. waited for a minute, then said, "You wonder what?"

"Duval's the mystery man here," I said. "After meeting him, and after what Joe Begay told us, I'm not so sure he's a bad guy."

"Those Simon Peters?" he said.

I nodded. "Remember what we heard those two saying when we were hiding in the bushes?"

"They didn't sound very spiritual, as I recall."

"They sounded downright cynical," I said. "Duval didn't strike me as cynical. I was looking for it, too. I mistrust all those spiritual guru types. I'm pretty cynical myself. But Duval seemed sincere. He didn't strike me as the kind of guy who'd hire cynics as bodyguards, either. There are plenty of true believers who can do that work. I'd like to know more about him."

"According to Joe Begay, there's not much to know that isn't known."

"Maybe not," I said. "But if there is, I know somebody who can find it out."

"Go for it, then." J.W. looked at his watch. "Me, I'm outta here. See you at martini time."

After J.W. left, I refilled my mug, found the portable telephone, went back onto the balcony, and called Charlie McDevitt. Charlie was my oldest and best friend. We went to law school together, and afterward Charlie ended up prosecuting federal criminals from the Boston office of the Justice Department, an easy, fifteen-minute walk from my office in Copley Square. Charlie and I used to play golf together, back before I gave up golf, and we still did a lot of trout fishing, and whenever we could, we did favors for each other. The recipient of the favor bought the favor-doer lunch. That was our deal, regardless of the magnitude of the favor.

Charlie's computers gave him access to all the data that the FBI, CIA, IRS, INS, and every other federal agency had stored away, and best of all, Charlie was generally willing to overlook all those pesky government regulations that theoretically forbade him from sharing information with trusted friends like me.

His secretary, a grandmotherly woman named Shirley who was a dead ringer for Mrs. Paul, the woman on the fish-stick package, was happy to hear from me. I dutifully asked after her grandchildren, and she brought me up-to-date on each of them, one at a time. Then she asked when Evie and I were getting married, as she always did, and I had to tell her again that we were enjoying things just as they were too much to risk rocking the boat.

Shirley didn't approve of unmarried folks having sleepovers, but all she said was, "Well, all in good time. I suppose you want to speak with the boss?"

I said I did, and a minute later Charlie came on the line. "Golf or fishing?" he said.

"I keep telling you," I said, "I've given up golf permanently. Right now I'm on the Vineyard, and believe it or not, I've been here for several days and only been fishing once. Didn't catch anything, either."

"So what's up?"

"You still willing to risk your career to check somebody out for me?"

"Since nine-eleven it's a little trickier to do," he said.

"But on the other hand, there's more information. Whattya need?"

"Guy by the name of Alain Duval." I told him what I knew about Duval. "He's got himself a small army of bodyguards he calls Simon Peters, and I'm wondering about them, too. One I'm particularly interested in is a guy named Frank Dyer." I told him what Joe Begay had told J.W. and me about Dyer.

"Give me your number and a couple hours," he said. "I'll get back to you."

"It's worth a plate of that fried calamari at Marie's," I said.

"The hell it is," he said. "It's worth prime rib at Locke Ober, at least."

"You drive a hard bargain," I said. "But you're on."

I spent the next three and a half hours sitting in the sunshine on the Jacksons' balcony, watching the birds and thinking about how good it would feel to drive up to Mike and Neddie Doyle's house on the hilltop in Hancock, New Hampshire, with Christa beside me. I knew J.W. and I needed a plan, but I figured he'd seen the layout and would know what to do. J.W. was good at things like that.

When the phone finally rang, I answered it instantly.

"Okay," said Charlie. "Here's the gist of it. First, Duval appears to be a straight shooter. He makes piles of money, declares it all, and gives a lot of it away to legitimate charities, all of which we have thoroughly investigated. There was one case several years back when somebody accused him of brainwashing their kid and holding her prisoner, like you were wondering about, but that was dismissed when the kid turned out to be nineteen years old, not a kid at all. She convinced the judge she wasn't brainwashed and made a convincing case that her father had sexually abused her and Duval had helped her finally find some peace in her life. It appears that Duval's acolytes come and go freely. I don't think we're missing anything here, Brady. Duval's on the up-and-up, and if your girl is being held against her will, it's not his doing."

"What about those Simon Peters of his?"

Charlie cleared his throat. "That's more interesting. Last year he had eighteen of them on his payroll, and I ran 'em all. Then I went back for the past ten years and ran all of them, too. Up until a few years ago, those Simon Peters appear to have been just members of his flock, your average lost souls who'd been with him for a while. It's like they became more-or-less-permanent members of his community, so he started paying them a small salary. They were helpers. Disciples, I guess you'd call them. Bodyguards, really."

"He needed bodyguards?"

"I guess he thought he did. As far as I know there was never an actual assassination attempt or anything like that. Maybe it was just Duval's way of making them feel useful."

"But it changed?" I said.

"Over the past few years, the old Simon Peters have been dropping off the payroll and new ones taking their place. These new ones, they're different. Ex-military, bikers, guys like that. Nobody with a record, but nobody you'd exactly think of as spiritual, either. Tough guys. Enforcers."

"What about Dyer? Anything special about him?"

"Aside from what you already know, only that he was the first of his type to appear on Duval's payroll, and his salary is bigger than the others. Otherwise, he fits that new profile."

I thought about what Charlie had said. "So," I said, "you'd think I was off base to suspect Duval of holding Christa prisoner for some devious scheme, or of planning to kidnap a child."

"You know as well as I do, you never can tell what somebody might do. History doesn't necessarily spell out the future. But there's nothing in the man's past to warrant that kind of suspicion, no."

"Dyer, on the other hand . . ."

"I'd say he's capable of anything," said Charlie.

Chapter Twenty-five

J.W.

Sometimes, the day before a hurricane reaches the Vineyard there is an odd, yellowish color in the sky and a curious quieting of winds and normal sounds. It's the famous calm before the storm.

Thursday was such a day. Compared with the earlier part of the week, things were abnormally quiet. It was as though the gods were napping before they awoke for the weekend activities. Janie and my children went off with Mattie and John to the beach and I took Evangeline to a rehearsal with Flurge and the Bristol Tars. I didn't see Spitz or Dyer, and even the preparations at the site of the Celebration seemed muted. Nothing notable happened all day and that night Janie again stayed at our house.

I didn't sleep well and imagined odd sounds all night long. But no boogeymen appeared, no Simon Peters came in through the windows. Beside me, Zee slept the sleep of the good. I awoke feeling oppressed. After breakfast I took Janie with me when I went to pick up her mother. As I drove, my eyes flicked between the road ahead, the sky above, and my rearview mirror. There were no planes or helicopters in sight, and though every car I saw got a serious look, none seemed to be following me when I turned into the driveway of the Skyes' farm.

While Jill or Jen Skye—you'd think I could tell them apart by now—took Janie to the barn to admire the twins' horses, I told Evangeline what Zee had seen and done the evening before.

"I think someone may know Janie's been at my house," I said. "I'm going to stay close to her today. Keep your own eyes open."

Her eyes grew worried and hard. "I never should have brought her with me!"

"No one will get her if I'm with her," I said, putting confidence in my voice even as I was thinking that there was only one of me just as there had been only one of Hale Drummand.

She ran a hand through her golden hair. "You stay close to her. Tomorrow night, when you're watching the show, I'll get someone to stay with her in my dressing room."

"I can stay with her. Zee wouldn't miss the show, but I can get along without it."

"A musical snob to the very end, eh? Well, let's collect Janie. Flurge and I have one last rehearsal this morning."

We drove to the performance site, and while Evangeline was rehearsing behind the closed curtain, Janie and I strolled and took in the final preparations for the Celebration.

At the sound truck Harry and Frank Dyer were at work. Harry gave us printed programs for the two nights of song, dance, and speeches and introduced Dyer and Janie to each other.

Dyer said, "Your mother is a wonderful singer. I'm very happy to meet her daughter."

His glasses prevented me from seeing if his smile reached his eyes.

Behind him was a panel filled with dials, buttons, and

switches. Harry followed my gaze and grinned. "Frank's taken on half my work and more. Won't even let me touch that panel. Says I got more than enough to do handling my own. He's right, too, and he's done a great job with the mikes and speakers. We've tested every system and they couldn't be better. I'm trying to talk him into going back to California with me when this gig is over. What do you say, Frank? You coming with me?"

"It's tempting, but I don't know," said Dyer, grinning. "I like living here on the island."

"He's a tough guy to convince," said Harry, "but I'm going to keep after him."

"A good man is hard to find," I said, trying and failing to catch a fleeting memory.

"You got that right," said Harry.

Janie and I moved on. The field had been prepared for an audience of thousands. The cables and wires had been covered, the lights were up, the huge speakers surrounded the grounds, and the TV and camera platforms were already in use because, I guessed, some creative characters were filming the preparations for the show as part of a future film. Security was everywhere, both in civvies and uniforms.

By midafternoon lucky ticket holders would be coming in and spreading their blankets on the ground as near to the stage as they could get. They would bring food and drink and secreted booze and drugs, and in the morning it would take an army of workers to clean up in preparation for the Saturday performance.

When Evangeline's rehearsal was over, she donned her wig and dark glasses and I took her and Janie to lunch at Nancy's, where we could look at the Oak Bluffs harbor while we ate. Around us there was much talk of the upcoming Celebration by people who didn't know that one of its stars was seated at the next table. You often don't see what's right under your nose.

That evening I hesitated before leaving them at the farm.

"We'll be fine," said Evangeline. "John, here, has shotguns for all, if we need them."

John nodded. "Every spare cop on the island is working security for the Celebration, but I think we can handle anything that might come up here."

Fortress Skye.

"I don't think anyone knows that you and Janie are staying here," I said to Evangeline, "but keep your eyes open and if anything unusual happens, call the cops and then call me. Don't play hero, John."

"I don't play a hero," said John, lifting his chin. "I *am* a hero." Then he smiled and said, "Don't worry. If I hear a single twig snap I'll be on the phone."

So I left and went home. At cocktail time on the balcony, Brady and I traded tales of our day and thought about what we'd seen and heard. I felt I should be doing something decisive and suspected that Brady felt the same. But thought, the cosmic foe of action, caused us pause.

That night, while Zee and Brady joined the thousands at the Celebration site, Joshua, Diana, and I watched a bit of the show on our little black-and-white TV. It was an event wrapped in the flag and full of sound and patriotic oratory. Washington notables ranging from ex-president Joe Callahan to the current vice president gave speeches between the acts of apparently famous musical groups and stars whose names I'd never heard of. The audience loved it all, but it wasn't enough to keep me or my children from going to bed not much later than usual. I left all of the outside lights on and kept my pistol under my pillow, and was still awake when Zee slipped into bed beside me.

In the morning I was up at my usual time and was well into the *Globe* before Zee and Brady showed up at the breakfast table. I waited until they were halfway through their first cups of coffee, then said, "Well, are you both ready for round two tonight?"

"Damn right," said red-eyed Zee, whose face lit up with caffeine and the promise of more fabulous music. "It was great! Evangeline's tickets were for VIP chairs. Best seats in the house! Tonight's show should be even better."

"Not for me," groaned Brady. "I've had as much of that kind of culture as I can stand. Those speakers will blow your ears off. I'm meeting Christa at the end of the show, but I'm staying out of earshot until then. Do you happen to have any aspirin?"

"What a pair of wimps you are," said Zee, bringing aspirin from the bathroom and setting the bottle in front of Brady. "I'm going back tonight even if you guys aren't. I've already arranged for Josh and Diana to spend the night with the Duncans. I'll bet Madge Duncan will be glad to use our extra ticket and go with me while Frank babysits. Madge is a little more in tune with the musical times than some people I know."

According to the *Globe,* the first night of the Celebration for Humanity had been a noisy success with only a few arrests of rowdy fans. Duval had been the first celebrity speaker. He'd welcomed the audience and had gotten them to observe a minute of silent meditation for peace before the Gits appeared onstage as the opening act and had blasted meditative silence into distant memory.

I wondered if Christa had been in the sound truck with Dyer last night. I thought about Charlie McDevitt's comments about Duval and the changing character of the Simon Peters. I wondered why Dyer made more money than the other Simon Peters. Was Duval a straight shooter, as McDevitt suggested? A womanizing straight shooter, perhaps, but a straight shooter nonetheless?

McDevitt believed that Dyer, unlike Duval, was capable of anything.

Memories were dancing on the margins of my mind. I tried to capture them and almost succeeded.

Brady and I drove to the Skyes' farm and took Evangeline and Janie to Menemsha Hills, where we walked down to the shore of Vineyard Sound. A gentle morning wind hushed through the trees, and the sun was climbing through a clear blue sky. We seemed far removed from evil, but I watched our backs anyway.

I thought about the dead fortune-teller. I thought about the late Ogden Warner. I thought about Hale Drummand. I thought again about Dyer.

We lunched on sandwiches and soft drinks at the Chilmark Store, then walked to Wascosim's Rock.

Everyone I saw looked dangerous before I looked again and saw that they were not.

When we got back to the farm Evangeline spoke to Mattie Skye, then the two of them came to us and Evangeline said, "Go home, J.W. Have a drink and eat something. Mattie and John are going to stay with Janie in my dressing room while I'm onstage."

I kept my voice calm. "I thought I was going to be in your dressing room." Brady nodded.

"A car came into the yard this afternoon," said Mattie. "The two guys seemed nice enough and as soon as they found out they weren't where they thought they were, they left. But . . ."

"So plans have changed," said Evangeline. "You two go have some supper, then come back here. Those men were probably innocent as doves, but if they weren't and if they come again tonight, I want you here waiting for them. Janie will be with Mattie and John in my dressing room. They'll keep the door locked and John will have his shotgun."

I ran that plan through my head. I didn't like it, but I didn't have a better one, under the circumstances.

"All right," I said. I took my .38 from my belt and gave it to Mattie, who looked at it with dismay. "Take this just in case John runs out of ammunition. If you need to shoot anybody, just point it at them and keep pulling the trigger as long as it keeps shooting."

"Good grief!" said Mattie, but she kept the revolver.

At home, Zee kissed us both. "The kids are gone and there are leftovers in the fridge. I'm out of here. Madge and I are headed for the Celebration!"

We ate and I got Zee's .380 Beretta 84F out of the gun cabinet. It had been her pistol of choice before she'd switched to the .45 Colt. It held thirteen slugs, which, I figured, should be enough. If I missed my target thirteen times, I probably wouldn't hit it on the fourteenth try. I put the gun in my belt and we drove back to the Skyes' farm.

No one was there. The Skyes' SUV was gone and there was a note from John and Mattie on the kitchen table saying they'd give us a report of their adventures when they saw us next.

As the evening turned to night, no one came into the

yard. No twigs snapped under the trees. We watched the Celebration on TV. With the sound turned down it was tolerable. We took turns going out and circumnavigating the grounds. We didn't talk very much.

"I don't trust Dyer," said Brady, out of the blue. "If Duval isn't involved with the bad business that's been going on, then Dyer is the guy who's left."

"There may be someone we don't know exists," I said.

He nodded, but stuck to his guns. "It's guesswork, I admit, but it's not all guesswork. Let's add up what we know about Dyer."

"All right," I said, and I ticked off the bits of information I had.

"You left something out," interrupted Brady. "Before he joined the Followers he tried other religions and he hung out with militia members."

"Maybe he's a true believer and he's finally found his belief as a Follower."

"Could be. We also know he makes more money than most of the Simon Peters and that since he became one himself, the old Simons have dropped out and a new bunch has taken their place. Military types who carry guns at least part of the time. What does that sound like to you?"

"Like Dyer's got a gang of trained killers and Duval, though he may not even know it, is paying its freight."

He nodded. "Something is rotten in the state of Denmark. Spitz is afraid of terrorists, three people are dead, somebody is apparently after Janie, you and I have been coshed and locked up, Christa wants to split but is afraid to do it openly, and everywhere I look, who do I see? Frank Dyer and the Simon Peters."

He glanced at his watch and that caused me to look at

my own. The Celebration was nearing its end and it was time for us to go to the site and help Christa liberate herself from the Followers so she could go home to her dying father and start life anew.

Start life anew. The phrase triggered the memory that had been eluding me. "Come on!" I said, getting up and heading for the door.

Brady didn't hesitate. "What is it?" he asked as we climbed into the white Explorer.

I drove fast through the flowing darkness. "It's Dyer," I said. "He told Harry the soundman that he lives on the island, but he doesn't. According to the records, he lives in California and only came here after Harry's regular assistant got himself smashed up in an automobile accident out there. When Dyer showed up at the sound truck here looking for work, Harry thought he was a gift from God, but it wasn't God's work, it was Dyer's."

"And according to Harry, he's wired the whole sound system," said Brady. "What in hell's he got in mind?" He gripped the handle above his door. "Put the pedal to the metal, J.W.!"

I did that, and in our headlights the highway raced toward us. We came to the driveway leading to the Celebration and I flashed my FBI ID card at the guards. They waved us through.

We'd almost reached the parking area when a dark Land Rover flicked on its headlights and started toward us. The road was narrow and I pulled off to the side to let the car pass. As it did, the parking area lights shining through the Rover's clear windows gave us a plain view of the driver and of a passenger in the rear seat.

"Dyer and Janie!" exclaimed Brady.

I gunned onto the parking area and threw a fast U-turn.

Brady was out of the truck in a flash. "You go after them!" he said. "I have to find Christa!"

I spun sand and raced after Dyer.

At the highway I saw headlights going toward West Tisbury and followed them. I felt like a tin man, empty of all emotion other than a cold fear that I might be pursuing the wrong vehicle.

The Explorer had plenty of zip and I closed rapidly until, to my relief, I saw that the car ahead of me was indeed the Land Rover.

I accelerated past Dyer, pulled in front of him, and slammed on my brakes. The Land Rover smashed into the rear of my truck and both vehicles slewed off the road and stopped.

My neck hurt, but I climbed out and ran back to the Land Rover. Steam boiled from its smashed radiator but its headlights were still on. I yanked the rear right-hand door open and found Janie, dazed, held safely by her seat belt. In the driver's seat, Dyer, his door ajar, also seemed stunned. I reached in and unsnapped Janie's seat belt and pulled her to me.

"You'll be all right," I said.

"Where's Mommy? He said he was taking me to Mommy!"

"She's fine," I said in the gentlest voice I could manage. "I'll take you to her."

I looked up and saw that Dyer had not only unsnapped his own seat belt, but was brandishing a pistol. He twisted and swung it back toward me in a clumsy arc.

"You're not taking anybody anywhere," he mumbled.

I pushed Janie down and dropped to my knees as he fired. Window glass exploded above my head and Janie cried out in fear.

Time seemed to slow down. I dug the Beretta from my belt as Dyer fired again and I imagined that I heard the slug whisper by my ear.

Then I straightened fast and shot him four times and he dropped his pistol and fell out of his open door onto the ground.

"Stay right here," I said to Janie.

I walked around to where Dyer was lying. There was blood coming out of his mouth, but he was still alive.

"You're pretty quick," he said in a bubbly voice, "but you won't be taking the girl to Mommy."

"Lie still," I said. "There's a cell phone in my car. I'll call for an ambulance."

"Too late for that," he said in a weakening, watery voice. "Besides, all the ambulances are going to be busy."

There was something near amusement in his tone and it gave me a chill. "What do you mean?"

I had to put my ear next to his lips to hear his reply. "I mean that Mommy and the pols and the movie stars and all the fucking fans are going to get more of a grand finale than they expect. When the first fireworks go up, there'll be an even bigger bang, and the whole crowd will go up, too, in pieces. Nothing you or anybody else can do about it."

His failing voice choked and ceased, and as I looked with horror back toward the site of the Celebration, I saw a thin trail of sparks rise over trees and the first starburst of the fireworks fill the sky with diamonds. All I could think of was Zee.

Chapter Twenty-six

Brady

After I leaped out of J.W.'s Explorer, I stood there for a minute in the parking lot. The image of Janie's confused little face peering at us from the rear window of that Range Rover was burned into my mind. So was the image of Frank Dyer's determined, snarly face behind the wheel.

I hoped to hell J.W. caught up with them.

I shook my head. I had to focus on Christa. If I didn't grab her now, I might never get another chance.

I started trotting toward the soundstage. I weaved among the acres of vehicles that were jammed close together in the big sandy field that served as the parking lot for the Celebration for Humanity. Ahead of me I could see the scaffolding behind the giant stage rising up against the night sky. It was illuminated by pulsing red-white-and-blue lights.

Somebody—it sounded like Evangeline—was speaking. Her distorted voice boomed and echoed from the speakers, but it was easy to hear the emotion in it. "We celebrate the harmony and love that unite all people in every corner of the world," she was saying. "We must lift our voices as one. Our message of peace and unity must be heard. So please, everyone, join us now in song."

Then instruments began playing, and twenty thousand

voices—performers and audience all together—began singing "America the Beautiful."

As I trotted along the side of the parking area, I saw that the stage was jammed with performers, all with their arms around one anothers' waists. They were swaying back and forth and singing their hearts out, and so was the audience.

Suddenly from somewhere behind me came the roar of an engine. I jumped back just in time to avoid getting run down by a speeding vehicle. When I turned to shake my fist at it, I saw that it was a green Range Rover.

A moment later, another green Range Rover whizzed past me, and two others followed closely behind that one.

Each of the four green Range Rovers carried several men dressed in black.

Simon Peters.

The phrase "rats deserting a sinking ship" passed through my mind.

I didn't know what kind of sinking ship we were dealing with here. But the Simon Peters appeared to be deserting it, and they were in an awfully big hurry. And Frank Dyer had been the lead rat.

He was capable of anything, Charlie had said.

If Dyer and the other Simon Peters were in such a big hurry to get out of there, I was pretty sure I'd better get Christa Doyle the hell out of there, too. And pronto.

I shoved my way past a clot of people beside the stage. Some of them wore uniforms. More security, I assumed. But they were singing, too, all caught up in the emotional fervor of the occasion, and they didn't try to stop me as I worked my way around the side of the stage area, amid cables and speakers and more singing people.

About then they began the second verse. I couldn't

remember how many verses there were to "America the Beautiful." Many, I thought. I wondered if they intended to sing all of them.

At that moment, without warning, Princess Ishewa's expressive face flashed in my memory. Explosions, she had said. Bright lights. Whatever her second sight had shown her had horrified her.

The images she had seen had gotten her killed.

I remembered that a giant fireworks display would begin at the finale, like cannons merging with the music toward the end of the "1812 Overture."

"America the Beautiful" was surely the finale.

Cannons?

Princess Ishewa's voice was speaking to me. I heard it clearly. "Stop Christa," she was saying.

Something forced me to pause and close my eyes, and inside my head images began to flash. I saw great explosions of fire, one after the other, as rapid as repeating gunshots, as loud as cannons. They were blinding against the dark sky, and huge clouds of black smoke billowed up into the night.

In my head I heard the screaming of twenty thousand terrified voices.

The images were vivid and real, more like memory than imagination. It was as if I'd seen it all before, as if I'd witnessed it in some other life.

Already seen.

Déjà vu.

Second sight.

I didn't believe in any of that. And yet I absolutely knew, though I couldn't say how, that Princess Ishewa was speaking to me, telling me that I had to get Christa out of there before they finished singing.

I began to run. I darted around the back of the stage, and in the shadows way off to the side I spotted the sound truck. That's where she was. I headed for it.

Suddenly a man in a khaki Park Service uniform stepped in front of me. "Hey," he said. He fumbled for a revolver that was holstered on his hip.

I skidded to a stop.

"Where are you going?" he said. He got his revolver out and pointed it at me. "No one's supposed to be back here."

I stepped close to him and put my hand around my ear. "What did you say?" I shook my head and frowned. "All this noise."

"I said—"

I hauled off and punched him as hard as I could on the point of his chin. His eyes rolled up, his knees buckled, and he went down without uttering a sound.

"I haven't got time to discuss it," I said. "Very sorry."

I picked up his revolver from where it had fallen and ran to the sound truck. The door was shut. I grabbed the handle. Shit. Locked.

I rattled the doorknob. "Christa!" I yelled. "It's Brady. Come on. Get out of there!"

I heard nothing from inside.

I pounded on the door. "Christa!" I called again. "You've got to—"

It didn't register consciously, but somehow I sensed that someone had come up behind me, and I managed to duck my head sideways so that the heavy, thudding blow landed on my left shoulder rather than the top of my head. It staggered me and instantly numbed my left arm. My instinctive reaction was to drop to the ground and roll away from the direction of the blow, so that the kick of the booted foot that was aimed for my kidneys glanced off my hip.

I managed to scuttle away and turn to face him, and I saw that it was one of the Simon Peters, the one who had stopped me at my car the first time I'd visited Alain Duval. He had a big, square automatic pistol in his hand.

"So it's you again," he said. He was grinning at me, as if he was glad to see me.

I'd managed to hang on to the revolver I'd taken from the park ranger. I was holding it behind me in my right hand.

"Why didn't you leave with the rest of them?" I said to him.

"Frank told me to stay with the girl. He's the boss."

"They've all deserted you, you know."

He shrugged. "I do what I'm told."

"Well," I said, "I'm telling you to let me talk to her. If you don't, we'll all die."

He laughed. "The only ones that're gonna die are her and you. You first." He started to raise his automatic.

A kind of cold numbness had come over me, and I reacted before I thought. I brought the revolver around and shot him before he could shoot me. My first shot hit him high on the right side of his chest, and a red spot blossomed just under his collarbone. It knocked him sideways, so that my second shot got him under his left armpit.

He staggered backward, crashed to the ground, and didn't move.

I pushed myself to my feet and went over to the Simon Peter, who had fallen in the dark, shadowy area beside the sound truck. He looked dead. I picked up his automatic and tossed it into the darkness.

Then I went to the front of the sound truck. I pounded

on the door. "Christa!" I yelled. "It's Brady. We've got to get out of here right now."

After a moment, the door opened and a man stood there. This one wasn't a Simon Peter. I recognized him. He was a technician who operated the sound equipment. I assumed he had no idea what was going on.

He frowned at me. "What's going on?" he said. "Who are you?"

"Is Christa in there?" I said.

"Well, sure," he said, "but—"

I put the muzzle of the revolver against his forehead. "Out," I said.

His eyes widened. "I can't just—"

I grabbed the front of his shirt and hauled him out the door. He went sprawling on the ground. I stood over him and waved the revolver menacingly. "You go for the cops, I'm gonna shoot that girl in there, understand?"

He nodded.

I leaned over him and pressed the gun against his nose. "I'm dead serious," I said.

He held up both hands. "Okay, okay. I won't do nothing. Don't shoot anybody, for God's sake."

I glowered at him for a minute, then turned back to the sound truck. I assumed that as soon as I went in, he'd scoot for the nearest cop. I didn't have much time.

I pushed the door open. Christa was sitting in a folding chair. She turned when she heard me and smiled. "Oh, good. Uncle Brady. It's you. I was afraid you weren't coming." I noticed that her eyes were vacant and unfocused.

"Christa, we've got to get out of here. Right now."

"I'm almost ready," she said. "Where'd Harry go?"

"Harry left like I told him to," I said. "Now you've got to. Come on. Before they finish singing."

She shook her head. "This is the finale," she said. "It's almost over. I got a job to do. Then we can go home. Right? We're going home?"

I was aware that outside the sound truck the singing throngs had segued into another verse of "America the Beautiful." How many verses could there be?

"We're going home right this minute," I said.

She clenched her jaw and lowered her head and looked up at me. "I gotta do my job first."

I looked around the inside of the sound truck. There were half a dozen computer monitors on one long table, and coiled cables lay everywhere on the floor. A big panel of lights and switches and levers took up the entire back wall of the inside of the truck.

"What exactly is your job?" I said to Christa.

She smiled. "Well, see, right when they finish singing 'America the Beautiful' the fireworks start going off, and that's when I'm supposed to take this plug here"—she showed me a thick electrical cable with a three-pronged plug on the end of it—"and I plug it in here"—she pointed at a socket on the panel—"and then I just pull down this lever. It's connected to all the speakers. Frank spent a lot of time hooking it up. It picks up the sound of the fireworks going off and makes 'em really loud. Pretty good, huh?"

I remembered something Joe Begay had told J.W. and me: In the military, Frank Dyer had disarmed land mines.

"You can't do that," I said to her.

"What do you mean?" she said. "Course I can. It's my special job. It's important. Frank says it's an honor."

Princess Ishewa's face loomed in my memory. I remembered the horror in her eyes, and I heard the explosions, saw the fireballs and billowing black smoke. The agonized screams of twenty thousand souls echoed in my brain.

I grabbed Christa's shoulder, pulled her toward me, and looked into her eyes. "What did you take?"

"Huh?"

"The drugs. What're you on?"

She smiled placidly. "Happy pills. I took my happy pills like a good girl."

"Let me see that cable for a minute."

"This?" She held up the heavy cable with the three-pronged plug on the end of it.

"Yes. That one."

She handed it to me.

"Cover your ears," I said to her.

"Why?"

"Just do it."

I put the cable on the floor, bent down, placed the muzzle of the revolver against the rubber plug, turned my head away, and pulled the trigger.

Inside the truck, it sounded like a bomb going off.

The plug had disintegrated.

"Oh, no!" Christa screamed. "Oh, my God! What did you do?"

"I think I saved twenty thousand lives," I said. I reached for her hand. "Come on. Let's go home."

She pulled away from me and crouched there with her hands covering her face. "You wrecked it," she wailed. Her shoulders were heaving. "It was my one job, and you wrecked it."

I went over to her, grabbed her arm, jerked her to her feet, and slapped her face. "Come with me right now," I said in the sternest voice I could muster. I slapped her again. "You must do what I say. Do you understand?"

She stared at me, and then the tears welled up in her dark eyes. She blinked a few times, then smiled and nodded. "Okay," she said. "We can go home now." She held out her hand to me, and I took it.

As Christa and I walked out the door of the sound truck, orange and green and pink lights began exploding over our heads. We stopped and tilted our faces up to watch. The *ka-booms* of the pyrotechnics mingled with the cheering voices of twenty thousand celebrants and shuddered the earth under our feet.

A man was standing in our path. "That's him," he said. "That's the guy."

It was the park ranger I'd punched on the chin. He was flanked on one side by a man in a suit and on the other by a uniformed policeman. I recognized the guy in the suit. It was J.W.'s FBI friend, Jake Spitz.

Spitz and the cop both had their handguns pointed at me.

"Some show, huh?" I said, gesturing at the sky.

"What the hell is going on?" said Spitz.

I looked at the ranger. "I'm sorry I hit you."

He rubbed his chin. "If I'd had my wits about me, I'd've shot you. I'm not very good with guns."

"Good thing for me," I said. I pointed into the shadow beside the sound truck where the Simon Peter I'd shot lay crumpled on the ground. "Did you see that?"

The cop went over and knelt beside him. He put a finger under his chin, then pressed his ear to the Simon Peter's chest. Then he looked up at us and shook his head. "He's been shot. He's dead."

"I did that," I said. "He came at me with a gun." I

looked at the ranger. "I used your revolver. You'll find it inside the sound truck."

"You've got a lot of explaining to do," said Spitz.

"I know," I said. "First, let's take a look at one of those speakers."

"Speakers?" He narrowed his eyes at me for a moment. Then I saw realization spread over his face. "Oh, Jesus," he whispered.

I nodded. I still had hold of Christa's hand. "Christa, here, might be able to help explain some things. And if you guys wouldn't mind, would you put your weapons away?"

Spitz shrugged and tucked his automatic into his shoulder holster. The policeman hesitated, then holstered his revolver.

"You guys carry on," said Spitz to the cop and the ranger. "Get an ambulance for that body and check out the sound truck. I'll take care of the rest of it from here." He turned to me. "Let's take a look at one of those speakers."

I followed Spitz over to a boxed loudspeaker on the very end of the stage. Spitz climbed up. I followed him. Christa waited below.

The performers filled the stage beside us. They still had their arms around one another's waists, and they were swaying back and forth, singing yet another verse of "America the Beautiful." Overhead the fireworks exploded in bursts of green and red and blue. The crowd was singing and swaying, too.

The speaker itself was about five feet tall by three feet wide. Its front was covered by some kind of fabric. "Got a blade?" I said.

Spitz nodded, reached into his pocket, and handed me

a folding knife. I opened it, slit the speaker fabric along two sides, and pulled it off.

Spitz peered in. "Holy shit," he whispered.

I looked. Nestled on the bottom of the box was an olive-colored object, roughly rectangular, about the size of a thick, hardcover book. It appeared to be made from plastic.

"Is that what I think it is?" I said.

Spitz let out a long breath. "Claymore," he said. "Antipersonnel mine. We used claymores in Vietnam for perimeter defense. Set up a couple dozen in a circle, aim 'em at ground level, wire 'em up, detonate all of them with the flick of a switch. Nasty suckers." He pointed to the back of the mine. Two wires ran from it and out the back of the speaker box.

"Those wires go to a central cable in the sound truck," I said. "How many speakers are set up here?"

"I don't know. Couple dozen, at least. I bet they're all armed with claymores aimed down at the audience, just like this one."

"They're disarmed now," I said. "I shot the plug off the master cable. Frank Dyer had it set up so a single switch would detonate all of them. It was supposed to happen right after the finale, at the beginning of the fireworks. That girl"—I pointed at Christa, who was looking up at us with a sweet smile on her face—"she was supposed to throw the switch."

"Goddamn terrorists," Spitz muttered. "It was our worst fear."

"Maybe not," I said. "Maybe it was just one terrorist. Maybe it was just Dyer."

"I fervently hope you're right." He peered at me. "But why?"

I shrugged. "He wanted to kill a lot of people in front of a worldwide television audience."

"Sure. Of course. But why would he want to do that?"

I shook my head. "Could there possibly be a rational answer to a question like that?"

Chapter Twenty-seven

J.W.

The following Monday, after I put Brady and Christa on an early-morning boat, Zee and I were having a late breakfast and sharing the *Boston Globe,* which was still carrying Celebration stories. I had the sports page and was reading an analysis of the Red Sox's latest loss.

"I see here," said Zee, "that as the result of close cooperation among federal, state, and local law enforcement agencies, a plot to kidnap the child of an unnamed celebrity was thwarted during the Celebration for Humanity."

"That's sort of true, at least," I said. "Any mention of a hundred antipersonnel mines set to blow up a significant number of our nation's most famous politicians and entertainers, to say nothing of a few thousand ardent fans?"

Zee shook her head. "Not a word. Only official praise for the high level of security during the event."

"That's probably wise. No need to scare people after the fact. Besides, it would be bad for the island's image if people found out that all really awful things don't happen on the mainland side of Vineyard Sound. Any remarks about the five dead people?"

"Yes, indeed. Let's see if they all get a mention here. It says that Dyer and Sullivan, the guy Brady nailed, were two of the kidnappers. Dyer was shot by an FBI man to be named later, maybe—that's you—and ballistics tests have revealed that Sullivan was killed by the gun of a local police officer who was working in close cooperation with the FBI. Drummand died heroically in a confrontation with the kidnappers, and Ogden Warner was killed by the kidnappers before he could interfere with their plot. Poor Princess Ishewa died in an ironic accident; a seer who didn't see her own death."

"Spitz told me that the latest theory is that Dyer killed Warner because he was afraid Warner would get him fired." I looked at my watch. "Brady and Christa should be on the road to New Hampshire by now. I hope things work out for the girl and her parents."

The previous afternoon Zee and I and the kids had gone off to the beach, leaving Brady snoozing on the couch and Christa conked out in the guest room. Before loading the last of our beach gear into the Land Cruiser, I'd said, "Do you think I should go in there and invite Brady to join us? Maybe I could tell him that the fish are running. That'll get him up in a hurry."

"You leave him alone," said Zee. "He and Christa were explaining things to the cops until almost eight this morning. They both need their beauty sleep."

True enough. After the Celebration, and after hours of questioning, a policeman had finally brought Brady and Christa to our place and both of them had collapsed and stayed collapsed.

I'd had some sleepless hours myself. A few minutes after I shot Dyer, the West Tisbury police, alerted by a passing motorist who had understandably ignored my frantic efforts to wave him down, had arrived at the crash site. They took Janie and me to their little police station by the mill pond. There, after they grilled me, looked skeptically at my FBI ID card, and exchanged telephone and radio calls with security people at the Celebration, I learned that there had been no explosion and Evangeline learned that Janie was safe with me.

The highways had been so jammed with cars exiting the Celebration site that the eastern sky was brightening before a West Tisbury cop managed to drive Janie and me home to our families.

At the Skyes' farm, Evangeline, Janie, and I had shared embraces and the wet eyes that sometimes come after a close shave. At my house a few minutes later, Zee and I had done the same.

It had been a morning for tears, but I'd shed not a one for Dyer.

The Sunday skies had been filled with departing planes bearing the rich and famous back from whence they'd come. One of these was Evangeline's chartered jet carrying her and Janie home to Scotland.

On the way to the airport, she'd stopped to say a whispered good-bye so as not to waken Brady, to leave us her photo inscribed with thanks and words of affection, and to invite us to come and visit her and Janie at their castle. Diana, in particular, thought the last was a splendid idea since she had a high opinion of princesses living in castles. Zee and I had limited our replies to thanks and good wishes.

"By the way," Evangeline had said, "I talked with my people at Cragmoor about an hour ago, and they tell me that the strangers who've been asking questions about me in the village have all disappeared. They evaporated after news of the successful Celebration and the thwarted kidnapping got to Britain. Bad news, from their point of view, at least, travels fast."

Now, Zee put her paper aside and found my hands

with hers. "I'm so glad we got through this. It could have been horrible! I get goose bumps when I think of what almost happened."

"Millions of TV watchers would have seen a live massacre, if there is such a thing, bloody enough to gladden the heart of every America-hater on the globe, but thanks to Brady, it didn't happen."

"John and Mattie feel just terrible about letting Dyer go off with Janie."

"How were they to know what he was up to? He knocks on the door and says hi to Janie. She says hi back because she's met him already. He says her mom wants her onstage for the grand finale and tells John and Mattie to go around front so they can see it. All three of them believe him. Dyer was pretty slick. He fooled a lot of people, including Duval."

"And you think he planned to get ransom money from Duval."

"Who else? Duval is her father, he's rich, and he would be alive and well in California, whereas Evangeline would be very dead on Martha's Vineyard. Dyer wasn't going to get any money from her. The way I see it, the kidnapping idea probably came first. That accounts for the strangers scouting in Cragmoor village. I figure Dyer saw it as a way to finance his political activities."

"Kidnapping for ransom is a popular fund-raiser for revolutionaries in parts of South America, I understand."

"Then the Celebration was announced and Dyer saw an even better way to advance the cause."

"But he didn't see any reason to cancel the kidnapping. A double hit on the corrupt West."

I nodded. "That's my take on it. Of course, Dyer isn't going to be making any statements about his plans."

"Because you and Brady stopped him, and you saved Janie."

"Yes. Just barely."

"How do you feel about what happened?"

"You mean about shooting Dyer?"

"Yes."

I had given that some thought. "I don't feel much except gratitude that I killed him before he could kill me. I was lucky. If he hadn't been dazed from the crash, I don't think he'd have missed me. It was like a duel in a telephone booth."

She squeezed my hands. "I'm so glad you were lucky. And I'm glad you don't feel bad. Dyer was a horrible person."

I looked into her deep, dark eyes. "I think he probably thought of himself as a good person. He was going to rid his decadent country of some of its most unethical people, then he was going to extract money for himself and for his private army of Simon Peters, from another rich, corrupt person who didn't deserve his wealth. I think most terrorists feel very moral."

"You're the one who should feel moral. You and Brady."

"You're my morality," I said. "You and the kids. You make me feel good. That's morality enough for me."

She grinned. "If Brady was here, he'd be saying, 'Spare me from this sentimentality.'"

I could hear him saying that.

When we'd come back from the beach, Brady was coming out of our outdoor shower wrapped in a large towel.

"Your couch has lumps in it," he said.

"The kids offered you the tree house," said Zee.

"The shower compensates for the couch. I love outdoor showers. I'm going to try to figure out a way to build one at my place."

He went into the living room to dress, and while he was gone, the rest of us took turns in the shower. We all loved our outdoor shower. It was big and airy and you never had to clean it. Brady was right to want one in Boston.

"Pa."

"What, Josh?"

"How much longer before school starts?"

"It won't be long now. Are you ready to go back?"

"Yes. I was glad when summer vacation came, but now I want to see my friends at school."

I could remember feeling the same way when I was a kid. "You're right," I said, pleased that some things never change in the ever-changing world. "It's good to go back to school in the fall."

"Pa."

"What, Diana."

"Do we have anything to eat?"

"I imagine we do." I went to the kitchen counter and got leftover breakfast bran muffins from the cooling rack on the kitchen counter. I always make a lot of muffins.

Their mother and I watched our children eat. I was happy.

The next morning, early, I had driven Brady and Christa to the boat. Brady and I shook hands.

"Try to make it down for the derby," I said.

"I can probably manage that," he said.

"Not a working vacation, just fishing."

"You got it."

I watched them go up the gangplank and into the ferry.

Above me the sky was a blue dome. There was a light

wind from the southwest. The sea was dark blue, the beaches were pale yellow, and the trees were green. The island was an emerald surrounded by a golden band, lying on a bed of rippling sapphire-colored silk. It was a microcosm of the larger universe, totally beautiful and totally indifferent and meaningless.

I drove home feeling blessed.

Chapter Twenty-eight

Brady

Monday morning Christa and I exchanged hugs and good-byes with Zee and the Jackson kids. Then we climbed into J.W.'s old Land Cruiser, and he drove us to the landing in Oak Bluffs, where we boarded the ferry.

We were going home. For Christa, it was the last leg of a long journey.

I was looking forward to seeing Evie. I'd called her Sunday night. She said she missed me. That was nice. She'd be waiting at Woods Hole for us. She'd drive us to my place in Boston, where Christa and I would get into my car, and I'd drive her to New Hampshire.

When the ferry pulled away from the slip, we found some space at the railing up front on the top deck. We leaned there side by side and gazed at the mainland of America.

I found I had no desire to look back at the green mound of the Vineyard as it receded behind us, and I guessed Christa felt the same way. It had turned out to be a place where evil walked, and for me, at least, it would take a while before I'd be able to see J.W.'s blessed isle any other way.

Maybe in a month or so, when the annual bluefish and striped bass fishing derby began. J.W. and I had a date for that.

"You doing okay?" I said to Christa.

She looked up at me, smiled quickly, nodded, then returned her gaze to the water and the sky and the distant mainland. I let it go. She hadn't done much talking since I'd found her in the sound truck on Saturday night. I couldn't imagine what she was thinking. She hadn't seen her parents for over two years.

I had a lot of questions I wanted to ask her, but I figured I could live without knowing the answers. She'd share what she wanted to share with whomever she wanted to share it. It was more important that she talk with Mike and Neddie than with me anyway.

Saturday night, after Spitz and I found the claymore mines that Frank Dyer had rigged in the speakers, Christa and I were taken in separate cruisers to the state police headquarters in Oak Bluffs, where we were deposited in separate rooms. Jake Spitz, Olive Otero, another state cop, and two other Feds whose names and affiliations I didn't catch took turns asking me questions. I assumed that my interrogators were moving back and forth between me and Christa, checking to see that we were telling our own versions of the same story.

They fed me coffee and I talked into a tape recorder. I never sensed that they intended to charge me with a crime, although I had killed a man that night.

One of the Feds told me about the minefield that Frank Dyer had laid out at the site of the Celebration. It was a lethal design. Dyer had set up the speakers so that they surrounded the area where the audience was sitting. Each speaker was armed with claymores, and each claymore was armed with seven hundred steel balls, a pound and a half of C-4 explosive, and a blasting cap.

The caps were wired to the fat cable that snaked into the sound truck, the cable that Christa was supposed to plug in at the beginning of the fireworks display. When she pulled the lever, the mines would explode simultaneously, each one spewing its charge of steel balls over a sixty-degree arc waist-high on a standing adult. It would've been the equivalent of a thousand machine guns firing at once.

Those mines, the Fed told me, have a killing range of about a hundred meters. Hundreds of people in the Celebration audience would have been killed, including all of the special guests and celebrities in the front few rows. Thousands more would have been maimed and wounded.

The Fed explained to me that claymores—and machine guns and rocket launchers and just about anything else you might need if you wanted to kill a lot of people—are readily available on the international black market if you can pay the price. Sooner or later they'd figure out where Frank Dyer bought them and how he smuggled them onto the Vineyard. There were, after all, only two ways: by air or by sea. Thousands of boats prowled the Vineyard waters in the summertime. A smuggler would have little challenge.

They finished interrogating us several hours after sunrise on Sunday. Spitz drove us to the Jackson house. I sat beside him in the front seat. Christa rode in back.

Zee was standing in the driveway waiting for us. She opened the back door of Spitz's car, and Christa stepped out. Zee put her arm around the girl's shoulders and led her into the house.

I turned to Spitz. "I've got a question."

"Only one?"

"Several, actually," I said. "Princess Ishewa. I feel responsible for her death."

He shrugged.

"Can you tell me what happened?"

"I don't see why not," he said. "We rounded up those Simon Peters. They were pretty talkative." He hesitated. "This is strictly between us, right?"

"Absolutely," I said.

He peered at me for a moment, then nodded. "That night—the night she died, the night after you showed her Christa Doyle's picture—she showed up at Duval's place. The princess and the guru knew each other. What led her there, I don't know. Second sight, maybe. She was hell-bent on rescuing the girl, thought all she had to do was ask Duval and he'd let her go. Anyway, she was stopped in the driveway by a couple of Simon Peters, including Sullivan—the one you shot—and they took her to Frank Dyer instead of Duval. The princess didn't know any better. Told Dyer she wanted to take Christa with her. Said she was having these terrible visions. Dyer promised her he'd talk with Duval about it, see what he could do. Told her to check back with him tomorrow. So she left, and Dyer sent Sullivan after her in one of those Range Rovers. We found it in Duval's garage. Had a big scrape and paint from that Pinto on the side."

"But why kill her?"

Spitz shrugged. "Simple solution to a complicated problem. If the princess had asked Duval, he probably would've let Christa go. He didn't keep people against their will. Dyer couldn't afford to lose Christa. She was a key player in his plan."

"So Duval had nothing to do with it."

Spitz shook his head. "Nope. It was Dyer."

I thought about all that. "It *was* my fault, then."

"You could look at it that way, I guess. But Frank Dyer was the bad guy. Don't forget that."

I looked at him. "Was he?"

"What to you mean?"

"Was Dyer the *only* bad guy?" I said.

He gazed out the side window of his car for a minute. Then he turned to me. "You're thinking about international terrorism," he said. "Al Qaeda or something."

"Logical thing to think, isn't it?"

"Sure," he said. "No evidence of it, though."

"Dyer was on his own?"

"He and his Simon Peters," he said. "They were loyal to Dyer, but as far as we can tell, none of them really knew what he was up to. Frank Dyer was just another damn fanatical assassin. Except on a grand scale."

"That's a profound relief," I said.

I started to slide out of the car, but Spitz grabbed my arm. "One more thing," he said.

"I'm pretty damn tired," I said. "You kept me up way past my bedtime."

"You shot a man dead," he said. "What the hell did you expect?"

"He was a bad man. He was about to murder me."

"Listen," he said. "This is a big story. It's bound to get out."

"As it should," I said.

He nodded. "As it will. But we want to get it right. We don't want wild rumors flying around. Do you understand?"

I shrugged. "I don't know much."

"You know a lot," he said.

"The truth will come out sooner or later."

"Yes," said Spitz. "It will, and it should. We just want to be sure it *is* the truth. Not pieces of the truth, not one man's version of the truth. The whole truth. We haven't got the whole truth yet. But we *will* get it. When we do, you'll read it in the newspapers, I promise you."

"And meanwhile?"

"Meanwhile, you'll probably see stories that you know are inaccurate. Trust us. And don't, for Christ's sake, breathe a word to anybody about those damn claymores."

I shrugged. "All I want to do is get Christa home to her dying father."

Spitz nodded. "Well, good. I hope it goes well." He reached over and held out his hand. "We'll be in touch."

I shook his hand. "If we're not, that'll be okay by me."

He held on to my hand and grabbed my eyes with his. "Believe me," he said, "we *will* be in touch."

I decided that Jake Spitz was a scary man.

When I went into the house, Zee put her finger to her lips. "Christa's asleep in the guest room," she whispered.

"Already?"

She nodded. "Out like a light."

"What about me?"

"Use the sofa. We'll take the kids to the beach for the afternoon so you can sleep."

That sounded good to me. I went into the living room, picked up the phone, and rang Neddie and Mike's number in Hancock, New Hampshire. When Neddie answered, I said, "It's Brady. Christa's with me. We'll be home tomorrow."

She hesitated. "Really?"

"Yes. Really."

Neddie didn't speak for a long time. Finally, she said, "Oh, Brady. I can't believe it."

"How's Mike?"

"He's . . . he's hanging in there. Every day, waiting to hear from you."

"I didn't want to call you earlier, give you false hopes."

"I understand. Thank you." She hesitated. "How is she? Can I talk to her?"

"Christa's fine, Neddie. She's been through a lot. She's sleeping right now."

"I want to know all about it."

"I think that should be up to Christa. She's ready to go home."

"I've got to go tell Mike right now. I'll see you tomorrow, then?"

"Tomorrow, yes. Sometime in the afternoon."

"Thank you, Brady."

"It's truly my pleasure," I said.

A little before three o'clock on Monday afternoon, I turned onto the long, dirt driveway that led through the woods to Mike and Neddie Doyle's house on the hilltop in southwestern New Hampshire.

"We're here," I announced redundantly.

Christa had been silent during the two-hour drive from my apartment on the Boston waterfront. She fiddled with the car radio now and then and kept her gaze out the side window. She had a lot on her mind. I didn't try to make conversation.

When the Doyles' house appeared through the trees at the top of the driveway, she said, "Please stop here, Uncle Brady."

I stopped.

"I don't know if I can do this," she said. She turned and looked at me, and I saw the apprehension in her eyes.

"I'm not the same person. They don't know me at all. I don't know what they expect."

"I'm sure it will be hard for all of you."

"I've been so awful to them."

"What's done is done," I said. "They're desperate to see you again."

"They really hired you to find me?"

I nodded.

She cocked her head, looked at me for a moment, then smiled. "You did a good job."

"Thank you."

She leaned toward me and kissed my cheek. "Okay," she said. "I'm as ready as I'll ever be. I think I'll walk the rest of the way. Do you mind?"

"You're not going to skip out now, are you?"

"No. I promise."

"Tell your parents I'll call them sometime this week," I said.

She nodded, then opened the door and slid out. She came around to my side of the car. "Thank you, Uncle Brady. You rescued me."

I waved my hand. "You're welcome, Christa. Any time you need rescuing, let me know."

She smiled, turned, and walked toward the house.

I sat there and watched. Christa was still thirty yards away when the front door opened and Neddie came running out. Christa hesitated, then ran toward her.

The two women hugged each other, and I could hear them both squealing and crying and laughing. After a minute or two, they linked arms and went into the house.

I smiled, then turned my car around and headed back to Boston.

RECIPES

Brady's Baked Striped Bass

(Serves four)

Brady loves to fish for striped bass with the fly rod. To J.W.'s consternation, he returns most of those that he catches. But once in a while he lands a "keeper" and actually keeps it, because he believes (though Zee disagrees) that freshly caught striped bass is the best-eating fish in the sea.

You need a fresh bass fillet. Brush both sides of the fillet with olive oil and lay it in a shallow baking dish. Sprinkle the fillet with crushed Ritz cracker crumbs. Cover with very thin lemon slices. Dot generously with hunks of butter. Add salt and fresh-ground pepper. Bake in a preheated 375-degree oven for 25 minutes. Serve with a robust white wine, a fresh seasonal green vegetable, and boiled baby red potatoes sprinkled with parsley. Delish.

BLUEFISH WITH MUSTARD/HORSERADISH SAUCE

(Serves four)

J.W. cooks this in Cliff Hanger *(reissued as* Vineyard Fear*).*

2 lbs. bluefish fillets
¼ c. mayonnaise
¼ c. Dijon-style mustard
1 tsp. prepared horseradish

Place fillets skin-side down on greased foil in baking pan. Mix remaining ingredients together and spread on fillets. Bake in preheated 400-degree oven for about 20 minutes or until fish is opaque and flakes easily. Remove fish to heated platter. Garnish with dill sprigs if desired.

Fish may also be cooked in broiler. Place about 4 inches from broiler unit and broil 7 to 10 minutes (depending on thickness of fillets) or until fish is done.

Neil's Crispy Onion Chicken

(Serves four)

Like many excellent recipes, this one is amazingly simple. Try it!

½ c. melted butter (or oleo)
1 tbsp. Worcestershire sauce
1 tsp. ground mustard
½ tsp. garlic powder
¼ tsp. pepper
4 chicken breast halves, skinned and boned
1 (6 oz.) can regular or Cheddar-flavored French-fried onions, crushed

In a shallow bowl, mix together first five ingredients. Dip chicken in mixture then coat with crushed onions. Place in a greased 9-inch-square baking pan and top with any remaining onions. Drizzle with any remaining butter mixture and bake, uncovered, in a preheated 350-degree oven for 30 to 35 minutes or until juices run clear.

ABOUT THE AUTHORS

Philip R. Craig grew up on a small cattle ranch near Durango, Colorado, before going off to college at Boston University, where he was an all-American fencer. He earned his MFA at the University of Iowa Writers' Workshop. A professor emeritus of English at Wheelock College in Boston, he and his wife, Shirley, now live year-round on Martha's Vineyard. His novel *A Vineyard Killing* was named a *Good Morning America* Bookclub selection in 2003. Other titles include *Murder at a Vineyard Mansion, Vineyard Enigma, Vineyard Shadows,* and *Vineyard Blues.*

William G. Tapply is professor of English at Clark University. The author of more than thirty books, among them twenty-one Brady Coyne novels, he is also a contributing editor to *Field and Stream* magazine. He lives with his wife, novelist Vicki Stiefel, in Hancock, New Hampshire.